More Praise for
THE TURKEY WAR

"A taut tale of tragedy mixed with history and small-town life. THE TURKEY WAR moves at a brisk pace, packed with charm and reminding us of Steinbeck."

Inside Books

"Unger writes in an active voice that propels his readers into the slaughtering plant and into a piece of forgotten history."

Argus Leader (Sioux Falls, SD)

THE TURKEY WAR

Douglas Unger

BALLANTINE BOOKS • NEW YORK

Library of Congress Catalog Card Number: 88-45066

ISBN 0-345-36402-3

This edition published by arrangement with Harper & Row Publishers, Inc.

Manufactured in the United States of America

First Ballantine Books Edition: January 1991

For my father, and those who fought with him; and for Walter Zeller, formerly of the Afrika Korps, without whose generous stories this book would not have been possible . . .

*Mine heritage is unto me as a speckled bird,
the birds round about are against her; come
ye, assemble all the beasts of the field, come
to devour.*

—Jeremiah 12:9

*In the situation in which you now find
yourself, there can be no other consideration
save that of holding fast, of not retreating
one step, of throwing every gun and every
man into the battle. . . . You can show your
troops no other way than that which leads to
victory or to death.*

—Adolf Hitler
*Letter to Field
Marshal Erwin Rommel
and the Afrika Korps*

During the years before the war broke out, Mose Johnson was known as a local expert on raising turkeys. Mose worked as the chief yardman at Buster Hill Turkeys. In those days before huge semitrailers were specially made for the job with hundreds of individual cages for the birds, turkeys were driven in to market on any kind of regular farm truck. Or farmers sometimes herded their big festive flocks right down the main street of town in a colorful parade until they reached the processing plant. Once there, Mose all but rode the birds down the loading chutes. Turkeys hacked at his stockpole with their beaks. He often had to jump into the chute with them, feathers flying, claws and beaks tearing small rents in his pants just over the tops of his boots. Mose counted and sorted the birds, took down the numbers from the scales and marked them on the proper forms. He followed those figures through the paper storms of the main plant office, double-checking to see to it that a farmer's payment came

1

up to the right amount. His yard crew moved the turkeys to designated pens to wait for slaughtering.

Mose personally inspected every flock. Before the war, there were at least seven different breeds of turkeys sold to Buster Hill's plant. Mose enjoyed watching the bright reddish browns, the swan-colored whites, the glistening blacks and grays—particolored flocks of large gangly birds spreading out through the high wire canyons of the yards. He paid particular attention to the hens. If he spotted a really good-looking hen, low to the ground, fat in the breast, and with the right kind of stocky conformation to her shape, Mose caught her up to check the vent. He cradled the big bird head downward in his arms. He probed his fingers in gently to spread the vent lips, inspecting her closely. If her lips were moist and a flush pink in color with a strong blue veinous tone, Mose went on to press his fingers in more deeply, stretching the slick membranous walls, working his fingers in one at a time according to his belief that three fingers or more and she's a good layer, less than three and she's a turkey for the oven.

Whenever he found a brood hen he liked enough, Mose culled her out. He let her loose in a breeding confinement he had built in one corner of the turkey yards. It was a fine pen, made of close-meshed wire and covered with good roofing tin against the rain, and it had two neat lines of heated wooden coops built up off the ground for brooding. It was Mose's pastime as well as his job to experiment with turkey breeding. He spent a good number of his free evenings in that pen, which he considered to be a kind of laboratory for his special birds.

By the late 1930s, Buster Hill Turkeys was winning prizes for Mose's work at the Wovoka County fair. Twice his birds went on to make the finals at the state fair. One wall of Mose's three-room house, which stood about a block upwind of the turkey yards, was almost entirely taken up with photographs of prize-winning birds that he had exhibited, each with a colored ribbon pinned to the frame. Those photos all showed Mose in exactly the same stance—the turkey beside him with head erect, breast pumped out; Mose with his cowboy hat pushed back on his head, leaning on his showstick as on a gentleman's cane, his face showing an expression that seemed both pleased and, from a set tautness of his mouth, defiant. He wore that same expression countless evenings after he had finished working his regular shift and was leisurely taking care of his special turkeys. Mose loved to watch the awkward way the little pullets pranced about their small enclosure, heads in constant motion like in some strange exotic dance. Beaks clattering in the long steel feed troughs, the flock moved as one unit across the ground he kept hard and clean, their quick dark eyes like a tiny nation in search of food.

One of the ambitions Mose had had for years was to create his own particolored breed of turkey and call it the Johnson. He started the venture with a huge Bourbon Red tom turkey he bought from a grower named Jake Ballock for the unheard-of price of ten dollars. That tom was one of the largest Mose had ever seen, weighing about forty-five pounds in his peak year. He stood waist high to Mose, a gleaming, rust-red bird that thrust his breast out and strutted proudly in his separate pen. He spread his white-edged wings and jumped up, wildly clawing at the dust. He stretched his red neck up and way out, then let loose a high prolonged gobbling at the hens, a sound that could stop a man in his tracks like a siren. Then he slowly began circling, wings reaching out. First one wingtip then the other began beating the earth in a fast dancing rhythm that lifted his body just a few inches off the ground as if he might take off in flight; then he started circling again, calling out to the hens, louder and louder. Finally, he would settle, huff out his red breast and fan his pure-white tail into the sun. The big bird stood planted there, head erect, showing himself proud.

Mose crossbred that Bourbon Red tom with his select

group of hens—the dark-gray Slate, the black English, the Narragansett with its bright coppery plumage, the pure White Holland, and the Bronze. The tom chased the hens around the yard. He pinned them to the earth in explosions of feathers so violently that Mose finally had to devise a "turkey saddle" out of leather and canvas for the hens, to protect them from that tom's beating them up, tearing their feathers out as he fought them to the ground, slashing at them with his beak, then just tossing them aside half dead when he was finished.

Every few weeks, there was a new hatch of poults that grew brightly mottled plumage. Mose's favorites were the gray-spotted copper, with which he took second prize at the state fair, then the dark-green English with a pure white fan, which won him third. His least favorite offspring was a kind of ugly red-and-white pinto turkey that developed wings long enough that he had to wire them together with a board across its back to keep it from flying out over the fence. This was even after he had clipped off the tip of the left wing, the usual practice for domesticated turkeys, so that if a bird tried to fly, it tumbled around in the air instead and flopped like a wounded goose right back to the ground.

Mose crossbred his crossbreeds season after season, keeping close track of them on graph-paper charts on which he drew their complete genealogies. His breeding project soon began paying for itself. He started selling particularly large and even a few especially decorative-looking toms and hens to local farmers, sometimes getting as much as four dollars apiece for them. That was more than enough to pay for all the feed bills and even to expand the company's small hatchery operation. Mose saw himself as improving turkey stocks all over the state. And he was, to some extent. But in truth, most farmers back then still looked at raising turkeys as something marginal, an extra little cash crop to help out with the bills.

Local farmers began to go in for raising turkeys more

seriously when a company called Safebuy bought out
Buster Hill Turkeys and created a subsidiary called
Nowell-Safebuy Turkeys, retaining Buster as president
and chairman for fat stock offerings and a generous sal-
ary. With plenty of Safebuy money to back him, Buster
Hill began to persuade farmers that their brightest future
lay in turkeys. He lured them in with what banker David
Whitcomb called "guts-and-hide loans" to get started,
"the loan it takes the lender a barrowload of guts to give
and if the borrower don't make out, everyone involved
stands to lose his hide."

But the chance of losing out didn't seem likely. Turkey
was widely considered a luxury meat back then. And any
cash at all to be had that easily seemed a blessing to
farmers. Even during the hardest times, when day by day
it was tough for some people to afford to eat at all, most
families in this country still kept at least one turkey holiday. Buster Hill convinced farmers that the last thing the
poor would ever give up would be their holidays, and that
the rich were sure to eat whole trainloads of turkeys before they died. So farmers began signing on with Nowell-
Safebuy, a few at first, then scores of them. But there
still wasn't enough production capacity at the plant to
keep up with the pace of demand, especially with the
new and ominous developments in Europe, which began
to drive up the price of everything. A new processing
and cold-storage facility started going up brick by brick
on the east edge of town. Business boomed. People were
moving into town faster than houses could go up for them.
Main Street was suddenly almost as full of things to buy
as anyone could dream of finding in Rapid City. What
more proof did a man need than that?

Nowell-Safebuy Turkeys soon became the town's lifeblood. The steaming turkey manure with its odor of am-
monia was particularly oppressive on summer days. The
piercing noise of the turkey yards was sometimes annoy-
ing, especially when it started up at night. But almost
nobody complained; these were signs of solvency, after

all. It was reassuring that thousands of huge, colorful birds in the Nowell-Safebuy yards called out in a grating discord as steady as the sound of traffic in a city. Except for those eerie moments when, suddenly, the turkeys fell silent, all of them. Acres of huddled birds were filled with quiet wings, all heads drooping mutely like in some communal rite of brooding silence. Then something happened. A horn honked down the street, the plant whistle blew, or one lone bird cried out in shrill alarm. The turkey calls rose again over the town.

Three months after Buster Hill officially opened the new Nowell-Safebuy plant, Hitler's tanks rolled over Poland and war was declared in Europe. The price of turkeys went up by one third. France was crushed the following spring. Newspapers carried photos of the ragged British wading out up to their chests into the sea at Dunkirk. The newsreel just before the umpteenth showing of *Banjo on my Knee* at the Arcade Bingo & Theater showed formations of Nazi soldiers goose-stepping through the Arch of Triumph as the people of Paris wept. Parts of London looked like the heaped-up violence in a twister's wake. Hundreds of torpedoed ships were going down with all hands in the Atlantic.

The price of turkeys nearly doubled. Along with them, the cost of almost everything else was skyrocketing. Farmers were looking forward to a boom year. Buster Hill was on the telephone making deals, as frantic as a gambler, or driving off for days at a time, trying to find enough turkeys just to meet demand. Labor was short. Wages rose quickly in response. Anybody with half a body and no brains at all could find work at the Nowell-Safebuy. A rail spur ran alongside the new Nowell-Safebuy loading docks, and it seemed to Mose the same endless train was pulling freight cars past them, engines booming, boxcars and reefer cars squealing and clattering along, that whole winding chain of prosperity slowed only by the delays on the slaughtering line.

"To hell with Hitler. To hell with England. If we can

just stay clear of this thing, then the whole damn country's going to get rich and us along with it.'' This was Buster Hill's advice to everyone. He wore a WENDELL WILLKIE FOR PRESIDENT button on his hat. He personally handed out hundreds of pamphlets advertising the Republican party's isolationist platform during the elections of 1940. ''That Lend-Lease they're talking about, maybe,'' he said. ''But let's not go changing anything else. When you're looking at a poker hand like this one, you'd have to be a damned fool to be drawing new cards.''

But change did come, and new cards were dealt to everyone. Even as commodity prices kept steadily rising, turkey production began to drop at the Nowell-Safebuy from lack of manpower. President Roosevelt pushed through the first peacetime draft in history, and it began to take the best workers off the farms and the slaughtering line. Young men began leaving Nowell to enlist even before the first inevitable bloody day. Pearl Harbor was really only the final confirmation of a monstrous and deadly change that almost everyone in this country knew had already happened.

This was further confirmed by the way the war went at first. Newspapers were filled with the worst kind of stories, the radio announcers' voices crackled with emergency; and in the weekly newsreels, the voice of Lowell Thomas grimly narrated one defeat after another: Guam overrun. Marines on Wake Island massacred. MacArthur cornered in the Philippines with eighty thousand men who were hopelessly fighting for their lives. The pitiful remnants of our Pacific fleet putting out to sea. Everywhere, it seemed that our boys were losing and Allied forces were on the run. London was on its knees. Hitler's tanks were waiting at the approaches to Moscow and Leningrad. Singapore was devastated. Malta and Crete bombed to ruins. Rommel's Afrika Korps ready to plunge deep into Egypt. . . .

Busload after busload, men were now leaving for basic

training. Mose would have enlisted himself, but he was too old, discouraged by the recruiter in Rapid City because he was just three years shy of the maximum age of forty-five; also, his right foot had an inflamed knobby growth on it that he could just barely and painfully squeeze into his boot. So he would do what everybody left around him was doing, his part at home, his full and strenuous effort to somehow pull this country up from defeat. But how much could he really do? The Nowell-Safebuy plant was growing so short of labor that first bleak spring of the war that thousands of locally raised turkeys had to be shipped all the way to Omaha for processing. Even with double shifts for everyone, the situation was getting worse by the day. Then there were the other obstacles. Both wages and prices were frozen for the duration by the new National War Labor Board and the USDA branch that became the War Food Administration. Attracting more workers by paying them extra under the table could land a company manager in jail. So Buster came up with the notion of "job reclassification," an idea similar to the way companies like the cigarette manufacturers were suddenly putting out brand names never seen before in "deluxe" packages to raise their prices. Common butchers on the slaughtering line were now called "processing technicians." Laborers at the wrapping and canning stations were "packaging mechanics." The teams of dockworkers shoving boxes of fresh or frozen or canned turkey into the railroad cars became "transportation agents." Every worker's job title was changed. Mose wondered about skirting around the laws like that; then it seemed that everywhere he looked, everyone else was doing the same. Candy bars in odd shapes and reduced sizes; the same with soaps, toothpaste, cereal, everything. Besides, he was a man who generally stayed out of anyone else's business. As it was, even with pay raised as high as $120 a month, the Nowell-Safebuy wasn't coming close to getting the job done.

That first bleak spring after Pearl Harbor, another, even

stranger change caught Mose up short. Maybe because of wartime price structures, more likely because it had been planned that way all along as part of Safebuy's efforts to expand nationally, Buster Hill announced an official shift in company policy for the buying of turkeys. "In order to achieve a national reputation for the uniform quality of our products," that statement explained, the Nowell-Safebuy wasn't going to purchase just any kind of turkey from now on. The only breed the plant was going to pay farmers for in the future was a large White Holland type developed by a government research team in a place called Feltsville, Maryland, and by a group of scientists at a land grant agricultural college somewhere in Texas. Any farmer who wanted to grow turkeys for the Nowell-Safebuy would now have to order crates and crates of peeping, three-day-old poults delivered express all the way from hatcheries in Texas by the railroad.

The Nowell-Safebuy breed-conversion plan was delayed for about a year, mainly because of the war's transportation crisis. Mose unloaded the first crates of the new Texas turkeys during the second and brighter spring of the war. That was about the time the battle for Guadalcanal looked to be turning in our favor. The Germans had been decimated at Stalingrad and were in disorderly retreat. Montgomery had broken out in Africa and captured tens of thousands of enemy soldiers. MacArthur was preparing for the invasion of New Guinea, and I Shall Return brand cigarettes were just then being test marketed to see if they might catch on and become popular. Hope was growing everywhere. And so far, not one soldier or sailor from this town had died.

Anxiously, Mose unloaded and looked over the first shipment of the new Nowell-Safebuy turkeys. They seemed to him exceptionally strange birds, and he followed their growth closely. They grew into huge, ungainly creatures with pure-white feathers, uniform six-pound breasts, and uncommonly small, dark-red heads.

Also, it seemed to him that these turkeys were bred for stupidity. When he experimented on his own with them, the toms hardly seemed to know how to mount the hens. Dozens of little yellow chicks had to be put into coops with the incoming shipments of tiny gray turkey poults in order to teach them how to peck. Otherwise, those poults would just stand there in piles of grain and starve to death. Then, during the pullet stage, they grew too fast and heavily for the strength of their legs, which were like wheatstraw compared to their bodies. Mose was dismayed as he watched them shifting weight from spindly leg to spindly leg, dumbly following the smell of grain mixed with the scraps of their own kind after slaughtering and fed back to them on a new feed-recycling program.

Mose crossbred the Nowell-Safebuy turkeys with his own particolored stock, and at his own expense too, since his breeding projects had been ordered terminated by the company. At first, almost none of the mixed offspring even survived until the pullet stage. Then, after repeated attempts, Mose managed to nurse several of the new poults through to maturity. He soon discovered that the birds that survived grew small red heads, stunted legs, pumped-up breasts, and pure-white feathers anyway, despite the colorful prize-winning turkeys that had fathered them.

One afternoon in late autumn of the first year of the war, Buster Hill called Mose up to the main plant office. Buster was sitting under the slow fans of his office windows. It was an unseasonably hot day, and Buster's bulldog face was haggard with fatigue. Across from Buster's desk, piled high with paperwork, Mose sweated. He was almost asleep, grateful for this chance to rest under the fans. He was tired. Everyone he knew was tired from putting in double-time hours ten straight months already because of the war's labor shortage.

"We need a man with your experience," Buster said. "We're making you production manager. We're giving

you responsibility on the shop floor for the whole operation.''

It took a long moment in the sleepy breeze of the fans
for Buster's words to sink in. Then Mose sat up and said
straight out, ''If you don't mind, Buster, I'll turn you
down. Any more to do and I'd be working myself to
death. I'm just a yardman anyhow.''

''It's a whole new job classification,'' Buster said. ''So
we can give you thirty bucks raise.''

''No,'' he answered after a minute. Mose stared at his
tough hands, covered with small, scabbed-over cuts. He
felt his legs already stiff because of this uncommon rest
after running all afternoon. He stretched them out, rubbing his muscles as he would a horse. The thought of
himself as general manager, as the man who ranged
through the plant making sure every phase of it worked,
the one who oversaw the unloading and feeding up in the
yards, the slaughtering, gutting, boning, canning, or
wrapping fresh and moving out into cold storage—the
idea of that kind of responsibility made him feel too tired
to move. Running eight hundred turkeys a day from the
trucks into the yards, culling some back to feed up for a
week or two, then all that carrying of grain sacks and
supplements, rolling out the heavy barrels of scraps from
the building to add to the feed, all that running around
for fourteen hours a day, six days a week ever since most
of the boys had been drafted—that was enough to do.
Also, Mose had always disliked the atmosphere inside
the plant building, which, depending on the work station,
was like either a bitter chilling fog or a sweltering rancid
steam bath of gaseous turkey manure.

''No,'' he said again. ''I'm sorry, but I don't believe
I'll take it.'' He rested his hands on his knees a minute
and turned his head, letting the fans cool the back of his
neck before he stood up to leave.

''You just stay right there and have a damn drink with
me. At least let's talk it over. I mean, what the hell,''
Buster said. ''It's not just the money.''

Mose sat back down again. He watched his boss pouring out his drink, a highly unusual thing for Buster to do during working hours. He thought again of how much he had always liked his dealings with farmers at his yard job, especially the chance to talk birds with them. Mose drank down his bourbon out of one of Buster's stained coffee mugs in one swallow. "Darnit now, almost every good worker we had is shipped out overseas," Mose said. "There ain't nothing a production manager could do to get things going. The men we got left, most of 'em have been on that line so long, their arthritis is so bad they can't even bend down to buckle on their boots!"

"That's just why we need you."

By Buster's tone, Mose knew there was something else going on besides the manager's job. Also by the way Buster was filling the mug again with his most expensive bonded bourbon. Mose squirmed in his seat, feeling like a schoolboy.

"Manpower," Buster said. "That's what we need. And that's just what we're going to get. Our first shipment of war prisoners is coming here in a matter of weeks. Germans. Captured Germans. They're going to send us the ones classified as anti-Nazi sympathizers someplace in Virginia, but even so, it was tough to get it arranged with the War Labor Board. That's Washington. Goddamned Washington. Washington thinks these prisoners just might solve our problems. And that's why we need you. You're one of the few men left who can handle the job, and the only one besides me who really knows the operation inside and out. Eleven years experience. Eleven years . . ."

"Come on now, don't you be fooling with me," Mose said and laughed. "Germans? The enemy? Right here in Nowell? Right here in this building?"

"First time it's ever been tried. Never in this country," Buster said. "You ever heard of that Lend-Lease? All that free food and ammo we shipped out to England? It's got something to do with that. Part of the way the

British are paying us back. It involves the whole damn war effort. It's orders from Washington. So you can see the position we're in. . . ."

"Come on, Buster, you know me. I ain't any kind of a manager," said Mose. "I'm just a yardman. And I don't mean to cross over."

Buster leaned back flatly in his oversized chair, its springs long since shot. He reached an arm like a whole ham off to one side and scratched at the ears of the bull-dog pup he had named Buster, after himself, stretched out by his chair. "This ain't so bad a place to put prisoners, either," he said. "Not if you really think about it."

Mose thought about it for the first time. He took off his work hat of panama straw, his big hands worrying at the brim, the same way he did after showing weight slips to his farmers. He recalled he had seen lines of German prisoners marching with hands on their heads in one of the newsreels at the Arcade Bingo & Theater. But he had never considered where so many prisoners might be kept. He looked around Buster's piled-up office, imagining the Nowell-Safebuy slaughteryards filled with Nazis like out of the newsreels. "Jesus, Buster," he said. "You put one of them in there and the boys'll likely *feed* him to the birds! And what about this town? Are we going to have actual German soldiers running all over this town?"

"Hell, we'll give you forty bucks raise," Buster said. "Fifty, even. Anything you want, and I mean it—damn the wage and price controls."

"The answer's still no. I don't want no truck with no Germans." Mose was moving to his feet, starting to turn away from the big desk to let Buster know he was ready to leave. "Go on and find somebody else," he said. "I'm just a yardman anyhow."

"You walk out of here now and you're fired."

Mose froze there a moment, the fact sinking in that Buster might be serious. Buster was giving him a look that could have burned most other men out of the room.

Slowly, Mose sat back down again, sweating, shocked. He reached out for the coffee mug. He felt the fans cooling his face, the delicious, sour fumes of the bourbon and his exhaustion slowly rising behind his eyes. "You can't fire me," he said slowly. "I could join the union with seniority right damn now. Laws or no laws, the boys would shut this place down if you fired me."

"Come on, damnit, Mose! How many of the boys are over there fighting? We lucky ones here at home got to do our part. And if you can't do your part, well, that's cause enough, even for the union. There's a war on. You know it and I know it. An army's got to eat before it can fight. Our boys overseas need turkeys to win this war. . . ."

Spring 1943. More than a year had sped by since the country had awakened in shock and thrown itself into the war's emergency. Near the big gate of the Nowell-Safebuy, Dale Rynning and the last of the plant workers left in town were gathered in a scattered gang, swinging lunch pails, finishing cigarettes before the morning-shift whistle. "Looky there," Dale said, scrubbing the butt of his Lucky carefully on his boot to save it. "That sucker out there is talking just like them Nazi scabs."

All attention turned toward the yards, where "production manager" Mose Johnson strutted back and forth like a nervous turkey in a corridor of wire.

"*Achtung! Steigen Sie aus!*" Mose practiced into the dawn. "*Ach-tung! Gehen Sie zurr* . . . Ah, damnit," he said. He pulled a tattered, army-brown phrasebook from the back pocket of his jeans. "*Zu-dreh-en, zu-fass-en, zu-greif-en, zu-geh-en* . . ."

He went through his list of *zu* words again, trying to make them sound right. He even gurgled the *r*'s a little,

15

the way he often heard his men pronounce them. *"Zu-schneiden, zu-tritt, zu-wagen . . ."* The words felt like one big mess in his throat, and he had trouble not blowing spit as he bent his tongue and lips into these foreign conniptions.

After Mose had run through the list of words he needed to practice, marked in the phrasebook by one of his prisoners, he checked his pocket watch. Either his watch was fast or the whistle was late this morning. Maybe its valve had stuck again. Also, the prisoner crew hadn't yet arrived. Mose saw Dale and the others still milling around at the big gate. Exasperated, he waved an arm at them to get to work in the building.

Mose practiced again. He knew he must look ridiculous, and his German still didn't sound right, rolled through a thick Missouri River twang he couldn't shake. *"Stei-gen-Sie-aus!"* he drawled.

Two grain trucks full of prisoners rumbled in alongside the plant building. The gangs of them leaned out over the rickety wooden trucksides, thin khaki jackets buttoned to the neck against the morning chill. There was an armed driver and a sidekick riding shotgun in each truck cab. One army guard in combat fatigues stood in back with each load of men. Before the trucks had stopped moving, the prisoners were jumping off into the cold, damp shadows of the plant building. Hugging their shoulders and stamping out the stiffness of the ride, they formed a short, ragged line in front of the building.

They were his men now. Mose had spent the last month showing the first batch of his prisoners of war how to herd turkeys out of trucks and down the loading chutes, how to cull the biggest birds off into wire pens, how to push the flocks ahead of them with long barbed poles and lengths of rope they whipped around behind the birds. He did his best to explain to the Germans, hour after hour, the USDA films on every phase of turkey processing, while an army sergeant named Hormel, from the

10th Services Command, provided a shaky and pretty much senseless translation.

The only real progress he had made was by showing them himself. Mose demonstrated how to hang the live, fattened turkeys on a moving line of steel clips overhead, fastening them by their big red feet. An older prisoner kept watch on that upside-down parade of white-feathered turkeys, most of them dead quiet but some gobbling like hell and beating their wings in violent explosions. Then, one by one, they were pulled through the electric-shock machine.

Just down from the electric shock, two prisoners were positioned on a low platform. Wearing glass face masks and oilcloth rain slickers, they reached small knives up into that line of stunned white turkeys carried along on the mechanized track, wings still, beaks opening and closing in reflex. They neatly sliced each bald blue throat just under the crop.

The birds were then pulled through the revolving rubber fingers and the high-pressure blast of the steam plucking machine, which loudly pounded away. Inside it they were scalded, bled out, washed down. Stripped-bald carcasses streamed out of its vaporous mouth in a continuous line like a bleeding laundry hung out to dry. Then they were carried on the track through a wide steel chute to the gutting and butchering and packing stations, where Dale Rynning was in charge.

Dale was a huge man of Norwegian descent, powerful enough to have pulled a one-bottomed plow around his father's field to prove, literally, he was as strong as a mule. His hands were incredibly large, his knife handles refashioned with wrappings of butcher's string so they were thick enough for his grip. He stood like a massive tree trunk, his arms seeming to reach out over everything in the butchering rooms. From the gutting stations, the hanging carcasses were dragged through the chill-down tank, a cold-water bath that soon became a whirling fecal soup. Sometimes Dale would reach his big arms into the

deep steel trough up to his shoulders and grab loose birds
that had fallen off their hangers or were gumming up the
works. Or when the tank had to be repaired, Dale would
lean his chest up against it, steady himself, grunt, strain,
and shove it off its mountings. Nobody questioned him.
Nobody got in his way. In the green-tiled, brightly lit
gutting and butchering rooms, the crew under Dale's
charge always worked with a steady rhythm, their knives
flashing with quick execution, slabs of turkey flopping
off the bones like wet rags on the tables. Dressed in white
caps and smocks, Dale's crew looked like a team of
blood-spattered surgeons.

The first prisoners assigned to butchering alongside
Dale and his crew were inexperienced, and he didn't have
much patience or ability to explain the work. Also, he
was waiting to hear what his union, the Amalgamated
Brotherhood of Butchers and Meatworkers, with its headquarters in Chicago, thought about its members working
side by side with German soldiers, men who a few short
months before were firing their rifles someplace in Africa, others just like them right now maybe even killing
boys from this town. Besides, how could the union go
for a new benefits contract when those nearly free Nazi
scabs were being shipped in by the trainload?

All forty-two of the union members left in town were
waiting for an answer from headquarters in Chicago. In
the meantime, Dale might have to work alongside the
prisoners but he wasn't about to show them the trade. He
left them bewildered, on their own, mostly, hardly knowing what to do or assigned to the dirtiest jobs in the plant.
Some sliced open the neck and ass ends of turkeys as the
birds tracked along on the slaughtering line. Others had
the job of reaching into the deep, slick cavities and pulling down the guts, two men beside them cutting loose
the gizzards, hearts, and livers and slopping the rest into
big metal drums. Dale showed his prisoners their jobs
only once. Then he spoke to them only to tell them to
get out of his way in a kind of guttural Norwegian that

anybody could understand. He kept the few union workers still left on his crew set apart at their own stations,
mostly boning out the breasts or wrapping whole turkeys
for the cold storage. In a crude, handwritten memo, as
an official union grievance to Buster Hill, Dale demanded
that "all good American-born patriots" be provided with
their own separate tables in the company lunchroom.

The three dozen prisoners assigned to the Nowell-
Safebuy that spring were from the first shipment of them
to arrive in the county. No one, including the U.S. Army,
could say how many more of them might be sent. But
there they were, Germans, the enemy, six of them on
Dale's butchering crew, men who had served as the most
efficiently trained killers in the world just several short
weeks ago. After only a boat ride, a train ride, and a
change into baggy uniforms with the letters POW painted
across their backs, it seemed like insanity that anyone
would put knives in their hands.

An army guard was posted near the gutting and butchering stations for the first few weeks. But it was soon
clear that he wasn't needed. The prisoners could hardly
manage the physical effort of the work itself. Almost all
of them were shattered men, moving slowly in a hunched-
over posture of defeat. They rarely talked, even to each
other, in their low German voices. Whenever they were
given instructions in English, they nodded their heads as
if they understood, at the same time offering polite, taut
smiles or shell-shocked stares of incomprehension. They
were terribly skinny from the past two years in which
they had fought back and forth and back again across
thousands of miles of desert, sometimes eating only by
capturing supplies from the English ahead of them and
later from the Italians retreating in blind disorder behind
them. Their teeth were still falling out, their bodies were
still pocked with scurvy sores. Most of them were from
units that had been abandoned on the southern flank with
nothing but salt water to drink, until they were finally
rounded up half dead, then made to march over the hell-

ish wastes toward Benghazi, many of their fellow prisoners dropping of sunstroke on the way. After quick processing and an ocean voyage on returning Liberty ships, told almost nothing about what was happening to them, they were sorted out and loaded onto trains in Virginia. The next thing they knew, they were unloaded at their remote camp in Wovoka County, near Belle Fourche. They sometimes gathered along the wire at the Nowell-Safebuy, looking out across the immense prairie that surrounded the town, their faces dazed and uncertain, still not sure where they had really landed.

When he saw how slowly the prisoners worked at their jobs, Mose Johnson stepped in. "Listen now," he said. "The only way a man can stand this kind of work hours on end is to make it automatic . . . *automatisch*."

A prisoner named Keller sometimes helped with translation. Keller was strangely young-looking among the rest of the prisoners, most of whom seemed prematurely aged. From a distance, Keller hardly appeared old enough to be a soldier. Up close, one saw he had been wounded, his milky blue, boyish eyes oddly incongruous to his nose, which was mashed over to one side of his face. Keller was eagerly struggling with his English, trying to help, but it was hard for him—the boy had a sad yet comical look when he spoke, his nose still healing and raw-looking, like a misshapen cull potato, and under it, a stark red scar splitting his upper lip on one side of his mouth. It must have hurt him to speak, whether in English or in German. His German was also different from the kind the others spoke—a form of dialect, he told Mose, called Schwäbisch, which came more out of the throat, his Adam's apple bobbing up and down with glottal, wide-open sounds—and filled with expressions that sometimes made the other prisoners laugh. But he was a willing, steady talker, knew English better than the rest, and it was clear the others all respected Keller, looking to him to find out what to do. Mose stood by, listening to Keller struggle with explanations to the men. "Like a machine,'' Mose continued. He picked up a turkey and used his knife in demonstration. ''*Zu-fassen* . . . and, ah, *zu-schneiden, schnell* . . . ah, *wie Maschine. Nicht war?* Got it? And, ah . . . Keller?''

Mainly with gestures, Mose helped Keller explain to the men that by making their work precise and automatic, they would greatly reduce the risk of losing their fingers. He showed them the white scars on his own hands, and his left thumb with one end of it missing. ''A man has to learn to take pride in his speed at this job,'' he said. ''At just how quick and sure he can work his hands. Here. All there is to it are five neat tricks with the knife. . . .''

Mose showed them how. But the jobs on the line were difficult and strenuous. It was possible to tell simply by the way a man's shoulders looked if he was a veteran at working turkeys. After ten years of hefting twenty pounds of bird with one hand and handling the knife with the other, a man would have a shoulder about twice its normal size, while the dampness and alternating heat and cold of the slaughtering line would freeze it arthritically up around the ear. This made the other arm, which worked the knife, seem longer, while it went numb from tendonitis. After about ten years on the line, most men couldn't close their nerve-deadened fingers into a fist. Like the other old-timers, Dale Rynning stood a little cockeyed and had a handshake that felt like a big cold fish. The best Mose could say of Dale was that he had never seen a man as fast at taking meat off the bones.

Down the line from the butchering stations was the canning room. Mose taught his prisoners there to be alert for defective or misaligned tin cans, which could shatter and fly off the machines like razor blades, whizzing through the air with enough force to take small chunks out of the concrete walls. A seasoned-looking noncom named Wenzel was chosen for the job of watching for bent cans on the conveyor belts. Feldwebel Wenzel focused on the monotonous rows of advancing tin cylinders with the same intense concentration he had recently used to train his rangefinder for the antiaircraft guns he had aimed at enemy warplanes. Mose checked on the sergeant hourly, passing him gum and candy and giving him a minute's rest from the canning line.

Out on the loading docks, Mose taught the small gang of prisoners to lift two heavy boxes instead of one by using the strength in their legs. He kept after them until his chain of busted-up and still pitifully thin prisoners was steadily packing carton after carton of canned and frozen turkeys into the railroad cars.

Mose was responsible, then, for the entire processing line. He made an effort to keep up his humor, as long as his prisoners worked at a regular speed, to shift the men around a little to cut down the monotony, and to give a little extra break time to the harder-working crews. Sometimes he even passed them candy, gum, and such, or a funny postcard or a pinup cut out of a movie magazine to take back to their camp. The pinups were popular among the men, and Mose used them as a kind of incentive. Throughout the morning, he would show the pinup around to all his crews, joking a little with them and pointing out the low-cut swimsuit and maybe saying, "Betty Grable"; or the brief, suggestive sarong on a beautiful, smoky body: "Dorothy Lamour"; or the nightgown-clad "Rita Hayworth," gesturing to them in the shared, universal language of male admiration. At the end of the day, he awarded the pinup to the prisoner he judged the hardest worker. He felt a real satisfaction watching the man showing off his prize to his buddies. Except for the stations Dale Rynning bossed, Mose noted the speed of plant production slowly picking up.

He was proud of the way he treated his prisoners, giving them time for a smoke or to take a decent shit break when they needed one. He even extended the noon meal a good ten minutes when he thought his prisoners had been working especially hard. Beatrice Ott and the women's auxiliary from the Church of Christ Reformed, who supplied the company lunch, tried to make the government rations into a fine meal—generous helpings of beans and spuds, the meat not always turkey.

But there were also his problem days. A machine suddenly busted a chain or blew a valve. Or maybe some of the prisoners simply weren't working enough to keep the line up to speed, the pounding monotony of the slaughtering and packing getting to them. Fistfights and minor scufflings would break out among his prisoner crews for mysterious reasons, German reasons Mose hadn't the slightest idea of and that caused a sudden shutdown. Then he pressed his crew hard to speed up the work when the line began to move again. Waving his stockpole like the avenging Nimrod, he was everywhere at once, shouting, *"Weiter machen! Weiter machen!"* in his strangely drawled German. *"Was ist los hier? Was ist los? Weiter machen!"*

Mose was telling them to keep on going, keep on moving that turkey, hour after hour, day after day and without breaks sometimes, because he couldn't rest himself unless the Nowell-Safebuy plant was producing a continuous flow of frozen birds or canned turkey into the railroad cars. There were days when Mose worked himself so hard that he felt on the verge of dropping to his knees like a collapsing athlete, wanting to close his eyes and fall into the darkness of total exhaustion. And if he hardly slept at night these days, well, he wasn't going to notice. Not now. Not the way the war was going. Exhausted as he was, he was going to work and work and work as though lives somewhere depended on it. He hadn't labored so hard or with such purpose since he had given up on farming. There was something else, too, that went along with the importance of his new production manager's job. Suddenly aware of his own example if only to his own small corner of this world, he swore he was going to be horse strong, bull tough and hog smart hour after hour, day in, day out. There was a war on. He was doing his part. So Mose kept at it well into the night, long after his prisoners of war had been trucked off back to their camp.

Mose cleaned off his boot soles on the welded row of horseshoes outside the Cove Café and came in through the door as quietly as he could. It seemed all the voices suddenly dropped. He felt watched from everywhere in the room. Even the few farmers in there lowered their heads and hunkered down in their booths, and the women—Carol McCann, Anita Foos, Mary Wasiolek, that Hogan girl and her little friend Rae—all of them quieted down. It was like everyone was suddenly listening more closely to the crackling war reports that filtered through the radio at the Cove, news that was on everyone's lips these days, their main conversation.

A storm of battles was following the invasion of Sicily. Japs were sneaking out of Guadalcanal by night and their ships were taking a pounding at a place called the Savo slot. MacArthur was pushing ahead with heavy losses through the jungles of New Guinea. The women especially listened up to the news, their faces set tensely, their eyes staring off with a sad, glazed look as if they feared their men had already died.

Mose tipped his hat to the ladies. They nodded at him in a friendly but distant way. More distant, he thought, since he had been kicked up into management. He sat down at the counter, his back to Dale and the other union workers, who were at tables along the big window. They began again in low voices. Mose hardly had to listen to know what they were saying.

"We been ordered to put up with this deal and we're swallowing it whole," said Dale Rynning. "Well, we may have to work right alongside them. Nothing to say about that. But damnit, it just ain't right. We still don't know just who and how much somebody's getting paid!"

"The company's got itself one corker of a deal," Irwin St. Louis was saying now. "They're shipping 'em in here like cattle. They're out to bust this union with them, that's what I say!"

"I don't see how we even need them," said Bruce McGovern, the cold-storage foreman, who should have retired the past Christmas. "Our women could be working in there. There's women working all over this country. Ain't a single one of us couldn't use the extra money, either. . . ."

"And what's going to happen to our goddamn overtime?" Dale broke in.

Mose had heard enough. He turned around and cut them off with a loud, open-handed slap on the counter.

"You all got plenty of overtime and you know it! As much as you can stand!" Mose let that fact sink in for a moment. Most of the men were finishing quick coffees and a fast supper before an extra evening shift. "That ain't the issue anyhow. Those prisoners are here because of orders from Washington. And look what you're doing. Our boys is dying overseas right this minute, and you sit there griping about your overtime!"

"We can't even talk to you, Mose," Dale said. "The fact is, Buster Hill is out to bust this union, and you sit there talking like some voice in a newsreel. C'mon, boys. He's crossed over. No sense dealing with this company man unless it's at a grievance meeting.'' Dale slowly raised his huge body out of his chair, left money on the table, and slammed out the door into the street, the others gradually following him.

Mose turned back to face the counter and took a few deep breaths to get a hold on his nerves. Mrs. Nilsen came over then, and Mose ordered the quick supper special that meatless Monday—some kind of noodles with cheese sauce and a bread-crumb crust. He drank his coffee. Then he swiveled around on his stool and said toward the booths in back, ''Well, hey there, girls, let's get on some music! Come on now. . . .''

He emptied his pocket of change and motioned to Carol McCann, who was always the first to take him up on his offer. She was a big, pretty girl about busting out of her work clothes. Carol seemed to be the leader of the flock of girls, with Anita Foos a few steps behind her on her way to the jukebox. Mose watched Carol plugging nickels into the slot, the other girls gathering around her, helping her pick out the songs. There was something high-strung and hungry about Carol; sometimes she grabbed on to Mose's arm and led him to the jukebox to help her make her selections. Also, he would catch her looking him over behind his back. So why me? Mose kept thinking. Still, he had a feeling that girl wanted to jump on a man like a dog jumps on a bone, as the old song put it. And Mose liked her, the way she chattered on to him about the chores of her day. She was all alone out there, raising turkeys on her family's home-place, and she would ask Mose's advice about feed balance, weight gains, maybe a new disinfectant for her turkey pens, while they stood together watching the mechanical arm in that glassed-in music factory weirdly moving along over the black files of records until it snapped one up and dropped it home. That girl made him feel . . .

Not once in the eleven years since his wife, Adelle,

had up and left him on his farm, not once in all those
years had he felt so stirred up by a woman. Tonight,
when Carol picked up his change and turned her hearty
young smile at him, he felt like a Black Hills pine long
ago gone brown that suddenly shoots out all over with
green. He watched her coming back from the jukebox
with the other girls, all laughing together as though they
were sharing a secret. Maybe it was all a joke on him,
he thought. Mose reminded himself about Carol. Her
husband, Jody, was out there somewhere in the Pacific.
Catching himself thinking about Carol in that way made
him feel deep in the worst kind of sin, Jody over there
fighting and Mose back here getting all heated up despite
himself about his wife. He just wasn't that kind of man,
never would be. Men like that deserved the wrath of God,
their cattle laid waste, their vineyards barren of any
fruit. But maybe something else was going on with her.
Every time Mose mentioned Jody, even just in passing,
there was a quick way Carol looked toward the door of
the Cove as if she could already see the poor man's ghost.

Song after song played on. There were two different
kinds of selections on the jukebox. Jimmie Rodgers and
his famous, "Will There Be Any Freight Trains in
Heaven?" The good old Carter family, always popular.
Gene Autry's "Poor Lonesome Cowboy," and the fine
dark voice of Roy Acuff singing out "The Great Speckled
Bird." Mose liked those songs the best, that music of
crying fiddles and wailing steel guitars which rang out
through the fuzzy speakers of the Cove's worn-out jukebox, young Jimmie yodeling high and sad and sweetly
about his lonely railroad blues, or the great Buddy Jones
singing "She's Sellin' What She Used to Give Away."
But the girls preferred the other kinds of songs, the Artie
Shaw band belting out "My Blue Sky," and Ziggy El-
man's spunky "Zaggin' with Zig." Carol McCann would
punch out the buttons for the nearly worn smooth grooves
of Cole Porter's "Just One of Those Things" or the
Jimmy Dorsey band's "I'm Glad There Is You." All the

girls had memorized the words to that one and sang along. Sometimes Mose might even be pulled into a slow, shuffling imitation of a dance with Carol or Anita, friendly and fatherly, as he had come to think of that dancing. Then there came the moment when he let Carol go with a little laugh and a brotherly arm around her shoulders after she maybe pressed too tightly against him. He would escort Carol back to her booth, tip his hat at the girls, say his thanks, and, feeling worlds better, scoot back up onto his stool at the counter where his supper was steaming.

Usually, Doc Monahan came in about then, after long hours spent running here and there all over the county. He was also putting in two extra shifts a week at the hospital in Belle Fourche, because of the doctor shortage. The Doc barely had time to slosh down two cups of strong black coffee before he checked the clock on the wall and ran out again, already late for somebody else. But when he had a few minutes, he generally sat at the counter over his supper and talked to Mose. What the Doc mainly talked about was money.

"I could have set up a practice anywhere and I'd have been a rich man by now," the Doc said. "Now look at me. Somebody's going to have to loan me two dollars for that gas tank out there. Or trade me for gas coupons. Here. I got plenty of those. A stack as thick as a pinochle deck. But what the hell good are they without the greenbacks?" he said. "Seems like everybody's waiting until harvest to pay me. I got so many bills for that office and that damned X-ray machine that I figure I've put out all the cash I earned in the last two months this week alone." The Doc drank his coffee quickly and signaled Mrs. Nilsen for a refill, already grabbing up his hat and bag off the counter. "Once this war's over, I swear I'm going to quit. Flat out," he said. "Maybe go to Florida. Or California. Sunshine. Sit on a beach somewhere."

"I know just how you feel," Mose said that evening. He pulled a fat roll of bills out of his jeans and peeled

off a few, which Doc Monahan stuffed carelessly into a
pocket of his baggy dark-blue suit. The Doc nodded once
at Mose, a little guiltily, trying to pass him a couple of
gas coupons under the counter as if they were some kind
of payoff. "Don't worry about it," said Mose. "One of
these days I'll come in and you can take care of that darn
bunion of mine."

"No thanks," the Doc said. "You let it go so long by
now, I'd probably have to cut off your whole damned
foot. My advice is to get out of those sharp-toed cowboy
boots for once. Get yourself some decent shoes. Those
things are ruining feet all over this country!"

The Doc was out the door in a hurry, on his way pock-
eting a handful of cigars from Mrs. Nilsen's Dutch Mas-
ters box under the cash register. Mose watched him leave,
thinking how things used to be when the two of them had
the time to play a game of checkers in a booth in back,
and Charley Gooch and some of the range boys might
join them for a few hands of poker or even whist. Or the
Doc and Mose would share a piece of pie and talk quietly
about Adelle, the Doc strongly advising him to give up
on her memory and start a new life.

The Doc had been a friend to them both after Mose
had married her and moved her out to his farm. Adelle
was so pretty back then. The sun was like a crown in her
hair, the moon laid out at her feet, as some old song put
it. That's the way he saw her then and still saw her, no
matter what had happened. The Doc regularly dropped
in at their little wheat farm when he was out on his
rounds. Just to look at Adelle, he said, made him feel
hopeful again after all the suffering he had seen that day.
A lot of people came visiting just to look at her. Mose
had been proud of the way other men used to treat him
when Adelle was around, like he was a king, a man of
uncountable riches.

The Doc always turned up unexpectedly, two and three
times a week, but the one time they really needed him
he had arrived too late. Adelle had come down with

pneumonia. She was so far gone by the time he got there that he and Mose loaded her into the Doc's big Chrysler and drove her off immediately to the hospital in Belle Fourche. She recovered in a few weeks. But Mose had always been sure it was the fevers, the way she had tossed around, delirious, her pretty little head cooking inside that oxygen tent like in the fires of Babylon. She came out of those fevers a changed woman. That was the way Mose saw it. It wasn't a month before she just up and left him on the farm. She grabbed on to the first traveling salesman that came through town, a man with the Mason shoe company. She even kissed him full on the mouth in front of everybody at the municipal bar, something people had gossiped over but nobody told Mose about until weeks after she had gone. He was the last to know. There was a rumor Adelle was shacked up with that man in a hotel in Cheyenne. By the time Mose heard about it, he figured it was too late. What would he have done anyway? Tracked them down in Cheyenne and maybe beat them both to hash? Or taken up his double-barrel Remington and shot the two of them lying there in sin, then likely do the same to himself? He didn't know what to do. He went about his chores on the farm, lost in grief. His one consolation was reading Hosea, *And she shall follow after her lovers, but she shall not overtake them; and she shall seek them, but shall not find them; then shall she say, I will go and return to my first husband; for then was it better with me than now. . . .*

Better then than now. But he was fooling himself. He always had talked too big a game when it came to Adelle. He had gone to St. Louis to visit a cousin of his and had met her at a charity dance. Then the dinners at her family's—an aunt and uncle in the wholesale dry goods business. Fancy meals over matching English china and monogrammed silverware, he dressed in his Sunday best and his mouth working, working, spinning tales across the table at her like he was the biggest landowner in the state of South Dakota. The fine soil there. The neatly fenced-in hayfields. His cattle. The solid frame house he was planning to build, which would even have a cedar-paneled sewing room just for her on the second floor. He described it all to her over the sweet wine in his crystal glass and in the full heat of his youth and imagination. And she had believed him. West seemed to be where a young man with ambition was aiming. Even for the late-comers, like him, lucky was the woman who went with him and could give him that much cause. They were married in a few weeks, in St. Louis, Mose throwing his money around at the wedding as if there were no tomorrow. When tomorrow finally did come, crates of Adelle's family's furniture and dishes and hope-chest heirlooms given as wedding gifts with them on the train, Mose had even come to believe in that vision himself. They sat together in a second-class seat, her pretty head resting against his shoulder, holding hands. They looked out through the windows at the neatly tilled farms of Iowa, with so many houses and barns and silos passing by and set into that landscape that they seemed like palatial towers in a single huge and well managed plantation of corn. Mose kept pointing out at all that settled prosperity as though to say: See there, I told you so. That's what it's going to be like. . . .

It was a ragged, marginal, small gray rectangle of soil that he owned. People said that even the buffalo had rarely dawdled here on their long migrations into eastern Montana and thicker grass. The nice painted house Mose had described so vividly was still in the planning stages. For now there was what was called a dugout house, a shallow cave he had shoveled out of a small rise in one corner of his dry prairie, then braced with timbers over which he had laid a roof of sod with a single rusting stovepipe shoved up through it. The first time she saw the place, Adelle sat down on one of her big crates of beautiful furniture and cried.

Mose had promised it would be only a year, two at most, before they had all they ever dreamed of. But one

year led to another, four years into five. The season they
maybe did have enough money to do more than get the
dugout partly walled in like a basement and a foundation
started, they took a trip to New Orleans instead. Then
came the winter when it rained more than snowed, the
poor clay soil so soaked with dampness that just poking
a finger into the dirt walls caused water to trickle onto
the floor. The mahogany veneer on the chest of drawers
Adelle had kept polished ever more obsessively began to
turn white in large spreading stains, the glued wood edges
peeling back. Then pneumonia just after Christmas, the
Doc's emergency visit, the hospital, and Adelle was suddenly gone. They hadn't even raised their voices once
during that winter; she hadn't said one angry thing in his
direction suggesting what might happen. One afternoon,
she caught a ride into town with Vera Hogan as though
she might do some badly needed shopping. Then she was
gone, not even saying goodbye.

Mose waited for her to come back, all that winter.
Even though she had given herself to someone else, he
still expected her to come back to him, would have taken
her back without reproach. He wrote a letter to Adelle's
aunt and uncle in St. Louis, saying as much, counting
on her to end up there with them. A reply came that her
family was shocked she had left him and were worrying
now because they had no news. Mose read Corinthians,
Hosea, long passages of the New Testament. If the Lord
could take such women back in forgiveness, who was he
to say no? But as week after week passed that winter, the
doors to his hopes stayed closed. By the time the weather
finally broke, it brought the end of hoping and of farming
for him. He started praying that her vines would go bare,
her mirth be taken from her. In a fury, one night he even
kicked Adelle's mongrel dog out of the house. It was a
dog she had doted on like a child. Half terrier and half
dachshund, it was the ugliest whining mutt he had ever
seen. When it kept scratching at the door to his dugout
that night, Mose finally took down his shotgun, kicked

the door open, and blew it apart. He tossed the pieces into a ditch behind the house and left them unburied. He had nothing but hatred for his land from then on, not able to look at its soil in his hands without seeing the seeds of some vile whoredom in it. He cursed his farm with his lips and with his deeds. All he wanted was to get as far as he could from that miserable cold sod house and all the work of trying to make a go of that piece of dry prairie they had once called their own.

He blamed the land itself; damned land, dry land. It was the work of it that had broken her down, hauling water up from the creek, bucket after bucket. She had even once been kicked half to death by his horses. He had carried her up from the little dugout barn, the bones in her pretty back cracked or maybe broken, because she had suffered pain in her back ever since it happened. He saw now how all the hoe handles and manure fork handles he had cut down to fit her were just about worn through from the pressure of her small, girlish hands. Mose was left hollow from that, like a man stuffed with hay, still propped up on his feet but all the spirit gone. And it was the land that had done it. Land that had once been as fetching and pretty to him as a woman. Like any woman, as it plainly said in Ecclesiastes, her heart all snares and nets, the taste of her more bitter than death.

One exceptionally promising day that spring, his winter wheat just poking its bearded heads up out of its stiff green boots, Mose destroyed almost everything. He knocked their pitiful earth house apart with a pickax and crowbars. He splashed kerosene over what remained and tossed in a lit rag, grimly looking on all that night as her few treasured pieces of heirloom furniture and everything else they owned burned down to embers. The next morning, he picked a few things out of the ashes—some charred dishes, a pair of boots that had somehow not been burned, a souvenir ashtray, blackened brass candlesticks—and with only the clothes on his back, he drove off in his Model T in the direction of town.

When Mose started working as a yardman for Buster Hill Turkeys, it wasn't for the money. It was for something to do. Steady work, good work, hard work, to take his mind off things. Later, his job became more than that. He grew interested in the birds themselves, and in helping farmers to weather the Depression years with the cash from selling them. He taught farmers how to breed them and raise them. He was also finding a strong new sense of himself, no longer out there just making a farm like almost everybody he knew but in on the ground floor of an entire industry. He was one of Buster Hill's most important sergeants, holding his own in a business that was fast becoming the lifeblood of the town. So it wasn't for the money. Whenever he had been on his own, it seemed he had always had just enough money. He recalled Reverend Ott preaching once, "Nobody who's a servant of God would ever want to be a millionaire. All that's worth praying for is just enough." Without even praying for it, Mose had more than enough. He got a fair price from Jim Claypool for his farm and bought a little house in town. It was just the kind of painted frame house with a porch in front that he and Adelle had always dreamed of building, cute as a lamb's ear, as she might have put it. He bought that house cheap, and there was enough left over for a bank account besides. He had his job, his house, money, the kind of circumstances he had always imagined would leave him satisfied, maybe more so now that he had been pushed up into management. But none of that was really enough. Eleven years later, it still felt strange to him, knocking around living alone in that storybook house. It was like a cruel joke had been played on them both; as if God had finally given them all they had ever dreamed but only after she was gone.

By midsummer of 1943, turkey production was stretched to its limits. Mose spent week after week in the growing heat of the season driving his town crew and his three dozen prisoners of war double time. After he ate his supper at the Cove, leaving his usual fifty-cent tip on the counter for Mrs. Nilsen and the rest of his change for a few more songs for the girls, he headed off to his small house. He drank a good three fingers out of a fifth of rye he kept in his bedroom, then lay down and rested for four hours of dreamless, tossing sleep. Then he rose again and splashed his face and armpits with cold water over the kitchen sink and changed into fresh work clothes. He stepped out across his neatly whitewashed porch and down its steps into the night.

The nights at least were as cool as a desert after the sun goes down. There was a constant chattering overhead of bats mixing in the darkness, chasing the insects that swarmed around the six bare bulbs of Nowell's municipal lighting system. Mose strolled slowly down the street, breathing in the summer air as much as he could before he entered the brightly lit plant building. There, he put in a slow night's work with Will McCarthy and two of the day-shift workers, all that was left of the Nowell-Safebuy's night maintenance crew. As the new production manager, Mose followed Will around, learning every adjustment, each cog and wheel and pressure gauge of the Nowell-Safebuy plant machinery, which was already breaking down. Sometimes he just stayed at it with screwdrivers and pipe wrenches, laboring alongside Will McCarthy until the sun came up and it would soon be time to start his regular shift all over again. It was all he could do to keep from dropping in his tracks from lack of sleep.

Then a week came when Safebuy executives from California, accountants and bankers from New York, long black cars filled with union bosses from Chicago, were all over this part of the country. War Food Administration officials and military brass came in from Washington too, driven around in official green army cars. Or all of them massed in conference teams with Buster Hill, up at the main plant office. While those bigwigs were off partying in Belle Fourche and Deadwood and even as far away as Rapid City every night, Mose and Will McCarthy were still at work in the plant building, patching and welding the slaughtering line back together again for one more impossible day. The men and machines they had just weren't enough to handle the volume. Worse, it seemed that all that week, Dale Rynning, Irwin St. Louis, Bruce McGovern and the rest of the union boys were intentionally slowing down the line. Turkey trucks were stacking up to the point where they blocked traffic on Main Street. The men were waiting for word from the Chicago officers on what action they should take. While they waited, they were letting the company know just who was boss.

All that week, a resentment steadily built inside Mose like a stoked-up furnace. He found himself cussing out everybody, shouting strings of four-letter English words into the bewildered faces of his prisoner crews. He tossed live turkeys around like sacks of rotten fruit. It seemed to him that nobody cared. In all their days of meetings with Buster Hill, their nights spent running all over the state in their chauffeured limousines, not one of the accountants, the bankers, the company men, the civilian officials or the gold-braid colonels, not even any of the union officers in their double-breasted suits, had done more than take a quick five-minute walk through the plant whose destiny they controlled.

The way Mose saw it, all any of them at the top seemed to care about was money. It was all big deals and high finance and blue-sky talk in cocktail lounges for them. Stock deals, bond deals, floating loans, concessions and kickbacks with the union boys, leasing and pricing manipulations with the railroads—all kinds of deals were made with the sole end of consolidating financial power. All their talk was as if bucks alone were keeping the plant running. Nobody once looked at the truth. Production was so slack and badly run by then that some of our boys overseas were cutting back the lids of C-ration cans and dipping their spoons into a corrupt stinking mash of pressure-cooked turkey guts. Nobody at the top gave one tinker's damn about production anymore.

"That there's my resignation," said Mose. He tossed a sheet of paper with his crudely scrawled statement on it across Buster's desk. "I quit," he said. "War or no war. You can find yourself somebody else to run that circus in there."

"Hang on now," Buster said. "We're getting us a new shipment of prisoners in two weeks . . ."

"It don't matter how many men you get. Not if you don't shut that line down right now for a complete overhaul. With the quality of what we're turning out, it's an act of God we ain't poisoned anybody yet!"

"We got that covered, I promise you," Buster said. "New equipment's on the way. We'll get you a full crew on and then some. And health inspectors. Anything we need. . . ."

"Not me. Not anymore. I just can't go on any longer. Not one minute," Mose said. "That there's my resignation, and that's all I got to say."

"But we're getting in two hundred men! More than a full crew! Almost three thousand prisoners for this one county. Can you imagine? It's like a miracle. Two hundred of them for us. Three hundred or so to work for Great Westward in Belle Fourche and Sturgis. Hundreds more for the Forest Service program in the hills. More than a thousand to help farmers around here work their beets, pick their corn, shock grain and everything else. So help's on the way, I promise you. Think of it, Mose. We're expected to deliver five thousand birds a day by June next year! Every day, five thousand of them." Buster repeated it again: "Five thousand birds." A white cord was pulsing steadily in his wrestler's neck. He was tapping his gold-plated pen, a tiny replica of a pool cue he had won in his youth, tap-tapping it on his desktop. "Five thousand birds," he said again. "That's one hell of a load of turkeys."

"Aw, that's just hogwash. There ain't enough farmers around here even to raise that many birds!"

"They're damn well going to raise them now," Buster said. "We got it all laid out. The War Labor Board, the War Shipping Administration, the Department of Agriculture, the whole plan. Word's going out right this minute. Farmers around here have got the choice of raising either sugar beets or turkeys. They try anything else, and the railroad just won't ship their crops to market. It's that simple. And you're a part of the plan, Mose. We need you now more than ever. We're getting the manpower in, and the new facilities, everything we want. So you just can't walk out on us now. No, sir. Not now. Think about it. Five thousand turkeys a day."

Mose stared off blankly through Buster's office window, calculating how much work that many birds would mean. A hot August wind was blowing up dust from Main Street, the street Buster Hill kept lobbying hard with this town not to pave, to keep taxes down. Grit and sand peppered the big glass panes and clouded over the view like a fog. "I don't know," Mose finally said. "Buster, I just don't know what any of it's about anymore."

"What the hell do you think *I've* been up to all week? Some kind of vacation? Time off? You think I've been dragging them city slickers around all over this damn country for fun?"

"None of that's my concern," said Mose. "All I know is I had a line to keep on moving. And to keep it going with some kind of quality. That's been near impossible so long now I can't even think when it was different. Even our boys in there, even them, they can feel it too. They're as good as on a slowdown right now. And there's nothing I can do about that. Nothing I can do about any of it anymore. . . ."

"But that's all settled! All of it! We been around and around clear to Washington over this. The Chicago boys are telling Dale and the others right now. Jesus, Mose, it's been so damned complicated. Months of mixed-up statements from the USDA, the War Labor Board, the army, the goddamned union. Everybody's been saying something different. And everybody's been screaming at each other over one thing mainly. You know what that is? Do you?"

Mose shook his head. He looked at his resignation, a little rumpled at the edges, sitting on a pile of other papers on Buster's desk. Who had ever bothered to tell him any of this?

"Payment for the prisoners, that's what," Buster said. "Can you believe it? Pay them? Pay *them*? Cash money for captured soldiers of the enemy? Hell, the union's been demanding all along that they be allowed to sign every prisoner on! Give them apprenticeship cards, full-scale wages, all the new benefits packages they've been shouting about—everything but voting rights!"

"The union did that?" He tried to think if Dale or anyone had so much as hinted at that kind of demand, and decided not.

"Hell yes they did! We had to threaten a national press scandal if the War Labor Board let them get away with it, too. You know what I'm saying? Look who's working your job on the home front, G.I. Joe. Take a gander at just who's pulling down your paycheck while you're eating mud and dodging bullets in some foxhole. So they finally gave in. Any regular union member gets to bump a prisoner out of his job anytime. They get a guarantee of no layoffs for the duration. And though we can't legally give them a pay hike, they pushed through a whole new package they're calling 'benefits,' fourteen cents an hour extra we pay into a new kind of pension fund. Then a full health-care package on top of that. That's what the unions are fighting for and getting all over this country, with wages frozen. So they got just about everything they wanted but that we have to pay our damn prisoners like they were members. It was Major Pierce, the officer who's going to run the new camp the army's tossing up—it was the major who finally got the union to compromise on just how much we *are* going to pay prisoners. He got everybody to agree to paying them just exactly the same wages earned by our own army privates, somewhere around twenty-one dollars a month. Token payment. Shelled out direct to the major's camp to help pay expenses. So a lot of that money's bound to be spent right here. We're going to see a good share of that cash right back in our pockets. A stroke of goddamn genius, if you ask me," Buster said. "What do you think? Ain't it a stroke of genius? Don't you think two hundred new men could get that line off its crutches in there?"

Mose didn't answer for a long time. He found himself looking at the caked bits of feathers and turkey manure on his boots, which had flaked off onto Buster's new orange carpeting. "So we're paying for them now," he finally said. "We're actually going to put cash in their hands."

"Damn straight we are," Buster said. "Top to bottom. Signed and sealed in Washington. Just what we need to pull this company out of the fire. Major Pierce is on his way to Virginia right now to take his prisoners off the boats. He's even including enemy officers in on the deal. The plan is to get them to help organize a more effective work force. So that'll be pressure taken off you, Mose. We might even be able to see our way through to some time off for you. Some kind of vacation. You need it. You look like hell. So all you got to do is hang in there with us just a few more weeks, I promise you. Just a couple more weeks and you'll get some time off and be back to us feeling like a new man. We need you, damnit. Things here couldn't be worse than what's happening now," Buster said. "We're going to miss our quotas again this month. We got the War Food Administration seriously on our ass. It's all we can do to keep the damn Democrats in Congress from putting this company straight out of existence. . . ."

"You can only push men so hard. Then you've got to let up on them," Mose said.

"Right now, letting up on them ain't good enough. Not for me. Not for this company."

Mose nodded his head once at that fact.

"It's our quotas, Mose. We're in it too far to get out now. Our government contracts . . ."

Mose began to imagine five thousand birds a day run through the Nowell-Safebuy plant. He wasn't sure the turkey yards could even handle the unloading of that many birds. The slaughtering line itself would probably have to double in size. Who in the world could manage all of that? Just the thought of it made him want to head straight down the street to the municipal bar and drink himself senseless.

"Jesus, Buster, how are we ever going to manage so many?" Mose asked, breaking a nervous silence in which

Buster seemed to be carefully gauging him from the boots up. "None of those prisoners are professionals. It's darn hard to break them in when they ain't had the experience. Then to think of all the problems with just showing things to them . . ."

Mose stopped talking. There was a new concentration about Buster that let him know the boss was already off on other concerns. Somehow, like an Arab trader, Buster had gotten just exactly what he wanted out of him without Mose knowing when. Buster's attention had already turned to his stacks of paperwork, putting his pool-cue pen to them. He would be hardly listening to anything more his production manager might have to say. One of his beefy hands picked up the resignation letter and held it casually out across the desk. Awkwardly, Mose stood up and reached for it, taking it and crumpling it in his fist. He stood that way for a long time, as though waiting for Buster to say something more. Buster continued shuffling through other business, reading the scattered papers on his desk as if Mose were no longer there. "Five thousand birds a day," Mose said finally, with amazement. "Five thousand birds . . ."

Six weeks later, a whole fleet of army trucks full of prisoners roared in alongside the plant building. The prisoners hung out over the olive-green trucksides, thin khaki jackets buttoned to the neck against the early-morning chill. Before the trucks had stopped moving, the prisoners were jumping off into the dawn shadows that fell over the turkey yards. They formed themselves into ragged lines in front of the building.

"Achtung! Steigen Sie aus!" Mose ordered, even though most of the prisoners were out of the trucks already. He barked it out once more, striding off down the line as though inspecting his crew. He stopped in front of young Keller, whom he had promoted to a "rover," a worker who ranged up and down the slaughtering line and jumped in on a job whenever he was needed. Keller was also still helping Mose with his German, and was every day more indispensable to him. He waited there for Keller's shaved bobbing head to finish politely nodding. Grinning lopsidedly, Keller said, *Ja, ja,* Mose was

getting it right this morning; even the accent was sounding better. Mose paced up and back, watching the last of the prisoners climb down out of the trucks as the small team of army guards gathered together in a disorderly way. The guards all looked as though they were commiserating with each other through the pain of a collective hangover. Mose tried his newest line, one about not trying to escape. *"Jeder Versuch zu ausbrechen will furchtlos sein!"*

"Jeder Versuch aus-zu-brechen," Keller politely corrected him, *"wird fruchtlos sein."*

"Je-der Ver-such aus-zu-brech-en wird frucht-los sein," Mose slowly drawled in his Missouri River German. A few shaved heads of the enemy began to nod at him jokingly in approval. Mose spun around on his high cowboy heels. He stood there for a moment as if breathing in the sight of his new men. His first full crew. Hundreds of them.

Some mornings, that was all there was to the routine—a few practiced phrases from Mose, the once-over head count by the guards, then his prisoners formed up into their gangs and dispersed to their jobs. But other mornings, Mose had to wait for the last of them to climb down from the lead truck. It was always the same man, an officer. As Mose waited, his prisoners shuffled around, at ease in the cool, almost chilly shadows of the plant building, no matter how many orders he practiced on them.

Hauptmann Hartmut von Ujatz looked almost like the other prisoners, almost as young as most of them, except that he was already gray, and his dark-brown work boots still had a factory polish on them. The Hauptmann stood in the truck a long time, conspicuously, as though he were forming up his Panzergrenadiers for one more assault under heavy fire across the rocky sea of the Libyan desert. His head turned stiffly, his eyes taking in each of his men. Without a word, the Hauptmann stepped down out of the truck. It seemed that at the exact instant his boots landed in the dust, the lines of prisoners snapped to attention. The Hauptmann didn't join in formation with the rest of them. Instead, he clasped his hands behind his back. The Hauptmann stretched his legs a minute, walking stiffly in a small, casual circle, then he selected his place on the running board of the truck and sat down for a moment like a king on his throne.

The Hauptmann was tall, painfully thin, square-shouldered, his face sunburned and unpleasant-looking, as if he had just taken in a noseful of something distasteful. Whenever Mose said even a few words to him, the Hauptmann refused to answer directly. He insisted on speaking through his orderly, a noncommissioned officer named Gruenwald, who followed him wherever he went. Gruenwald clicked his heels and gave a smart little bow toward Mose. The orderly answered any of Mose's questions or pleasantries of the day in perfect British English, not even bothering to translate anything that was said for his Hauptmann. Gruenwald accepted cigarettes, candy, or gum on the Hauptmann's behalf, the officer's attention always off somewhere, as if nothing Mose could say was his concern. "My Hauptmann has been assigned here as an observer," Gruenwald had explained the first day. "According to the rules of his internment, he may refuse to have communication with anyone other than on an official and military basis. He wishes me to thank you on his behalf for your generous attentions. He asks only that he be left alone. Such are his orders. But I am here, at your service whenever needed, you see, in case any sticky business should come up."

Most of the week, the Hauptmann was off observing the other prisoner crews, the ones at the Great Westward Sugar refinery and on the farms. Mose heard that he acted about the same to everyone. The mornings the Hauptmann decided to appear at the Nowell-Safebuy, that was the way it proved to be. Rules were rules, but Mose still thought it was strange that when he politely approached the Hauptmann, tipping his hat at him and trying to say hello and such, the man merely dismissed him with an irritated look and a hand gesture like someone waving away flies. Each time, Gruenwald quickly appeared and stated again that his Hauptmann wished only to be left alone.

Mose would feel at his right hip, where a heavy, army-issue .45 in its button-flap holster rode clumsily against the bone. The pistol was part of the new security plan required by Major Pierce, since there were now more German soldiers with knives in their hands at the Nowell-Safebuy than there were able-bodied men left in the whole town. But the gun only made Mose feel doubly nervous. What use would seven bullets be if those prisoners really did decide to rise up or escape?

Each morning, Mose stood in front of the gangs of his prisoners and listened to the sounds of the plant machinery gearing up. Dale Rynning and the union boys, all of them with new titles now, like "foreman" and "team leader," and paid accordingly, were usually already at work inside the building, clearing their stations for action. The dozen army guards began to file down the lines of men, gazing sleepily at each prisoner number, then checking it off on their clipboards. This process took at least fifteen minutes. The guards were part of Major Harry Simpson Pierce's skeletal force from the 10th Services Command. They didn't look at all like soldiers. Shirttails out, puttees flapping at their boots, most of them seemed as if their only function in the war was smoking cigarettes. The oldest of them, Sergeant Hormel, was ancient, assigned there because he spoke a kind of broken German from his youth in Milwaukee. The way Mose saw it, the day after Pearl Harbor, the U.S. Army had probably shipped these soldiers just as far from the front as it could get them. He had to stand by impatiently in front of his hundreds of milling prisoners, watching the guards count and miscount each morning, wasting the war effort's precious time.

Finally, one of the guards would shuffle over to Mose

with the clipboards. Mose signed his name to the daily
lists. Then, give or take a dozen or so, two hundred prisoners of war were left to his exclusive charge for the
shift. Most of the guards strolled away to their card games
at the tables in the company lunchroom. Others went
back to the fleet of grain trucks that pulled out of the
turkey yards, rumbling off to the Orman Camp to pick
up new loads of prisoners assigned to labor in the surrounding grain and sugar beet fields.

The prisoner gangs formed up and moved off to their
jobs. Mose would feel more at ease. But he sometimes
wondered whether, if any emergency really did happen,
the company lunchroom was close enough that a loud
shout or a gunshot could bring the guards running from
their cards in time. But given the kinds of soldiers they
were, maybe everybody was better off with them out of
the way. And what real need was there for guards? Where
was there to escape to but the thousands of acres of beet,
grain, and turkey farms that surrounded the town for more
than thirty miles? Though it wasn't true, prisoners of war
at the Orman Camp had been strongly briefed that local
citizens would recognize prisoner haircuts and uniforms
and as likely shoot escapees on sight as run them in.
Beyond the farms, to the north, east, and west, there
were literally hundreds of miles of next to nothing—most
of it rolling dry-grass prairie, some of it like the Bad-
lands, where even range animals had trouble surviving.
To the south lay the Black Hills, in those days mostly
wilderness. An escaped prisoner might manage to sur-
vive until winter there or with lots of luck find means to
the distant Mexican border. It was like once they had
landed here, they were penned up on a tiny island in the
middle of this country, a lonely and isolated place of
several hundred farms and a few thousand people, surrounded by an immense ocean of grass. Where could
they possibly get to from here? How could any of them
be fool enough to think of escape? But there wasn't so
much as a rumor of escape from Major Pierce's intelli-

gence staff at the Orman Camp. The war was over for these men, who were dazed, broken, defeated, humbled. It was enough for most of them just to be physically recovering from the deprivations they had suffered. Still, they were soldiers. They did what they were told.

That autumn was one of the most chaotic Mose could remember, a few short weeks on which it seemed the whole future of operations depended. On the radio, in the newspapers, and in the weekly newsreels shown one night only as they passed through on the Jack Rabbit Bus Line, it seemed the same kind of disorder was happening overseas. A month before, though considered a victory, the campaign in Sicily had allowed thousands of German soldiers to escape across the Strait of Messina. Allied troops invading the beaches at Salerno and the Volturno River were soon bogged down. The Eighth Air Force lost 60 B-17s and their entire crews in a single disastrous raid over Schweinfurt, deep inside Germany, climaxing a week in which 148 planes were lost. A few weeks later, the 2nd Marine Division was taking a thousand casualties a day, fighting inch by inch for a palm-covered island called Tarawa, a chunk of real estate no bigger in size than an average turkey farm. It was soon clear enough what was happening. Yellow telegrams with word of the dead and wounded were arriving at front doors all over the county.

While the pace of battle was picking up everywhere overseas, the three thousand German prisoners, most of them a mere few weeks after being captured, had been shipped into Wovoka County, arriving in fancy Pullman railroad cars complete with Negro porters serving their meals. The crews of prisoners were organized into groups that worked at the Great Westward Sugar refineries, at Nowell-Safebuy Turkeys, for the U.S. Forest Service in the Black Hills, and on the hundreds of small farms that surrounded Nowell. Meanwhile, other crews of prisoners were involved in a frantic race against the coming winter to toss up the buildings of what amounted to a whole new town called the Orman Camp.

The camp soon grew more populous than Belle Fourche, the county seat. It consisted of about 150 plywood-and-tar-paper barracks, each holding about twenty men and heated by a big coal stove at its center. The black shabby buildings were laid out in parade formation across a piece of prime bottomland along the Belle Fourche River and surrounded by a roof-high barbed-wire fence with the strands set so far apart that any maverick calf could have easily crawled through. There were guards' quarters set at even distances around the perimeter but no towers, no fixed machine guns, not even dogs to raise an alarm; the guardhouses were just a bunch of wood-and-tar-paper shacks at the wire's edge, in which the guards lived just slightly better, and in time worse, than their prisoners.

At the Orman Camp, it was soon evident that these Germans knew how to work, and how to make do with whatever they had. Even before winter came, large vegetable gardens around each building were laid out, plowed, the soil sifted with German precision. At the center of the camp, the prisoners built a larger, all-wood building, which served as the camp store and the PX for Major Pierce's guards, and in time it was packed with more goods than the town grocery had seen in years. Next to the store was a large canvas tent with a wooden floor, which the prisoners had stitched together to serve as a huge beer hall, a movie theater, and on Sundays as their church. Just behind it squatted a small metal building that was a post office and camp hospital, the American flag flying on a stocky lodgepole off to one side. During that first prairie winter of blizzards and subzero temperatures, further plans were made by the prisoners. In the spring, a little branch of the Belle Fourche River was dredged almost overnight by the work of thousands of shovels, then dammed to make a large, deep swimming pond. Behind the pond, the prisoners marked out an area that they sod-busted, plowed, leveled, then seeded to grass, all done with hand tools. When the grass camp up, they ran ruler-straight lines of lime that marked out an area about the size of a small cornfield, then set up two white rectangles at either end. It was the first soccer field in this part of the state. The local sports until then were rodeo, baseball, basketball, skating, and curling, in that order, and people who motored by on the high bluff that overlooked the Orman Camp sometimes pulled off the road awhile just to watch this funny-looking game in which two dozen men seemed caught in a perpetual manic dance with an odd-sized leather ball.

By summer, the Orman Camp looked more like a tar-papered lake resort than a prison. Makeshift canvas sun umbrellas and scrap-lumber lounge chairs were set up along the grassy shores of the swimming pond. At the center of their little lake, the prisoners anchored a red float with a ring of brightly painted buoys decorating its sides. When a visiting general came from Salt Lake City for his summer inspection, Major Pierce and his guards commandeered the lake from the prisoners, the general and his staff persuaded to join them on the float for a swimming party. Crepe-paper streamers billowed around the general in the breeze. As the prisoners looked on, there was a brief panicky moment when the float threatened to belly over under the assembled weight of the general's staff and their cases of beer, until they shifted into a more balanced arrangement. Later, the prisoners were gathered up and marched to the main compound, accompanied by brisk music from a visiting military band. In front of them all, the general pinned a medal on Major Pierce's uniform. Rifles were fired in salute. Then the general gave an address that commended Major Pierce on his exceptional organization, on the exemplary achievement of the 10th Services Command in building and running the Orman Camp, calling it a model of the U.S. Army's humanity toward its prisoners even in the face of the deeds of their homeland, whose evil, he informed them, was unequaled in history. The only thing that maybe saved a riot from breaking out among the prisoners was that the general's translator was so inept. Good German translators were almost never used by the army for its stateside prisoners of war; anyone with any competency at all was sent far closer to the front. So most of the general's speech was incomprehensible anyway, and the translator mixed up his use of the word "evil," in this case meaning to say "evildoers," or *Übeltäter*, for *Übertäter*, which came off as something like "overdoers unequaled in history." In a polite if confused way, most of the prisoners finally ended up applauding.

No matter the general's words and the mixed-up communications, their treatment was certainly worlds better than any of these toughened Afrika Korps survivors had expected. Rumors had spread among them that prisoners sent to England were forced to work like slaves in cold, damp ports, subject to frequent beatings by their guards and quartered in unheated warehouses, where they died of pneumonia by the scores. The Orman Camp was plywood cold in winter and tar-paper hot in summer, but there was always plenty to eat, and though the prisoners worked hard, it wasn't unwillingly. Most of them were required to labor about 150 days out of the year on the beet and grain farms or in the Black Hills National Forest. The more skilled jobs, at Nowell-Safebuy Turkeys or at Great Westward Sugar, were in high demand, not only because of the steadier money but mainly because they provided something to do through the long prairie winters.

Winter was the hardest season for prisoners. Some of the skilled, year-round jobs were even bought and sold, or won and lost in card games, as were the places on day-labor parties into the hills for coal and firewood. In winter, most prisoners had only their camp chores to do. They braced in idleness against the howling weather of the plains, listening to the few crackling radios they had built from parts or somehow smuggled in. Camp monotony was broken by the occasional flickering movies, mostly war propaganda, at which they laughed openly during the unrealistic combat scenes, whistling and hooting and stamping their feet at bumbling and scar-faced Hollywood Nazis and at half-blind banzai Japs. They quieted down and let out pitiful moans anytime a beautiful actress appeared on the screen. One night, after nearly a year of putting up with stupid and slanted films of their "evil master race," they were shown a movie called *Above Suspicion*. Soon after the first Hollywood Gestapo agents appeared, the projector had to be shut off to quell the beginnings of a loud prisoner demonstration, though Major Pierce wasn't sure if it was the fake-looking Nazis or what he always considered the disappointing hawkish beak and birdcage body of Joan Crawford that had set them off. The major never again allowed any war film or film with Joan Crawford in it to be shown at the camp, which left the prisoners stuck with movies like *Andy Hardy's Double Life*. The comedy *Roxie Hart* was shown so many times that the prisoners were soon reciting the meaningless dialogue in their thick accents before the lines were spoken. But at least it had Ginger Rogers, and they could recast her beauty in new cinematic dreams of their own. Then they scattered back to their confining barracks and resumed their endless card games, passing around the few censored books, magazines, and newspapers they were allowed, some men using them to practice the English they were slowly learning.

That first autumn while the Orman Camp was going up, Mose Johnson worked hard with his hundreds of new prisoners sent in every day to the turkey plant. Each morning for two weeks, he assembled his new workers in the company lunchroom. He had never made a speech in front of so many people in his life. He felt tongue-tied, nervous, embarrassed. Nothing he had learned about the first few dozen prisoners who had been working for months by then seemed of any use. Even with the little German he could manage, he still had to talk to them mainly with hand gestures. Young Keller and a few of the others helped with translation to explain the USDA instructional pamphlets and short films on the modern methods of slaughtering, cleaning, boning, canning or freezing, packing and shipping, of turkeys. As Mose talked along, the prisoners often simply lounged back in their chairs, most at best pretending they understood, some joking quietly with each other, some falling asleep.

One morning, as Dale Rynning was completing a slow demonstration on the boning out of turkey breasts, Mose finally snapped his pointer stick over his knee and whipped both pieces across the room at dozing prisoners. With Keller translating, Mose told them he would see to it that their wages were docked fifty cents a day per man if he caught anyone else sleeping through a demonstration. He was shocked to see many of the prisoners begin to laugh when they caught on to what he had said. Laugh! He'd give them something to laugh about. "All right, you got it!" he said. "Fifty cents a man docked for today!"

After a short film on personal hygiene for food-plant workers, as Mose was leading his groups of prisoners out onto the shop floor to begin introducing them again to their stations, Keller politely approached him. Keller was bobbing his head up and down and smiling in his usual lopsided way, which gave him a look a little like that of a loyal hound dog. "Pardon me," he said. "But I think I must explain something. You said in there fifty cents today taken from us! We laugh not because of you, I want you should know it. We laugh because each day we are paid ten cents!"

Mose stopped there with Keller, for a moment not getting what the man had said. The crowd was noisy all around them, filing out onto the shop floor, then slowing down and waiting in disorder for Mose to push on through and take the lead. "Ten cents," he said then. "You mean that's all the cash Major Pierce puts in your pockets?"

Keller eagerly nodded.

"Hell's bells," said Mose. He meant to ask Keller more, but the way the crowd had begun spreading out aimlessly through the plant building took his attention. "C'mon boy," he said. "Let's just get out there and show them how to do their jobs."

Later that afternoon, Mose was happily surprised by how well the day was going. Every single prisoner was at his station, working along, the slaughtering line moving at a more than acceptable speed. He decided to drop the idea of docking their wages. As he thought more about what Keller had told him, he also considered the fact that the Nowell-Safebuy wasn't the only company or farm that was paying out nearly eighty cents a day per prisoner for an eight-hour shift. There was Great Westward Sugar, the U.S. Forest Service, and almost every beet farmer he knew. . . . So where was all the money going? After the shift whistle blew and his prisoners were trucked off to their camp, Mose decided to find Buster Hill at the plant office and bring up this question of prisoner wages.

"The fact that some sonofabitch is smart enough to get his piece of this war don't change a thing," Buster said. "We're lucky to get these men at the price we're paying. I heard just this morning that because of union pressure, meat packers are shelling out two bucks a day

for prisoners down in Omaha. Two bucks! Can you believe that? So let's not go asking too many questions. You
can figure out for yourself what's going on. And look at
it this way. If we open our big mouths and put Major
Pierce's ass in a sling over this, you can be sure every
officer in his chain of command'll want in on the fran-
chise!''

Mose left the plant office thinking that the only people
really getting shafted on the deal were his prisoners. And
his prisoners were clearly grateful they were paid anything at all. They were given more than they could eat at
the Orman Camp, toilet things, soap, medicines, generous ration coupons to buy cigarettes—everything they
needed. What more could they possibly want? Ten cents
was ten cents, damnit. Ten cents was at least enough to
pool together to buy the makings for beer, and a few
assorted luxuries including extra coffee and cigarettes,
black-marketed to them by their guards. And, of course,
sausage.

Mose discovered on the second day of working with
his full crew that the prisoners had a powerful appetite
for sausage. At their lunch break, a chunky young man
assigned to cold storage started moving around excitedly
in front of Dale Rynning's sandwich, pointing at it and
calling to his buddies, *"Wurst! Es gibt Wurst hier, gell?
Wurst!"*

The word caught on down the ranks of men sitting at
tables eating their company lunch of beans and turkey.
Crowds of prisoners gathered around to get a look at
Dale's sandwich. Dale was sitting at one of the tables
reserved for the regular employees and a few army
guards, set apart from the others. Nobody realized what
all the commotion was about for a moment, and one of
the guards even cautiously started to reach for his rifle.
When Dale saw what the stir was about, he laughed
loudly at the prisoners, opened the bread of his whopping
hoagie, and dangled a piece of sausage up like fish bait

at the crowd. The lunchroom filled with a deep-throated sound of amazement as in the presence of a god.

Mose mentioned this incident to Beatrice Ott. The next day, Beatrice and the women's auxiliary of the Church of Christ Reformed managed to round up enough sausage all over town so that each prisoner had a taste. It was mostly antelope sausage—there was hardly any pork sausage around. But the prisoners didn't seem to mind the difference. They came out from lunch in extra-good spirits and worked along happily that afternoon.

Word soon got out about sausage. Charley Gooch and his rancher friends, aging sheepmen on their big spreads set as far as fifty miles out into the parched grasslands, all began to hunt antelope both in and out of season. The range boys set up a tractor-driven grinder at the Gooch place and stuffed in antelope after antelope, including some of the bones and almost everything else, seasoning the meat in the old range-style fashion—black pepper, green pepper, Mexicali red peppers, bucket after bucket of fresh-ground wild sage, plenty of salt, and a coffee can of vinegar for good measure—then they packed that mess into casings and started shoving yard after yard of sausage links into their makeshift smokers.

Sausage quickly became a fine side business. There was never enough of it during the war. As the months wore on, local farmers increased the number of hogs they raised and lined their pockets. Before that regular pork sausage could hit the market in any quantity, Charley Gooch and his range boys went boom and then bust. The last big shipment of antelope sausage came in that next winter, when a small caravan of Cheyennes from the Wind River reservation brought in ten thousand pounds of it, which they sold for a high price to Major Pierce's grocery store at the Orman Camp. By that time, Charley Gooch and his boys were all but out of business, except for mutton sausage from old ground-up killer ewes. It had taken less than two years of wholesale hunting before antelope became almost an endangered species in Wovoka County. Some people say they never did come back in their former numbers.

Ten cents was ten cents. Prisoners at the Orman Camp spent whatever money they had on sausage and other luxuries—the few magazines they could get, store-bought items like gum and candy, the makings for the beer they brewed, and other things. Some prisoners even managed to save up their dimes and money they earned from farmers for extra work, and they put together packages of store-bought canned food, coffee, sugar, wool caps and socks, and little trinkets they crafted during their idle hours. Those packages were wrapped up, addressed, and sent off to their suffering families in Germany. With the help of the International Red Cross, some of the gifts got through to their beloved fatherland, and a few of them even to the people they were intended for. It must have been part of our government's policy to let such shipments go through. The German people had been told that American cities had been bombed to rubble and our economy was broken. Imagine the disturbing surprise when the first of such happy little gift boxes were opened in desolate Berlin.

No matter what money the prisoners were paid, the Orman Camp seemed like a paradise after the devastation most of them had barely survived. In their minds, the fact that they were still alive was nothing short of miraculous. Mose hardly heard a complaint from his prisoners. Not even the expected griping at the sun or cold or at the monotony of their jobs. But he did notice something else, a quiet brooding that came over them at times. Some of them were locked for weeks in a dark, storming sadness when it hit them that everything was over, all of it for nothing, that the most they could do now was to grieve and pine away for their country, their women, their homes.

Keller told Mose that the train ride alone—thousands of miles from Norfolk across what seemed to them an overwhelmingly limitless country in all respects—was enough to convince most prisoners that the war was already over. From what they could see out the train windows, especially all the cars that some of them had counted, in numbers they found incredible, along with the modern bridges, the paved highways, the tall smokestacks in what seemed even the smallest towns, it was clear to almost all of them that life in America was very much better than in their homeland. Mose was surprised to hear this, imagining such a powerful enemy as Hitler's Germany to have every miracle of science, tall buildings, a life as comfortable as in St. Louis or New Orleans, the farthest Mose had ever been from home. "You have so much of all things here in America," Keller said. "If the German soldier knows this, then perhaps he would not so long fight on. That little corporal Hitler," he added then, a bitterness in his voice. "*He* should be made to ride a train across America. . . ."

Like most of his hundreds of fellow prisoners at the Nowell-Safebuy, Keller considered his job there to be a great privilege. After reflecting about that, Mose wasn't at all surprised. Every night, his Nowell-Safebuy crew went back to their camp and heard the stories of the other prisoners, the ones who were spending long shifts howing row after row of sugar beets, weeding, thinning, then at harvest painfully bending over for hours on end, cutting the dark-green beet tops under a sun so hot that time of year that the Sioux had declared it both merciless and holy. Men like Keller soon concluded that, though strenuous enough and surely more dangerous, working turkeys wasn't half so exhausting.

Mose's prisoners were astonished they were paid any money at all for working. Still, it didn't seem right to him that anyone should be making a killing off prisoner labor from the war. Mose stewed and worried and didn't like that one damned bit. But he finally came to agree with Buster Hill. The best thing he could do about a situation in which he was powerless was to leave well enough alone. His job was to keep the slaughtering line moving. And from the first few weeks of his full and green prisoner crew, that line was turning out more turkeys each day than anybody had ever expected. So he would keep his mouth shut, and that would be the end of it. Their money was no concern of his. One evening, though, Mose grew curious enough to take out a piece of paper and a pencil at the Cove Café and make some calculations. He figured the take was close to half a million dollars a year out of the prisoner payroll.

Another holiday season was on its way. Thanksgiving was frantically arriving. Christmas was just down the street. The demand for frozen turkeys so far exceeded production that the line at the Norwell-Safebuy during the first days of autumn suspended the canning and boning operations. Local supply still wasn't enough; tens of thousands of live turkeys were rushed in from as far away as Minnesota and Colorado to be processed, wrapped whole, and shipped off at once in railroad freezer cars. Most of the early-autumn cargo was bound for San Diego and a string of freighters known as the Great White Fleet, refrigerator ships commandeered at premium rates from the United Fruit Company for the duration. They were mistakenly repainted too light a shade of U.S. Navy gray, which made them easy targets for submarines, then they were packed to the hatches with turkeys bound for our boys in the Pacific. As the holidays grew nearer, many thousands of birds were loaded as if they were high-priority secrets onto army trucks that pulled into town day and night, then raced off to an air base just outside Rapid City, where cargo planes, along with hundreds of air force bombers—B-17s and B-25s fresh off assembly lines—would make quick and sometimes unscheduled landings to take on so many tons of turkeys that the birds were stacked like cordwood up to the machine gun turrets, then they were flown off in all directions, most of them bound for overseas.

More than a million and a half of our boys were overseas by then. And more were on their way, seasick and miserable in Liberty ships, bucking the rough seas toward England to begin training for the invasion of Europe. News from all fronts was filled with hope. The battle for a rotting jungle called Bougainville was in full swing. The fleet was massing in the Marshalls and preparing for assaults on the inner defense lines of the Japs. Hundreds of thousands of troops were dug in over in Italy for the prolonged terrible siege of Monte Cassino. Bombers were striking deep into Germany; the first daring night raids were dropping their deadly cargoes on Berlin. The way Mose saw it, our boys were doing one hell of a job bottling up Tojo and the Nazis. They deserved the best this holiday season. It would likely mean the last hot meals and days of rest many of them would live to see.

People in town and on the surrounding farms threw themselves with increasing energy into doing their parts at home. In the exhausted evenings at the Cove Café, the radio was turned up to full volume. Women traded ration coupons back and forth like bidding points at games of bridge. Then they pushed back the tables and did slow, awkward dances cheek to cheek with each other to programs such as the *Hit Parade*, weeping over lyrics like "I'll be seeing you, in all the old familiar places," and "I'll be home for Christmas, you can count on me. . . ."

There was suddenly so much work in town and so many turkeys that two full shifts a day of prisoners were thrown onto the Nowell-Safebuy slaughtering line. Even so, they weren't even half enough to take care of the rush. Early

blizzards that year didn't make things any easier. Mose
stood before the huddling gangs of prisoners in harsh
prairie winds that blew the snow and ice in stinging blasts
into his face. His hundreds of new prisoners jumped up
and down in front of the Nowell-Safebuy, trying to stay
warm, rubbing their wet gloved hands together in that
prairie cold so sharp that every time another gust of wind
came up, almost anyone let loose an involuntary moan.
Those prisoners were ill prepared for the weather, dressed
in military-issue coats that were too thin, and not all of
them yet with knitted caps, sweaters, scarves, and some
still in footgear busting out at the seams. But sorry-
looking as they were in the subzero cold, whenever their
Hauptmann was with them they lost most of the appear-
ance of a defeated army. They stood at attention for him,
as stiff as a line of raketeeth. He left them standing that
way for minutes after they had suffered through the daily
head count by the army guards. Then they clicked their
heels. They saluted him before they dispersed on the
double to their jobs.

Mose had never seen men as good at their jobs. It was
amazing to him and to everyone. They had clearly been
handpicked at the Orman Camp for this kind of work.
Mose figured the Hauptmann must have been responsible
for that. Most of the prisoners had been captured with
little booklets on them called *Soldbucher*, soldier books,
as thick as passports, which in painstaking German fashion accounted for some of their background and every
important detail of their military lives. Who could even
so much as read more than a few words in "Milwaukee
Deutsch" at the Orman Camp? Sergeant Hormel? One
or two others? There were so many hundreds of thousands of prisoners of war all over this country by then
that it seemed the army had simply thrown up its hands
and left them mainly to run themselves.

Most of the assigned prisoners had had industrial experience in their homeland, many even at meat packing—
there were journeyman butchers among them, and cooks,

machine operators and mechanics, men who had worked in canneries and as longshoremen—and any soldier who could be so identified with a related trade in Germany was selected and assigned to a roughly corresponding job at Nowell-Safebuy Turkeys.

Striding off down his lines of prisoners, Mose looked out for the ones who remained from the few dozen or so he had trained himself. He was glad to see that Feldwebel Wenzel still kept his job. And young Keller was there too, on Mose's insistence, as he still depended on him to interpret. As for the others, Mose regarded them with a genuine awe. There were groups of them with the thick fingers and strong hands that marked their trade as meat cutters, men who were easily giving Dale Rynning and his union boys a run for their money gutting the birds and boning turkey breasts. The machinists, engineers, and mechanics among them had taken it upon themselves to disassemble and reconstruct the overhead turkey conveyor system so that it was about sixty feet longer yet was speeded up by about one-third. Then there were the longshoremen, thick leather bands supporting their wrists, leather thigh pads sewn to their pants like bale-bucking patches, metal box hooks hanging from their belts, men who despite the fact that they were still recovering from wounds and illness could pack box after box of turkey into railroad cars as if they were all in some kind of training for the Olympics. It soon seemed clear that Nowell-Safebuy Turkeys would by all signs meet its quota of five thousand birds a day long before anyone expected. The new prisoners were working so fast and well and were seemingly so happy with little supervision that Mose sometimes had to remind himself that he was still the man in charge. Each morning, he stood taking in the sight of his new men, waiting for the shift to begin. He checked his pocket watch. *"Achtung!"* He ordered them to get to work, his tone more friendly than commanding. *"Gehen Wir schön jetzt zur Arbeit! Gehen wir jetzt! Weiter machen!"*

Then one morning the sound of his voice barely carried across to the building in the whipping wind of a blizzard. An army guard, teeth chattering, gave Mose his stack of clipboards for the day. Mose watched as the guards all peeled off as quickly as they could, to go warm themselves in front of the oil stoves in the plant offices. His mouth went suddenly dry at the thought that he was now in charge of so many men.

"Achtung!" Mose Johnson shouted at them. They milled around in front of him in scattered gangs, waiting in the wind and snow. "All right you men!" he shouted. "Let's get out and work them turkeys!"

The prisoners hardly moved. They finished last cigarettes, still out there waiting, suffering in the cold. Hauptmann von Ujatz was still in his truck, his attention distracted by some minor detail he was talking over with his orderly, Gruenwald.

"All right now, let's go! Let's get a move on!"

The prisoners showed no reaction. Mose paced back and forth in the paralyzing cold. Unconsciously, he lowered a hand to the holster flap in his pistol. What was he going to do? He looked in the direction of the Hauptmann, way off down the line in the blizzard, hoping to catch his attention. What kind of man was this? The Hauptmann finally squinted back toward Mose, conceding a small bow in his direction as if he were dressed in a tuxedo or something and greeting Mose from across a ballroom.

The one morning a week that the Hauptmann now observed the plant operation, his routine was always the same. He was the last to step nimbly off the wooden truckbed. As soon as his boots landed on the ground, all the prisoners at once snapped to attention. No matter how cold it was, the Hauptmann made them wait. He walked a few apparently purposeful steps in either direction, gray head turreting up and back, a general inspecting his troops. This ritual seemed to take longer every week. Mose felt as if he sweated more each time, no matter the weather. His shirt was soaking through under his sheepskin coat, his fingers were slick with perspiration under his gloves, his heart pounded until he felt the sound of it echoing through his body like in an empty metal drum. The Hauptmann appeared to finish his inspection. He crossed his frail arms over his chest, standing there with snow devils gusting all around him like he never felt the cold. Then he raised his left hand, just the hand, a quick little signal. As though the prisoners could see that hand through the backs of their skulls, they clicked their heels, saluted sharply, then dispersed at once in tightly ordered squads into the building. Mose tensed even more at the sight of that scattering double time.

There was also the strange business with the Hauptmann's chair. It was an olive-drab folding canvas chair like something out of the movies. Periodically through the day, Gruenwald ordered a different man off the slaughtering line to carry that chair to a warm area inside the plant building. It was generally set up with its back against a wall somewhere, off out of the way. The line worker who moved the chair did so stiffly, a nervous expression on his face. The chair was ordered into position by Gruenwald, then often adjusted, maybe just a few feet to one side or the other, as if there was always an exact place where it should be folded out. Before sitting down, the Hauptmann exchanged a few words with the enlisted man, words that never seemed pleasant to hear. That line worker answered him in a crisp and obedient tone of voice before he clicked his heels, saluted, and was dismissed back to his job. This chair-moving ritual happened seven or eight times a day, the Hauptmann and his orderly followed around by yet a different scurrying line worker, to whom the officer always spoke as though interrogating a criminal.

There was another odd business that went on every morning the Hauptmann came with his men. Signs went up over the prisoner work stations, at least one in every big room on the slaughtering line, folding cardboard signs in fancy black German lettering. Mainly just two different phrases were written on them, repeating themselves along the walls: *Freude durch Freude* and *Eigennutz vor Gemeinnutz.* Keller translated them for Mose as "Joy Through Joy" and "Self-Interest Before Common Interest," slogans that were suddenly all over the place on inspection mornings and that seemed to make the men laugh in a snarling, cynical way as they were hung up. Certain prisoners smuggled the signs into the plant and hurriedly fastened them up before the Hauptmann finished sitting down in his chair, as if they were all some kind of elaborate show for him. Then just as the whistle blew at the end of their shift, those signs came down. They didn't turn up again until the next time the Hauptmann visited the plant. The signs bothered Mose. What did they really mean?

"I get what they say," said Mose after Keller had translated for him. "But just what is that 'Joy Through Joy'? It just don't make any sense."

"It is very difficult to explain," Keller said. "All over German factories, we have similar signs, ordered there by Hitler. *Kraft durch Freude*—'Strength Through Joy.' Or, for example, *Gemeinnutz vor Eigennutz,* just the opposite of this one. Do you see their meaning now? Our patriotic work slogans turned around. When the Hauptmann comes, we put up these signs because we know they make him happy. It is like a good joke for him. It is just his way. Then we take them down. There are some who believe such signs are not loyal to Germany. The rest of us don't want any trouble. No fighting among ourselves," Keller said.

Mose still didn't understand completely; he couldn't figure much of anything about the Hauptmann. Especially not the way the man sat down in his chair, stiffly, like a general at a parade, as dignified as though he were still in full uniform, despite his cheap and baggy set of khakis with POW painted crudely across his back. Also, the Hauptmann was terribly thin. It looked to Mose like some inner misery was gnawing the meat off his ribs from the inside. His face was deeply furrowed, weary-looking, the skin sagging around his smart eyes, which seemed to have seen too much. He looked like a seated scarecrow. He chain-smoked. That was his main activity. The hollows of his cheeks blew in and out with smoke, an expression in his eyes as though he were staring through the thousands of miles toward his home. Sitting there, supposedly as an official observer, the Hauptmann hardly appeared to notice the men on the slaughtering line. Then, abruptly, he signaled for Gruenwald, who would listen to his instructions, then hurry away, often merely to pull yet another prisoner off the job to move the chair to a different section of the plant.

"I don't like it one damn bit," Mose said one after-noon to Buster Hill. "Look here. It's against regula-tions." He leafed through an olive-drab pamphlet titled *U.S. Army Regulations on Enemy Civilian Aliens and Prisoners of War*, which one of the guards had lent him. " 'No enemy officer should be allowed to fraternize or otherwise engage informally with enlisted prisoners,' " Mose read. He flipped to another page. " 'All enemy propaganda, songs, and slogans should be strictly forbid-den whenever possible. . . .' "

"That book you got there's already out of date," Buster answered. "Nobody uses that damn thing anymore. Why in hell can't you just leave that man alone?"

Mose was following Buster through the plant, the little bulldog dancing around at Buster's heels. Buster tipped his hat to his prisoner crew at the boning tables. They returned his greeting with Hallos and Gut afternoons. The little dog nosed around under their feet for scraps or hopped up with his stocky front paws at their legs, beg-ging for tidbits. The prisoners called the dog *der kleine Churchillhund* and made other jokes about it that Mose couldn't catch. All the while, they never skipped a beat in the swift movements of knives and hands. Buster rolled up his sleeves, grinned at Mose, and bellied up to the

boning tables, ready to show off some of his old turkey
know-how from his days spent butchering in his con-
verted blacksmith shop. Buster deftly took up a knife and
pulled a turkey off one of the moving steel hangers overhead. With several quick, circling knife strokes, he
peeled the fat breast off the bones like sectioning a fruit.
The prisoners all around him stopped their own fast work
just long enough to watch, nodding and grinning at Buster
and saying things like *Ja, ja, sehr kräftiges,* one of them
blurting out, *"Ein wirchliches Direktor Gefolgschafts-
mann,"* which made all of them laugh.

Very workmanlike? A regular manager follower? Mose
translated to himself. What could the men mean by that?
To Buster, they must have seemed like friendly signs of
approval. But Mose heard something else in their tone.
Maybe that was what bothered him most. Everything in
the plant—the Hauptmann, the way these new prisoners
were, even their laughter—it all had shades of a dark
meaning that gave him the willies. Buster stepped back
from the table looking pleased with himself, wiping his
hands on his slacks. He stood watching over the shoulders of his prisoners a minute longer, as though letting
them know that he personally kept track of what they
were doing. Then Buster slapped a few men on their
backs and gave the whole gang a thumbs-up sign. Mounds
of pink boned meat rose on the tables at an even faster
pace.

"You can't say that man doesn't do his job," Buster
said as they continued on together through the plant. They
stopped again in the canning room. Mose watched
through the curtains of steam that rose up out of the huge
pressure cookers, long steel cylinders with gauges and
valves, which looked kind of like fighter planes without
wings. Turkey partly roasted in the low-steam ovens was
packed into the cans, then cooked inside them under a
dozen pounds of pressure. Small groups of perspiring,
shirtless prisoners cracked the hatches on the cookers
and started moving the racks of canned turkey out onto

the conveyor belts to the labelers and the boxing room. Forklift loads of boxed cans were being run out to the loading docks at dangerous speeds. Their faces perspiring in the cold, the men on the snow-blown loading docks were packing box after box into the railroad cars as if they were racing for a prize.

"It just don't feel right somehow," said Mose, "It don't look right, either. That man just sits out there. And for all the world, I'd swear he's up to something. Anybody can see he's the one giving orders. Now that ain't right, damnit. That's flat out against the rules!"

Buster pulled off his hat, cooling himself a little in the cold, using his shirtsleeve to wipe the sweat off his forehead. "We just might work up to six thousand birds a day by June," he said.

"Yessir," answered Mose. "We surely could."

They moved back through the plant, Buster having to pick up his little bulldog and carry it in his arms because it kept trying to run off to the butchering rooms. Mose waited there feeling foolish, searching for words, not at all sure what more he could say. The both of them stood for a moment, the steady noises of the plant all around them like a single huge engine loudly rumbling under their feet. Then Buster Hill decided for him.

"Just look around us," Buster said. "Take a good long look. You ever seen anything like it? Nobody works like they do. Nobody I've ever seen. That man's doing his job, damnit. That's all you or me or anybody should care about. So just sit on your hands, Mose. Sit on your hands and stay out of his way. Ignore that stuck-up sonofabitch and let him do his job. That's an order." He started up the stairs to his office, his dog in his arms. Then he turned to Mose again and said, "I'm beginning to think the only trouble we're likely to see from here on out is laying *them* off, when our own boys start coming home."

January. The year that brought with it more hopeful news. That winter, the German armies had disintegrated on the Russian front. The Allies landed troops at the Albano hills south of Rome and, finally, that imperial city seemed within reach. MacArthur had finished cartwheeling his way across New Guinea and the surrounding islands, and was setting his sights on his promised return to the Philippines. Allied air forces in Europe began the nonstop pounding of the German heartland, day and night, reducing its cities to fire storms and ruins. The few vivid seconds of seeing the city of Hamburg hit by a hurricane of fire on the Movietone newsreel before the showing of *Crash Dive*, with Tyrone Power, at the Arcade Bingo & Theater cheered almost everyone in the audience. Mose was happy enough that our boys were doing the job over there; but he was glad, too, his prisoners were spared seeing such a fire storm, that they were allowed so little news. Turkey production had never been higher, meeting a mounting quota now set at thirty-five hundred birds a day. Factories everywhere were rolling at their peak. Labor was still so tight that in that same newsreel, the manager of a bomber plant was shown refusing to allow Dorothy Lamour to gather up her war-bond pledges inside his factory. That "sarong girl" had already raised so much money for the war effort that the amount had been declared a national secret. The manager had the gall to stand there and say straight into the camera, "When any good-looking woman walks through the plant, it costs us a thousand man-hours of labor. Dorothy Lamour might cost the country half a bomber. . . ."

But when would it all end? The news that really hit home was that fourteen of Nowell's sons had already lost their lives, equal to half a graduating class from Geoffrey Nowell High School. Reverend Ott was gathering the scattered families of his congregation about every month now for memorial services for a local boy at the Church of Christ Reformed. Mose took time off from his work at the plant to stand among the crowd, mainly women, reaching out his arms to support the grieving, feeling in them that desperate and bitter sense of carved-out loneliness that could never be filled. There was something else too, a sense that they clung to him at the coffinless gathering before the altar like he was any man, surely not himself, Mose, and any man at that moment, at that final giving way to grief, might just then fill their baffling, intense, irreplaceable desires for the man they had loved.

That was the way he felt the Saturday one of the Claypool brothers was remembered. Private Joseph Claypool was a training casualty, so his body was shipped home for burial at the National Cemetery in Sturgis. Having an actual body there to deal with seemed to make the death all the more real. So many more people turned out to mourn him that Mose arranged for a green army bus from Major Pierce to transport the crowd. Sometime during the potluck funeral reception at the church's coffee room after the graveside service, it seemed Alice Claypool had done everything but hang her arms around his neck, even as Mose was trying to remember just exactly when it was he had actually met her husband. She should have known Mose better than that. He had his own knowledge of grief and loss. That Saturday, as always, Mose helped lead the crowd of mourning women out to their battered farm trucks and their old rusting cars, out into the violent winter in these streets, which could turn their tears to ice. He held them like a brother one last moment at their open car doors, kissed their cheeks, sent them off through the drifting blizzard to their empty homes.

Mose crossed the rutted, unpaved street, bent into the cold wind. In a total exhaustion, he moved his winter boots toward the municipal bar, where he sat alone on the stool next to the wood carving of a once famous opera singer whose name everyone had forgotten, a beautiful painted woman that swept up and out from that bar like the figurehead of an old wooden ship. Mose sat there and ordered whiskey after whiskey, drinking through his own sense of grief renewed, thinking only of one woman, remembering how it felt once to sleep together with her on nights such as this under their patchwork quilts so warmly that most times they forgot to get up and toss more coal into the stove. He knew what it was like to lose a love that would never let go. Adelle, so briefly once his dearest Adelle . . .

He awoke Sunday morning not remembering who must have helped him home. His limbs ached in all their joints. Dazed, head throbbing, he felt his skull was packed with steaming rags. Worse, his kidneys flamed up again from their stones. Half blindly setting his cowboy coffee on the stove to boil, he thought only of that, how the pressure gathered inside, his kidneys pumped up and burning like two lit torches in the muscles of his back. During the week now he could hardly whip himself out of bed and stagger off to the Nowell-Safebuy in the bitter darkness. But once at work, he was so busy he didn't have time to think of or even feel pain. What was keeping him going was looking forward to Sunday, that one workless day, a voice in his head saying over and over: If you can only make it until Sunday . . . if you can just get through to Sunday . . .

Each week he planned to sleep in, but he never did. He awoke in his bedroom at the usual time, just before dawn. His body whipped itself out of bed automatically, in painful motion already before he caught himself and remembered it was Sunday. He sat there in pain for a minute. He breathed deeply a few times of the chill air from the window he kept partly open, punched his feather pillows full again, and propped them and himself up against the wall. He lazed there, rolling a smoke one-handed, watching it dawn in his backyard. He thought of his few Sunday chores—church, his housecleaning, the bag of dirty laundry to carry to Anita Foos, just up the street. Sometimes he noticed the window was streaked with grime, reminding himself to get out there and wash windows the first warm Sunday that came along.

His headache increased with each deep inhale of smoke but he kept on smoking. He gazed off around his bedroom, noticing the pretty robin's-egg-blue wallpaper with the little flowers printed on it, the exact same pattern that Adelle had once dreamed about and circled in the catalogue from Montgomery Ward. It had once made Mose feel close to her again to see it all around him, lovingly ordered, cut true with his razor-sharp penknife, the sheets pasted up so that the pattern exactly fit. So she might see his forgiveness; so she might live at peace in this room when she came home, as he had long convinced himself she one day would. Then he had noted the few ragged edges to it, up near the neatly painted but smoke-yellowed ceiling. That, too, he had abandoned in bitterness. When was it? How many years now? He promised himself for the umpteenth time, war or no, finally to pick up that load of aromatic cedar and finish off the bedroom trim. To do it just the way she would have wanted it. Doing it that way now, the way she had once described such a room, would somehow make an end of it; he would enjoy the fruits of his vine all the more knowing she would never taste them.

Sundays, his thoughts were always the same. For twelve years now, twelve years alone, twelve years since he could finish anything. He smoked, lying back, letting his hangover crash over him the way he imagined breakers would on a beach. He felt as tired as though he hadn't slept at all last night. It was like somebody had carried him to his bed after a long night's work and there he was, still lying awake, and now he'd have to drag on his clothes all over again. Mose stood up then, tossing his smoldering butt into a porcelain ashtray in the shape of a can-can dancer with *Mardi Gras New Orleans 1927* across her belly, partly covered by a gray crust of ashes. Adelle had playfully bought him that ashtray from a Negro on the street. Then, back in their tiny hotel room, she had raised her skirts, kicked up her legs, danced for him. . . .

Mose shuffled slowly out of his bedroom. His bunion ached. He put the coffee on to boil. Every hour he had worked that week seemed to cry out in his limbs as he moved. The torches in his back were turning up their flames. Just as on any working morning, Mose threw open his back door with a loud slam against the siding. He felt a kind of satisfaction at the sound, a small portion of angry movement he allowed himself. His habit had never been to use the toilet first thing in the morning. Out on his farm, Adelle used to scold him for it, but then way off in the gumbo like that, who was there to see but her? Then it still always made her laugh the way he pulled his brown Stetson work hat off its hook by the open door and put it on, then stood there barefoot in his union suit, breathing in deeply, testing the air of the new morning. He stepped out onto the back porch like that. He unbuttoned the flap of his union suit, reached in at his pecker all curled up there like a pig's tail and shook it out. He closed his eyes. *Oh, shit, not again now* . . .

He cleared his throat of the phlegm that was always

there these days, spitting it out in racking coughs. His eyes still closed, he tried to chase away any thoughts of work, reminding himself again that it was Sunday, finally Sunday. But this only made him feel more vividly that in less than twenty-four hours now he would be out there, working turkeys again. When had he started dreading his job that he had once been so glad to have? When had he lost his energy for it, the sense it was somehow linked to a different future?

One Sunday, he had found himself standing in the street in front of his house. There he was, looking at its good frame lines, the peaks of its shingled roof, at the well-trimmed lawn, the little picket fence he kept whitewashed and looking new. For a lot of years, he had even planted tulip bulbs along the sidewalk every autumn. Standing in the street, he suddenly wondered who were the people living inside. He imagined a man, a woman, their children in the yard, their dog barking along the fence at the postman. That's what almost everybody he knew was working for, that was why they were over there fighting. And that was enough to want from this world. Looking at that house, nobody would have thought a man was turning gray inside it, all alone.

Tomorrow was Monday. The Hauptmann's inspection day. Maybe that was part of it, that now his job came down to the same slow burning vision of that Hauptmann already sitting out there as if in some blind, limitless space. Mose was in pain again, his face set into a strained grimacing as he aimed a long smoking trail into his backyard but it was more like he cussed and burned it out of his body without meaning to. Adelle would have been scolding to hear him like that, raging and cussing up some violent energy at how many more hours, days, months, years were still left in this war, already seeming endless to him, longer even than his arteries as he jittered up and down with the intensity of his pain and cussed it out, *ohhh shit ohhh shit the sonofabitchin' sonofabitch. . . .*

Mose opened his eyes and let the deep freeze of the morning take him on, steam rising off the patch of yellow snow in his backyard. He rolled his head around as if he was searching the sky, easing the tension in his neck. He loved that moment in the mornings. He didn't give a damn even if the neighbors might see him, though no one ever could because of the tall hedges on all sides of his backyard. It was only then, mornings, a few leisurely moments of relief in which he was sure there was no greater satisfaction for a man, when, as his friend Charley Gooch had put it, "He can face the morning with cock in hand and the sanctuary of his thoughts."

Mose cleared his throat and coughed his lungs clear. He shivered in the cold, smelling the fresh coffee on his stove. He turned back into his house with thoughts of breakfast at the Cove Café, awake now, fortified, ready to put on his shirt and bolo tie and Sunday best, hopeful that the rest of his day wouldn't go downhill from here.

Over his pancakes at the Cove, Mose studied Reverend Ott's lesson for that Sunday. He was often a lay reader, now that Deacon Margrave had become a chaplain in the navy. Mose was always honored to do the reading, using his good strong voice which filled the church to the rafters. He sat at the counter with his Bible propped up next to his breakfast and went over and over the gospel of the week, mouthing the words to himself. It was one of the passages the Reverend Ott had chosen to help comfort this town during the war's hard times. Strong words, firm thoughts, an offering of invincible and prayerful faith in final victory: *And the Lord went before them by day in a pillar of cloud, to lead them the way; and by night in a pillar of fire, to give them light; to go by day and by night: He took not away the pillar of cloud by day, nor the pillar of fire by night, from before the people. . . .*

One afternoon, Keller came running up to Mose in a state of high agitation, spluttering out words in English so fast Mose could hardly understand. Keller grabbed him by the arm and started dragging him toward the canning room. "Come now! Fast!"

In the canning room, added to the deafening pounding of the machinery was a high shrieking sound of disintegrating metal. Shattered bits of tin cans were flying all over the room like shrapnel. Many of the prisoners there had taken cover at their stations, their arms crossed over their faces. *"Dreht es zu! Dreht es zu!"* Mose shouted. A piece of sharp tin grazed his side. "Shut her down! Shut her down now!"

Somebody had sense enough to throw the main breaker switch, and the booming wind of the conveyor belts, the plunging bass drum of the canning machines, the long clattering track speeding along with the hanging carcasses of fresh-slaughtered turkeys, slowly came to a stop. The plant filled with an unnatural silence.

One of the turkey cookers still boiled away, the jet of steam blasting through its pressure valve steadily increasing. Behind it, Feldwebel Wenzel was oddly positioned, his body pitched forward into the big conveyer system that led to the press that stamped the lids on the cans. Keller was the first to get to Wenzel. The man's face was as gray as leaded tin. At first it wasn't clear what was wrong, his body was positioned so close up against the conveyor system. With a sickening turn inside, Mose saw that one of the rollers had sucked in the man's right arm and most of his shoulder.

"Kommen Sie mit! Hier! Schnell! Schnell!" Mose shouted at some of the men to join him from the canning line. Scraps of half-processed cans with turkey stuffed into them had landed everywhere, making the concrete floor as slippery as a skating rink. The prisoners trying to get to Wenzel skidded around on the greasy scraps, some of them sprawling to the floor. "Come on now! Quick! Let's back this damn thing up! Keller!"

Keller let go of Wenzel's head, which he had been holding in his hands, stroking the forehead and cheeks, talking to the man in a soothing voice. He helped Mose get a team of prisoners to grab on to the conveyor system, pulling the belts back like a team of human mules. How in hell could this have happened? The man must have reached his arm all the way in. But what was he reaching for in there? Wenzel screamed. His crushed arm was pulled back through the rollers with a sickening noise, whipping back out like a flattened fire hose. His body fell into Keller's arms and jerked a few times, convulsing, then slipped through them to the floor, his eyes wide open but turned to glass.

"Back away now! Back up! Give the man some air!" Mose knew what to do. "Get some cold rags on his face and get him breathing!" he shouted at Keller. "And don't you move him till I get back!"

Mose took off on the run. He rushed out of the plant building into the snow-packed streets, crashing along off balance over the ice and trying not to go sprawling. He ran that way past the municipal bar, the Baker Hotel, the Cove Café, his breath rasping in his lungs. It was only fifty-fifty that the Doc would be in his office. Then he saw the cars parked outside and he slammed through the door and jumped through the packed waiting room straight into the examination room. A half-naked Lonnie Anderson ripped her feet down out of stirrups and rolled over on the big steel table with a shout. . . .

In the canning room, prisoners were sitting around in grim little gangs, most of them as far away from Feld-webel Wenzel as they could get. A few army guards had joined them, looking on indifferently from the doorway, smoking. Wenzel lay limply on the floor, soaked in blood, a big wet towel now fully covering his face. Still out of breath, dragged all the way on the run and in his shirtsleeves, Doc Monahan found the man's good wrist and curled his fingers around it. He took out his stetho-scope and made sure. "Jesus damn Christ," he said. "Any damn fool can see the man is dead."

"But that arm . . ." Mose started to say, then stopped.

"Shock," Doc Monahan said. "Looks like shock to me. Or maybe a coronary. A blood clot. What in hell happened?"

Keller raised a hand, gesturing in the direction of the conveyor belts. His face was gaunt, white; his mouth was taut, even the red scar on his upper lip gone almost pale, his blue eyes distant and totally cold.

"You'd think with all the damn money this company spent on new equipment, somebody would have thought of just one goddamn safety guard!" The Doc threw his stethoscope into his black bag. "It's a shame, that's what it is, a damn crying shame."

"Today," Keller said suddenly, a quivering in his voice. "He get news. Here," he said. His hands shaking, Keller reached carefully to the dead man. He unbuttoned the flap of a shirt pocket and pulled out a letter. He un-folded a thin, tissuey page and took a long time going over the words, lost for a moment in them. "It is written here . . . his home city . . . Bremerhaven . . . bombed to ruins. His house was destroyed. Nobody has news of his wife and children." Keller looked at the Doc and then at Mose, as if this all somehow explained something. "He was not well this morning."

"Somebody told me the air corps sometimes drops leaflets," said Mose. "Maybe they were evacuated. . . ." A long moment passed. The three of them squatted in silence around Wenzel's body.

"Too late now," Keller said then, the first to speak.

"Damn straight," said Doc Monahan. He rose to his feet, tucking his bag under his arm. "You go on and show Buster Hill just how this happened," he said to Mose. "Tell him this is no problem of mine. Tell him to get the army to handle the autopsy and the papers, I'm too damn busy. And next time make sure they're at least still alive before you come busting into the office and scare my patients half to death!"

Buster Hill was away from the plant that day, gone off to Omaha for some kind of regional meeting of meat packers with the War Food Administration. Mose was in charge, and there was work still left to do. He motioned for the army guards to come in. The way they shrank back from their job, trying to pick up the poor man by grabbing at his loose uniform like they were afraid to touch him, drove Mose to cussing. "Shit fire, pick him up! He can't bite! Get a move on!"

They gingerly set their hands on the man and lifted him, trying not to look, letting him crumple in the middle. He dragged the floor as they carried him out that way, all broken and folded up, careful not to get blood on their uniforms. Mose looked at his pocket watch. It was late in the afternoon. Buster would likely climb all over him in the morning for it, but he thought there wasn't any sense in starting the line up again. "Wash it down now!" he shouted, but he didn't need to. His prisoners in the canning room were slowly moving for the hoses, and a team of them had already started unjamming the crumpled tangle of metal from the jaws of the canning machinery.

Keller sat slumped down against a cement-block wall, staring blankly into space. The dead man's letter was still in his hand.

"You all right, boy?" It took a moment before Keller heard this and looked up at Mose.

"Maybe I don't feel so good," Keller said.

"You look like hell," Mose said. "Come on with me. Come on now and let's get us some coffee."

Keller started to move to get up, then stopped and sank back down. He looked at the letter in his fist, surprised, as though he noticed it there for the first time.

"Come on now, boy," said Mose. He reached down for Keller's arm, helping him to his feet. "Come on now, let's get out of this stink. Let's get out into some fresh air," he said. But Keller didn't seem able to move. Mose slipped the letter out of his hand, carefully folded it up, and buttoned it into the pocket of Keller's shirt.

Out in the cold, in the cloudless winter twilight in which the sun still shone yet seemed as far from the earth as it could get, angling toward the southern hills, Mose led Keller off to a deserted section of the turkey yards, the both of them shivering, having forgotten to find their coats. "I used to keep some whiskey out here," Mose said as they neared the tiny section of the yards that was its own separate pen, covered by rusting roofing tin and with a number of small turkey houses set against the wire. A few of his special turkeys still remained out there, despite Nowell-Safebuy policy, and as Mose approached, they rushed out of their little brood houses and began hungrily searching the metal troughs for their evening feed.

"Here we go," Mose said. He reached in behind the feed bin and found the half-full bottle of rye he had long ago stashed there. He led Keller inside the small enclosure, and they huddled against one of its tin walls, out of the wind. "This'll warm us up," he said.

"Thank you very much." Keller tipped the bottle up and swallowed three big gulps. A few turkeys began to approach them, moving in cautious circles, scratching at the frozen earth. Mose drank down a quick swallow and passed the bottle back to Keller, who this time took one long pull that left it nearly empty. The sun was sinking now, drawing its orange scarves back into its pockets, and they stood there for a long time, watching the changing light. "He was my friend," Keller said. "Two hundred and ten were in our original artillery group. Only seven of us were left by the end. We were transported here on the same boat. . . ."

"It just happens sometimes," Mose said. "Hands, arms, slipping on the floor and breaking bones . . ."

"He was happy to be here. To be alive so his children might one day know him."

"Hands mostly. Ten years in there and most men can't even close their fingers around their paychecks."

"Hitler left us in the desert with nothing. No food. No water. No bullets. Berlin just tossed us into the trash heap and left us to die. . . ."

"I'm sorry. None of it's our doing. None of it's our fault," Mose said. "It's all one hell of a screwup. That's it. That's all we know. Somewhere along the line, this whole damned world just got all fouled up. . . ."

"*Ja, ja. . . .*"

Turkeys came closer now, beaks bent low to the ground, quick dark eyes watching for any movement, one of them even trying a fast peck at Keller's shoelace then jumping back with a flutter of its wings. The boy let loose a sound that might have been a tiny embittered laugh. He poked one of his heavy work shoes ahead a little, shaking the laces, and the turkey pecked at them again and danced back warily. It was a huge turkey, old and ragged-looking and with half its reddish feathers molted in balding patches. Still, it strutted in front of them like it was as proud as ever, then it settled its bony carcass low to the ground, reached its bald blue neck high and let loose with a hoarse-sounding imitation of how it had once called out like a siren to the hens. Then it presented itself, fanning out its red-and-white tail once more surprising than a peacock's but filled with big spaces now, feathers missing, a sad and pitiful show.

"*Truthahn . . . Truthahn . . .*" Mose repeated like it was the first time he had ever practiced the word for a tom turkey.

"*Ja, ja. Truthahn . . .*" Keller said.

It was almost dark now. The two men watched the old bird for a long time, finishing the few drops in the bottle, feeling a strong, sad emotion, and it was as though they shared a deep and sudden agreement on something profound.

The night took over from there. Mose never even thought of bringing Keller back to the waiting trucks and packing him in with all the others like cattle to be driven off to the Orman Camp. He just signed Keller's name to the night-shift list as he had dozens of times before. Though the holiday rush for turkeys and the need for emergency swing shifts was over, a night crew of prisoners still stayed on at the Nowell-Safebuy to help Will McCarthy with maintenance. So with the both of them feeling the fog of the whiskey and the stinging and now sunless cold reddening their ears and faces until they couldn't stand it anymore, it was easy to toss all caution aside.

They stood together and watched the loads of prisoners leaving, truck engines groaning off into the wintery night on their way back to the ''Fritz Ritz,'' as most people in town had started calling the Orman Camp. Mose found an old sheepskin coat for the boy, one that didn't have POW painted across its back. The two night-shift guards didn't even notice as Mose led Keller past them toward the big chain-link gate topped with barbed wire and straight for the wide-open streets of the town. Keller hesitated a few steps at the gate, stopping to look back at the Nowell-Safebuy plant, all lit up like a huge ocean liner in the eerie blueness of the starry evening. Just one more step and he would be free, unconfined by guards and wire for the first time in almost a year.

"Come on now!" Mose said loudly. He threw an arm across Keller's shoulders and dragged him out into the street. The boy laughed then, nervously, his eyes wide, a big smile on his mashed-up face. "Let's just damn the rules and go on and have ourselves a time!"

A good time for Mose always started at the Nowell municipal bar, the one saloon in town, owned and run by the town as its main source of revenue. He led Keller through the rattling glass door and straight up to the bar, where Dolores Moss, an appointed official more powerful in many ways than the mayor, tended to her bottles and taps and the bright displays of jarred sausages, hard-boiled eggs, potato chips and pretzels in their wax-paper bags. It was a weeknight. The place was nearly deserted, save for a few of the union boys who were stewing over their beers. They always took a booth toward the back, partly to be next to the pool table, mostly because Dolores Moss usually sat them there so their blood-spattered coveralls reeking of butchered turkeys wouldn't drive her out of her own saloon.

"It's nice in here," Keller said. He hopped up on a barstool just the way Mose did, a kind of two-handed vault.

"Never heard this old sty called nice before," said Mose. "This place is generally rough. Been here ever since Nowell was a cow town. Nothing here but this saloon, that hotel across the street, and a big corral out by the railroad tracks. Herded steers in here thousands at a time!"

Mose was loud, too loud. Dolores Moss glided over to them with her firm and disdainful expression already on her face, the same one she used when she was ready to cut somebody off. Mose clapped Keller around the shoulders like he was his best friend. "What'll it be, boy! Whiskey? Beer?"

"Maybe a little beer . . ." Keller said. There was a sad expression on his face and in his voice. Nothing could take away what had happened.

"Dolores! Two whiskeys here! Two beers!"

Dale Rynning was with the union boys in back. If Mose hadn't been so loud, maybe nobody would have done anything. But it was too late now. Dale rose up out of his booth like a bear coming out of its den. His huge shadow suddenly filled the mirror behind the bar and one of his arms fell across Mose's shoulders as heavily as a haunch of beef. "Just what in the hell's going on here, Mose?" Dale tipped back and around in his big rubber boots. He had been drinking steadily since the early shift whistle. "You know better than this," Dale said. "Go on and tell me what this Nazi scab's doing here stinking up the place."

"Get your hands off me," said Mose. "Right now."

Dale didn't make a move to lift his arm.

Keller downed his beer in one quick swallow. "Here. We go now, sir. . . . "

"Nobody's going anywhere," Mose said.

"Come on, Dale," said Dolores Moss. She was already reaching under the bar for her sawed-off Louisville Slugger. "Let's keep it friendly now."

"You know who this is? This is a Fritz here. A goddamn prisoner. Since when do you serve liquor to the Nazis? I'll bet this sucker ain't even old enough to drink!"

"That right Mose?" Dolores asked. She looked closely at Keller for the first time, the same kind of scrutiny she used to give reservation Indians who came in begging for free drinks.

"He ain't any Nazi," Mose said. "Tell 'em you're not a damn Nazi, Keller!"

"I'm sorry. . . ." Keller saw the look Dale was giving him and stopped. He turned his face toward the foggy zinc surface of the bar, his body tensed as if he was ready to jump, but Dale's huge mass was in his way.

"This is business. Strictly business," Mose said. "The man here's my interpreter. We got business to discuss!"

"It's against the law, that's what I say. Besides that, me and the boys don't drink with no Nazis. Not here. Not anywhere." Dale leaned on his arm a touch more, increasing the pressure just enough to squeeze Mose's chest against the bar so that it was hard for him to breathe. "This here is ours. American territory. Maybe they can work the plant because that's the way it's got to be. But you can't go letting them run around this town. You get me, Mose? So why don't you go on now and talk your business someplace else!"

There are times when, faced with unreasonable force, a man just doesn't have any choice. Talk alone can't get him out of it. Thinking things through ends up appeasement. Action alone makes the difference. Rapid and decisive movement. Quick reflexes overcoming force with force. And this Mose did. He whipped one hand to his hip so fast that before Dale had time to so much as reach for it, there was a big heavy pistol shoved into his belly. "A man was killed today," Mose said. "This boy's friend. Hell, my friend too. Everybody knew him. One of the belt rollers on the canning line chewed his arm up to the shoulder. Reached in too far. That's what happened. Then he died. Just up and died. And here you are just about to do the same. You get your hands off this second or, I swear to God, I'll make it two in one day."

Dale's arm came up and he stepped back, opening and closing his huge fists. Dolores Moss was jumping for the telephone and starting to dial the sheriff. Keller was trying to put a hand on Mose's wrist, muttering rapidly in German, already off his stool and on his feet. Mose just sat there, pistol raised, a tense grin on his face as he yanked the gun away from Keller's reach. "Just finish up your drinks, boy," Mose said. "We don't have to worry about this tub of guts now. No, sir. Not you, Dale. Buster's been waiting for any excuse, anything, just to fire you straight out of there. Well, you got it now. Don't you bother to show up tomorrow. Don't you bother to show your face there ever again."

"Out! Out of here now!" Dolores Moss had hung up the phone, getting the county dispatcher but not raising Sheriff Meeker, who was likely sitting drunk in his patrol car out by his speed trap. Or he was off into the gumbo, chasing down ranchers whose sheep had strayed through the fences onto the roads. "Don't you ever bring that thing in here! Damnit, Mose! What did you go and have to do that for?"

"We're gone," said Mose. "My friend here and me are on our way. Come on, Keller. . . ."

"I'm sorry. I did not know . . ." Keller started. Then he bobbed his head around, meekly finished his drinks, and cautiously started inching for the doors.

"Sell me a bottle and we're out of here," said Mose. He holstered his pistol and turned back around on his stool, money in his fingers so fast it was hard to imagine where he'd got it from. "Here you go, Dolores honey. . . ."

"Don't you think you've had enough?"

"We'll stay then. Right, Keller?"

"This is it," she said. "The last time. I ought to have you arrested, damn you." Dolores slammed a bottle of the cheapest she had on the bar and took the money. Mose shoved the fifth into his coat pocket, already on his way to join Keller in the street.

Keller wanted only to head straight back to the Nowell-Safebuy, shaken by the violence and the whiskey, disgust in his voice as he marched ahead of Mose and said, "You take me out, we get into trouble. I don't want trouble. You don't know what they can do to me! Bread and water and for a month locked up!"

"Don't worry," Mose said, catching up, clutching drunkenly at Keller's arm. "Nothing's going to happen."

"Fine for you to say," he said. "You could get me in very big trouble!"

"You mean the pistol? You mean this?" Mose clumsily reached at the button-down flap of the holster for his .45. Keller grabbed his wrist, holding it fast.

"*Ja, sicher. . . .*"

"This ain't nothing. Not here. Not in this town! Ain't a month goes by when somebody don't go for his gun," said Mose. It was true. Guns were common in this country. Often even a minor argument at the bar meant that at least one of the offended parties rushed out to his pickup in a cowboy rage and pulled his rifle down out of the rack. Usually, they just shot up each other's cars or trucks. Headlights were blown out. Windshields were starred with bullet holes. Or sometimes they cruised by a house in the middle of the night and put a single potshot through the living room window. It was amazing that, at least in recent memory, nobody could recall anyone actually shooting anyone else. If things got so far as two men squaring off with guns, well, a few shots were generally fired. Charley Gooch used to joke that boys in this country grew up playing cowboys and Indians with real Indians, real guns, and live ammunition. Charley was a half-breed Sioux himself, and he still joked like that. But it seemed as if they played a dangerous game of seeing just how close they could shoot at one another and still miss. That was about it—a few shots fired off, some broken glass—until Sheriff Meeker finally showed up to arrest both men and slam them into the county jail in Belle Fourche until they cooled their cowboy heels.

"Hell, what happened in there ain't nothing," Mose said. "Ain't nothing at all. Come on now, boy! You haven't even had your supper. It's too late to get anything back at the Fritz Ritz, so come on now. At least let's get ourselves some coffee!"

Before coffee, Mose uncapped his new bottle and

leaned with Keller against the darkened windows of Gamble's Hardware. Keller barely tasted the stuff at first. He was down, low down, and Mose couldn't stand to leave him off like that. So he kept urging him on, telling him what a time they were having, how often could a boy get out and howl like this? When would he ever get the chance again to get out and really see this town? "Don't you worry about nothing," said Mose. "You think old Wenzel would want you to just stand around and cry? Would he? Hell, no. He'd want you to get good and drunk, that's what he'd want. That's what *I'd* want, if it had been me. Hell, it could have been any one of us. So come on now," he said, passing the bottle across and just about pouring it down him. "You want to see some girls, boy? How long's it been since you even looked at a girl?"

The Cove Café was about a third full with its usual weekday crowd of mostly women. Carol McCann was there, looking nice in her jeans and in a sweater so tight Mae West had nothing on her. There was pretty little Carol Hinkle, blond and freckled and sitting with that Hogan girl, both of them smoking cigarettes, eyeing the door and ready to stub them out in case one of their fathers came in. Andrea Scott was there too, her hair done up in piled braids, her coffee cup turned over on the saucer in front of her as she sipped at her Mormon icewater. A few old beet and turkey farmers were at a booth in back—Pearly Green, Jim Fuller, and Will Hartley, with his cap pulled low over his eyes and likely talking politics. Even now, during the war, he was pushing the idea of forming a beet-farmer cooperative, starting up a little refinery, competing with Great Westward Sugar at its own game, if he could only convince enough farmers to take a look at their hole cards and go in with him.

They were easygoing people, friendly and open-minded, most of them. They didn't seem to think anything at all was really wrong when Mose slammed into the Cove Café with Keller and took off the boy's coat for him so that everyone could see the POW letters painted on his back. Most of them had worked in their fields right alongside similar prisoners. War or no, in these parts the way any man worked was the way they judged him. The prisoners had developed a powerful reputation for being hard workers. Some farmers had done much the same thing for their prisoners as Mose was doing. They had gone out to the dusty hay wagon on brutal summer days with bottles of beer and gotten to know them. They had taken them into the shade of their porches and sat them down for lemonade and iced tea and mainly with gestures tried to have a conversation. Some of them had even invited selected prisoners into their homes.

"Hey, Mose," they said, watching him come through the door like nothing at all was unusual. Then Will Hartley piped up first, "Who's that you got there?"

"This here's Keller!" Mose was in a gregarious mood, pulling Keller down to their booth and introducing him proudly. "My right-hand man. Talks English better than you talk farming!"

"How do you do," Keller said shyly. They shook his hand all around.

"So you speak English! Wish I had one of those," said Jim Fuller. He launched into one of his regular stories. "Last harvest, one of those damned guards left his rifle leaning right up against my fence. My prisoners didn't know what to do. They didn't want to pick it up, you know, so nobody'd get the wrong idea. So one of them comes at me in by the silo, waving his arms and spouting off some kind of jibbering nonsense so fast I thought maybe somebody was hurt or something. That's what I thought. Then he makes his arms like he's holding a rifle, you see, and he goes *pow, pow!* Just like that. *Pow, pow!* And that really gave me a scare. Then I follow him out and there they are, all of them, gathered 'round that damn half-rusted rifle hung on the barbed wire and not knowing what the heck to do with it!"

Everybody laughed. It was the tenth time they had

heard that story, but they still laughed. Even Keller laughed with them a little. "All the time at camp," he said. "Same thing. The guards leave keys, and rifles, just the same. One of them even one day forgets to pick up a whole group of us. They spent the whole night in a field. . . ."

"Some soldiers, huh?" said Will Hartley. "It's a wonder we're starting to win this war!"

"What do you think?" asked Pearly Cyrus Green. "I mean, what do you really think?" Keller stood uncomfortably by their table a moment, not getting what Pearly was asking. Pearly said it again, more insistently. "Do you think we're winning this war?"

"Go on, boy, tell 'em," said Mose. "Tell 'em just what you think!"

"In my position, it looks to be true," Keller said. That made the whole table chuckle at him.

"In his position . . ."

"Damn straight. What would you think if *you* was in his position?"

"But come on now," Pearly said. "What do you really think? Are we winning this war or not? Straight from the shoulder now!"

"Well, we really do not get much news," Keller said. "And I would not want to say. Not when we really don't know. . . ."

"You're shittin' us," said Will Hartley. "You can't get away with that. Not here!"

"Come on, boy, give it to 'em straight. I'd like to know myself," said Mose.

"Come on now! Are we winning this war or not?"

"All right," Keller said after a moment. The words sounded like he was letting out a breath he was holding. A few tables down, even the women were listening now. "Pardon me for saying it. I mean no offense here," Keller said. "But to my thinking, it is not so much that the Allies are winning the war against Germany. No. Not that. It is Hitler that is losing the war. It is his war from the beginning and he is losing it, and all the people of the world are suffering.'' Keller paused a moment nervously, as if he was testing their reactions. Nobody even stirred so much as his boot, waiting for the boy to go on.

''This is not only what I think. This is what Field Marshal Rommel thinks too. And almost all our officers in Africa. . . .''

''You're shittin' us,'' said Jim Fuller. ''Rommel? *The* Rommel? You can't tell us he ain't no Nazi!''

''No!'' Keller said. ''Rommel is a soldier, yes. Surely. But that is what we heard he said: 'This swine heap is for Hitler's war.' That was when we had to lie down in the sand and fight to the last bullet. No retreat allowed! One of our generals, von Thoma, he puts on his best uniform, all his medals. He has been ordered not to retreat. So he stands by his burning tank this way and he lets the English capture him with a curse for Hitler. 'It is all for Hitler and his gang of thieves,' he says. 'This is lunacy,' he says. That is what it is. His stupid orders. All for that one crazy man who could never get past the rank of corporal. And I think our General von Thoma was right. Look at us. So many thousands. Perhaps the best soldiers in the world! We could have won the battle for Africa. We could have won many times if Hitler had let us. But no. He decides to throw the best army in the world straight into the trash heap!''

Keller kept on talking. He talked most of that evening. They sat him down at the table with them at the Cove Café, ordered him two big hamburgers, French fries, and coffee, which Mose Johnson kept spiking with his bottle. They asked him questions, pushed him, coaxed the answers out of him. Keller told his story. Nobody in this town had ever heard such a story as his, and before long the women had moved to a closer table. Mrs. Nilsen had turned off the radio—Phil Spiltany and His All-Girl Orchestra with their *Hour of Charm* show direct from Hollywood. Mrs. Nilsen propped herself up on her elbows on the counter across from the booth, attentively follow-

ing every word. Mose turned a chair around and sat that
way, holding himself up on its backrest. Carol McCann
scooted in next to Mose as if to listen more closely,
reaching out her coffee cup for him to spike and pressing
tight against Mose's arm at the same time. Keller kept
on. Whenever he tried to stop, people prodded him along.
They wanted to know all of it from him, just what it was
like, the real story, the one that they had been told only
in the smallest bits and pieces, which had somehow
drifted to them mixed in with other news. Where was he
from? What was it really like over there? Just how had a
nice boy like him ended up way out here?

"I am not a professional soldier, you should know,"
Keller said. "Most of us are not. Some of our officers,
yes, but the rest of us, no. I saw the war coming a long
time, in 1935. Military was ordered by Hitler for all
young men. Many of us see the direction this would take
us. So I think to myself, Well, go to join. Why not? Two
years completed in service before a war might come, and
it is finished. You are done. You do not have to go again.
So that is what I did."

They pulled out of him that Keller came from a family
of clockmakers in the foothills of the Alps. He wouldn't
say exactly the name of the town. "You tell too much,
and who knows? Somebody finds out clocks are made
there. Then the enemy thinks maybe they make timers
for artillery shells. The bombers come and your family
loses its house," Keller explained.

He went on about his town, the factories there, the
surrounding farms and forests. From what Mose could
get out of it, it seemed that during all the chaotic years
before Hitler, there was little work, hardly a job to be
had in his town. All the factories were in a mess in Germany. Many had closed down during the highest rates of
inflation ever recorded anywhere on this earth. "Whole
wheelbarrows full of marks! This you had to pay for one
loaf of bread and a piece of miserable sausage!"

Then the Great Depression all the world over. Almost

nobody Keller knew had work, money, enough to eat. "Just about the damn same over here," said Will Hartley.

"*Ja, ja,*" said Keller. "But that is when the Nazis begin their dirty business inside the trade unions." Keller told them how gangs of party members went to union halls, where lines of the unemployed were in violent moods, and handed out brown shirts and billy clubs. These unions they termed the "germ cells," and strikes were called. Workers were exhorted and bullied to take to the streets under Fascist banners. The issues were food, shelter, jobs, and building up national industries once again in the face of what Herr Hitler in his screaming speeches was calling "foreign treachery."

"Anybody out of work long enough believes in promises that can't be delivered," said Will Hartley. "Sounds to me like that's what happened."

"Worse than this," Keller said. "Workers massed in the streets. They drag people out of their houses with clubs to force them to vote for National Socialism. And what was it did we get? Some jobs, sure. But with Hitler, what were we paid? A few marks, that's all. Maybe six American dollars a week. Taxes like a sickness. And all we heard at the clockworks were orders from them. 'The National Socialist worker must know that the prosperity of the national economy means his own material happiness.' These slogans. Everywhere. We had to know them enough to say them in our sleep. 'The National Socialist state knows no classes. Only citizens with equal rights and equal duties. And alongside them in the factories and on the farms, state subjects who are absolutely without rights. . . .' "

"No rights, that's just it," said Will Hartley. "Nothing for the workers. That's what we're really over there fighting, damnit!"

"Who the hell cares about rights unless their belly's full? Go on and tell me that," said Pearly Green.

"Don't give us none of that hogwash, Pearly!"

Will and Pearly were about to get into one of their regular rows until Keller cut them off.

"But what he speaks is true!" Keller said. "We have a saying in Germany. Let me think a moment. It goes: 'The hungry dog pulls the cart home faster.' That is the way it was. So . . . yes. Things were better. At least our dinner pails had something in them now. The workers, they just keep their mouths shut. But where were our unions? Gone. No strikes for higher wages. Anyone who tried to strike was fired. They could never be hired again. Later, they were taken off to camps. And where were our leaders? In big cars with the factory owners. All in the party now. All wearing swastikas. All getting rich making guns and tanks and bombs. Even one of my own cousins became very rich. We thought he was crazy, but he saw what was coming. He sold his mother's house and started a small factory for boot polish. . . ."

That was when Keller quit his clockworks job in disgust and joined the army. He spent months drilling with wooden sticks as rifles, then he was sent into the artillery and taught how to use a rangefinder, set timers on dummy antiaircraft shells and pump them into the chambers of training cannons made of telegraph poles. His unit was made to goose-step past mass Nazi rallies in Stuttgart and Nuremberg. Then just when the real guns began to find his unit, all of them sent in after Hitler's repudiation of disarmament treaties, Keller was out of the army again. "I want to earn enough money so that I might marry. I look around my town and it appears impossible to do that in Germany. So I get good luck. I have good experience in a clockworks. So I get a job finally as a watch salesman for a Swiss company. In just three months, they give me a transfer to their office in China. . . ."

China! Who in this town had ever known anybody who had been to China? China was the place boys were told they would find themselves if they dug holes too deep. "It was like ants," Keller said. "All over. So many people. But it is a wonderful country, China. So much to see there. Maybe the best thing that has happened in my life. Even when the Japanese came, many Germans and Swiss were still there getting rich. There is no place better than China to sell watches. . . .''

As a young man in China, Keller came into his own. He described being pulled around in rickshas through Shanghai, and playing tennis and croquet on British lawns. He had fine clothes made. He joined a foreign merchants club, where he sat drinking good Chinese beer with Englishmen, Dutchmen, even the French. He lived in the international district with the other Europeans, learning their languages, discussing the world situation like a gentleman, wondering at the madness of anyone's daring to disturb a system in which supply could never conceivably meet demand and it seemed that everyone was getting rich. Then the smoke of war grew thicker even there. The Japanese extended their cruel administration, their bombings, their prisons. Hitler swept through Czechoslovakia in the name of German ''living room.'' His armies stood poised on the border of Poland. ''Everyone was sure that the French and English would once again back down,'' Keller said. ''They had been morally weak so far. And still, they were weak in their military. When the war did come, we did not expect it like it happened. I had an English friend in Shanghai, a salesman of bicycles. The day the war broke out, we wondered together what to do. His father had been lost in the first war. So he thought he must go to Hong Kong right away to enlist in the British army. But me? Why should I go anywhere? My time in the army was served! But they found me, all right. All Germans had to renew their travel permits to stay in China. Our consulate was very efficient. My name was on a list. So my permit was denied. The Gestapo took away my sample case of watches. I never saw it again. They kept me at the consulate like a prisoner for a week. Then they made me swear the oath to Germany and to Hitler. I was in the army all over again! They put me on a boat for Germany.

It was a German boat. But we flew a flag of Argentina all the way. Our captain knew Spanish. Some of the crew were told to grow mustaches and dye their hair black. When a British ship came close enough to see us, an alarm sounded. These crewmen all had to be on the decks. . . ."

Once back in Germany, Keller was sent straight into a fighting unit as an artilleryman in the Afrika Korps. He was given a khaki-colored uniform with sets of long and short pants, canvas and leather boots, a light greatcoat, a pith helmet both awkward to wear and totally useless against enemy shrapnel, a steel helmet, a leather bandolier, a pack, and two canteens. He was shipped with his unit by railroad into Italy. Then, in Trieste, when he and his comrades expected at least enough supplies to feed themselves decently before their highly dangerous crossing of the Mediterranean on troop ships, tens of thousands of cheap paper editions of *Mein Kampf* were passed out to them instead as if they were Bibles. According to Keller, these tons of books later became useful. The Nazi high command hadn't realized just how terribly cold the nights could be in the North African desert. Afrika Korps uniforms were designed for a *Blitzkrieg* campaign under the sweltering Sahara sun. Before these mistakes could be corrected with heavier greatcoats, each weighty and ponderous volume of Hitler's vanity was used for about ten minutes of warmth in makeshift heating stoves.

"From the beginning, we had almost nothing to eat," Keller said. "We drank coffee made from salt water. The Italians, they brought in chefs from restaurants. With them were brothels, in buses parked in the rear. They had lemons, good food, good water. We had few shipments of supplies. My unit, we came to live by taking what we could from the Italians. Even on the ship going across, we broke into the stores and filled our cannons with Italian lemons. That is the way it was. We had almost nothing. Only enough shells for a day or two of fighting at any time. And our tanks had no fuel. Every time a British tank was knocked out, if they could, our men rushed up, even under heavy shelling. They took what fuel they could get from it with hoses. Many died doing this. Then Tobruk. The Australians. The New Zealanders. It is a wonder before God they could hold out as they did. We even used our antiaircraft shells on them. It was my job to set the timers. To find the right range so the flak would burst over their heads. I felt very bad about that, but there it is, war, and you're the one who has to do it. They would have done the same to us, after all. We captured their supplies. We lived from English tinned meat and biscuits. It was very, very bad at Tobruk. Every day, shelling and more shelling. But Rommel was with us. He was drinking his coffee made from salt water too. He came to my unit once. He sat down with us behind our big guns and remarked how good was the food the English put in tins. It was only since he started eating it that he could shit something solid again. . . ."

Keller fought with the Afrika Korps for two years, forward and back, then forward again, thousands of miles across the broken, rocky desert from Tripoli to El Alamein. He grunted and strained with his crew, moving an ammunition truck that pulled its tons of 88-mm antitank and antiaircraft cannon on wheels across the wastes where the truck and cannon often bogged down in the sand. Or they had to be bridged across gulleys and cuts in that landscape that was like ocean waves of rock and sand. And it could storm in the desert at any time, blindingly, grit choking a man's breathing, working its way into truck engines, into bearings, wearing out even the hardest steel machinery in no time.

It is one of the oldest facts of modern warfare that artillery fire always draws the same from the enemy: big guns fighting big guns long before they get the chance to level their barrels at approaching tanks and troops. Of the 210 men in Keller's original unit, only seven who had

boarded the troop ship with him at Trieste were left alive
by the time they were abandoned in the desert at El Alamein with orders to fight to the last bullet. Some of
them died of pneumonia from cold desert nights, of sunstroke in the terrible heat, a few from intestinal illnesses.
But the majority of his comrades in arms were simply
blown to bits by enemy artillery shells. And toward the
end, by almost ceaseless bombs and cannon fire from
enemy air raids.

"We followed our orders," Keller said. "We stood
and fought to the last bullet. I remember the night that
order came through. We could have retreated from El
Alamein. We could have saved ourselves. Or we could
have done what the Italian company next to us did. They
had the same orders as us. All that night, we hear them
firing off their guns into the air until they run out of
ammunition. No bullets left! Then they raise a white flag.
But not so with us. We keep fighting. The next day, we
fired our last shell from our last working gun. We destroyed the gun so the British could not use it. Then we
waited. It was my job to go ahead a little and try to see
where the British were going to come from to capture us.
We wanted to be ready, no surprises, and surrender to
them without being killed. That's how I got this," Keller
said. He raised his right hand up to his mashed nose,
reaching for the end of it as if he was still amazed it was
no longer where it should be on his face. "Always in
battle, I stick my nose out first," he said with a little
laugh. "You can see what I get for that. The way it happens, I go to look for the British we know are coming,
and my nose pokes out. Somebody shoots a bullet. It hits
a rock in front of my face and a piece of the rock smashes
my face. So there it is. I think I am not very nice to look
at anymore. My mouth too, but that is not so serious. So
there it is. Not so pretty for the women anymore. . . ."

"You look fine to me," Carol McCann said, smiling
at him. Keller stopped talking. He looked around the
table for a moment, embarrassed, not able to raise his

eyes toward the women. A long moment passed. "Really. He looks just fine," Carol said. "Like somebody who's maybe been boxing too long, that's all. Ain't that right, Mose?"

Mose didn't answer. Others at the table all did, reassuring Keller that he looked just fine but the boy knew better. Carol was clutching at Mose's arm by then, leaning close against him, and for some reason, he wasn't moving out from under her soft implied embrace this time. Mose just passed the bottle around the table again, Jim Fuller reaching for Keller's empty cup and giving it a healthy pour. "Thank you very much," Keller said. He drank the stuff down, grimacing at it. "You are all very kind. Especially the girl is kind. But maybe I talk too much now. Maybe now I go back so I can be in time for the truck to my camp."

"There's still time," Mose said. "Forty, fifty minutes anyway. Go on. What happened then?"

"That's right. Tell us what happened."

"I don't know," Keller said. He looked at them all around the table then, grinning a little awkwardly, maybe showing his appreciation, maybe something else about him too, wondering if he had said too much. If he had talked like this at camp, some prisoners locked up with him would have called him a traitor. But what harm could telling these townspeople do?

"You are very kind to me," he said. "When we were captured, none of us expected kindness. There are some among us who still say we are soldiers, that we must keep up our spirit to remain loyal to Germany. But how can we? How can we with such kindness?" Keller waited a moment for someone to give him an answer, but nobody could. "If I talk like this at my camp, someone would surely want to fight with me. But you have been kind. And I will tell you all I know. That is how it is with me," he said. He finished his drink, waiting a long moment as if unsure if these people understood. But how

could they? How could anyone know who hadn't been
there?

"Even the British were kind to us," Keller continued.
"The British we had been fighting for two years. And
we cut them to pieces many times. I remember the way
I am captured. I am holding my shirt up to my face because I am badly bleeding. One British soldier all alone
comes. He sees the situation. He looks at our ruined
guns. He sees us coming out from behind the rocks. Our
arms are raised to surrender to him. He says he takes us
prisoner. We are all scared, the Britisher worst of all. He
keeps moving his rifle to point at each of us. He doesn't
know what to do. It looks like he might shoot. Then he
sees we have already thrown our few rifles and pistols
into a pile, and there are no bullets. Keeping the rifle
raised at us, he looks over the pistols carefully. He puts
the best one in his belt to take with him. But before he
does that, he raises his arm and motions toward from
where he was coming. He is very easy about it, this Britisher. He tells us to walk that way with our hands on our
heads until we come to a place where they are gathering
prisoners. But we are not so sure about this. Is he not
going with us? Is nobody to go with us?

"No, he says. He is busy. We'll have to get on by
ourselves. How far? we ask him. He doesn't know.
Maybe six miles. Maybe eight. Where, exactly? we ask
him. He doesn't know. The truth is, he is lost. He was
separated from his company during the night. Where do
we think his unit might be now? Which way do we think
he should go? So we show him through our field glasses
where the British will be. If they are not there now, they
are sure to be there in an hour. He tells us thanks. Then
he comes over to me. He says he is damn sorry and gives
me a bandage from his kit. He sprinkles powder on it
and wraps it around my face. He gives us cigarettes. He
gives us each a small sip of water. Then he goes off, all
alone, in the direction we tell him. He waves at us from

the top of the hill. So we put our hands on our heads and start walking. . . .''

It was late in the evening, hours past the time Mrs. Nilsen usually closed down the Cove Café. The youngest girls, Carol Hinkle and Marge Hogan, had already reluctantly left for their long drives home. It was only the few farmers, and Mose, Carol McCann, Andrea and Mrs. Nilsen, gathered around Keller by then. And it was soon clear how drunk the boy had gotten when he tried to get up out of his seat and knocked into the wall and nearly tottered over.

Pearly reached out and steadied him. Everyone laughed. Everyone shook his hand again. ''Hell, this one ain't half bad,'' they said. ''Ain't he all right? He's damn near white as we are,'' they said. They thanked him for his story. Congratulated him for being alive. They said good night.

''How about a dance for the boy,'' said Mose. ''Come on, Carol honey, dance with him! Let's get on some music now. . . .''

''No time,'' Keller said. ''I get into trouble if I am not back with the others.''

''Time, hell,'' said Mose.

''You'll have to do your dancing outside now, boys, because I'm closing,'' Mrs. Nilsen said.

''We go back now, sure,'' Keller agreed. He weaved around on his feet. ''I thank the pretty lady very, very much. . . .''

''Just one turn, boy . . .'' Mose said.

''I go now,'' Keller insisted, whipping around quickly, then walking off unsteadily in the direction of the street.

''Some other time then,'' Carol McCann called after him. She followed Keller out into the street, tagging close at Mose's heels. Jim Fuller chased after them with Keller's coat. But the boy was already half up the street to the Nowell-Safebuy plant, moving fast in a snaking pathway over the rutted snow. Jim handed the coat to Mose.

Then he, Will, Pearly and the others climbed into their pickups and started their reluctant engines in the cold.

"Why don't *you* offer me a dance sometime?" Carol asked meekly, dogging Mose up the street.

"Keller!" Mose called out. "Wait up, boy!"

"Come out to the place sometime," Carol said. "I could sure use a hand out there. Anytime. Things just ain't running right. It's all so much to have to do by myself," she said. But Mose was way up ahead of her by now, tracking Keller down, and he left her standing alone in the street.

She watched the black moving shadows of the two men joining each other near the plant building. She saw them link arms, sliding off balance on the ice. They laughed, a deep sound that rang out in the cold air as loudly as the first organ notes in church. Then they somehow managed to catch their bearings, skating on the ice, and disappeared back through the big wire gate, their dark laughter fading eerily after them.

"Damnit, Mose, you should know better," Buster Hill said. "Taking a prisoner without any guard right into the bar like he was anybody! What the hell got into you?" Buster was livid, foam on his lips, so agitated it looked like he was ready for a stroke.

"I thought it was the right thing to do," Mose said. "A man died in there, you know. The boy's friend. . . ."

"It ain't the first time. It ain't gonna be the last time, either," Buster said. "It's dangerous work. Everybody knows that. It goes with the territory. And that sure ain't any excuse to go breaking the law, goddamnit!"

"Yessir," Mose said. He stood in front of Buster's desk, hat in hand, eyes fixed on the floor under the desk, where Buster's bulldog was chewing on a knucklebone, worrying it around with its paws. Mose was badly hung over. He felt every cracking of the dog's teeth on the bone like a rifle shot. "What law?" he asked finally. "What kind of law is it against?"

"How the hell should I know," Buster said. "It's rules,

that's all. Army rules. Same as the law as far as you're concerned. But that ain't the point, damnit. You just don't go squiring a prisoner around in full view of everybody straight down the street. It makes folks damned uncomfortable. It gives us all a bad name. And you certainly don't go firing Dale Rynning over it! Not when we're near worked to death as it is. Not when we got to make five thousand birds a day by June!''

"I didn't mean to do that," Mose said. His headache throbbed. "I'm sorry for that. He don't get along with the men, that's all. Dale's just not fit to be in charge of a crew. That butchering room's got the highest accident rate anywhere in this plant. Cut fingers, cut hands, prisoners slipping around and going ass over teakettle on the cement." Mose stopped talking a minute, his hangover washing through his body in waves. "Jesus, Buster, he keeps them so damn jumpy it's a miracle nobody else has been killed in there."

"You just leave Dale Rynning to me," Buster said. He was on his feet, and he turned to look out his big windows for a moment. There was a warm snap just before spring, and the streets were so muddy that cars sank up to their hubcaps in the melting snow ruts. Mose couldn't take the intense sunlight through the windows. He squinted his eyes, turning them back toward the bright-orange carpet, which wasn't much better. "Can't fire him anyway," Buster said after a minute. "Not unless we want the union on our ass, and we don't want that, no sir. Not now. The War Food Administration meeting down in Omaha made that real clear to us. Any of our boys comes back from overseas, we got to fit them in as agreed. Just when those prisoners are really working like a team, we got to give in to the goddamn union. Pull prisoners off the line and put our own boys back on. Full wages, and raises in the form of benefits included. Either that or we got to find new jobs for them someplace else."

"Seems to me that's only right," Mose said.

"Right? Who in hell's talking about right? Of course

it's right. Hell yes that's just what we're going to do. I just can't imagine it working out. Take a soldier been through it all over there fighting the damn Germans. What do you think's going to happen if we put him right alongside some Fritz on the slaughtering line?''

"Jesus, Buster, I never thought of that," said Mose. It was true. How could anything like that possibly work? Dale Rynning cussing them out in Norwegian all the time was bad enough. "What are we going to do?"

"Five thousand birds a day," Buster said. "That's what we're going to do. The War Food Administration don't know any more about working turkeys than a pig knows Sundays. But we're still going to meet our quotas." Buster turned back to Mose, reached out and shuffled through the disordered piles of papers on his desk in search of his glasses. He put them on, then riffled through his papers again, the half-cut, ill-fitting lenses tottering on the end of his smallish nose like a small empty oxen yoke. "Here," Buster said. He shoved a map of Nowell across his desk. "We're going to start up a jobs project. Out west of here, along the highway, right at the old Jennings place. The company's been planning a hatchery, including a fertilization and research facility. Why not just start it up now? Throw our union boys on to build it. Then we'll make sure to keep the project in the building stage as long as it takes."

Mose inspected Buster's map. It looked like a kind of battle map he'd seen in movies, complete with big arrows pointing around every which way. He saw how the old Jennings place had been parceled out into squares, with the frontage along the highway blacked in. Then, on an attached page, Mose saw the drawing of a simple brick building with shrubs and trees and a fence all around it, and the Nowell-Safebuy logo on a big sign planted on its neat front lawn. "I don't know," he said after a minute. "What happens if the boys don't want to lay bricks? Won't they call that the same as a lockout?"

"We'll give them a raise enough to keep them happy,"

Buster said. "By working on construction, we can re-classify their jobs to get around the wage freeze. What else can we do? We can't just throw them in there on the line, damnit! Then once this war's over, it's another story. How many of the boys are going to complain when there's three hundred of them lined up at the door for jobs?"

Mose nodded his head once at that fact.

"We get the project going, then we'll see if we can take Dale Rynning off the line and set him out there lay-ing bricks," Buster said. "But that's likely to be a while yet. And we'll need somebody else, maybe Bruce Mc-Govern, somebody who knows what to do when there's a breakdown. So until that happens, you keep your mouth shut. Get along with that sonofabitch. Any more friction between you two and you're both fired."

"Yessir," said Mose. He waited a moment for Buster to say something more. His headache pounded in a steady rhythm like machinery ripping through tin. Then he re-membered what he had come into Buster's office for in the first place. "Listen," he said. "About a safety guard for the canning belts. We got to get somebody in there to figure out what to put on. Maybe a steel panel. Maybe something else. We should get it done right now."

"We got the safest and most advanced equipment in this industry," Buster said. "Accidents are bound to happen. Along with logging, this is the most accident-prone business in the world."

"But listen now, just one minute. I was just thinking how we might get in an engineer. . . . "

"We'll see what we can do," Buster said. "Just don't expect anything overnight. In the meantime, put a card-board panel up there and a warning sign."

"But, Buster . . ."

"We'll do what we can, damnit!"

"Yessir," Mose said. He tried to imagine how to rig up a cardboard or maybe a plywood panel as a guard in the meantime. "That boy Keller didn't come in this morning. Likely as hung over as I am. As soon as he comes in tomorrow, I'll get him painting out a sign in German and then rig something up myself.''

"Keller?'' Buster asked. "Which one is that?''

"The boy,'' said Mose. "You know. The one who talks English good enough to help. The boy I took out last night. Damn good worker too, and the way he talks . . .''

"Sure, him. That's right. That's his name,'' Buster said. "Well, you'll have to find somebody else. Major Pierce marked him down as an attempted escape. He's locked him in solitary for a month as an example.''

"What?''

"Major Pierce phoned in this morning,'' Buster said. "Somebody told him all about it. The sheriff was called, you know. Could have been one hell of a mess if he'd been there to arrest you both last night.''

"But he never escaped!'' Mose shouted. "He never escaped! I took him out myself! Put him in the truck myself! Jesus, Buster . . .''

"Hold on now,'' Buster said. "And get your hands off my desk, you'll mess up my papers. . . .''

"But, Buster . . .''

"The boy's in no trouble, so just relax a second,'' Buster said. "Major Pierce knows the prisoner didn't escape. He explained it all this morning. His commanding officer over in Salt Lake City was thinking about cutting down on his guard staff because there hadn't been any escapes. Not one. Not even anything like one. So he just wrote this boy up as one so he could justify keeping a full staff on. You see, the major doesn't want to be caught with his pants down just in case there ever *is* an escape.''

"Jesus, Buster . . .'' Mose felt like a horse had kicked him. "The boy didn't do anything. He don't deserve this. He's a good worker. . . .''

"The major said he's in solitary as a warning to the others,'' Buster said. "But he's cut out the bread-and-water part of it. He's got three good meals a day, books, everything, even a radio. It's all just for show. So don't you worry. The major said he'd be back on the line fit as ever in a month. And he asked us to back him up on the escape story if it comes down to it. So it's a good thing it happened. I mean, how many hundreds of them are in there right now? What in hell would we do if something really happened? Think about it once. Do we really want the army to cut down on the number of guards just in case?''

"But, Buster," Mose said. He felt he was on the deck of a hay wagon, bucking over ditches. He sat down, sick to his stomach, words reeling in his head too fast to speak them. "I'm . . . it's my fault . . . and we need him . . . the poor boy . . . not fair, damnit . . .''

"Nobody blames you for a thing," Buster said. "Not me, not the major, not anybody. We're even grateful to you. Sometimes a man needs to go one step too far just to find out where the line's really drawn. So you were the one to do it, it happened, and it's all worked out just fine. Could have turned out a lot of other ways. The major was even saying if it was somebody else, a man we didn't need too much, he'd like to have written up charges of aiding and abetting. Federal charges. Then dropped them, of course, before the FBI got into it and the whole mess ever got into court. So we're damned lucky this time. We know just where that line is now," Buster said. "Think about it, Mose. It's all worked out just fine for everyone.''

Buster's attention focused again on his map, and on a sheaf of papers attached to it, which he seemed to be mulling over, page after page. Mose was on his feet, turning and ready to leave; then he spun around again, Buster not even noticing as he approached the desk. Mose stopped there a moment, looking down on his boss, breathing in and out of his nose, as steady as a boxer. "It ain't just fine," he said. It was only then that Buster saw him. He squinted up through his reading glasses with a surprised expression. "You hear me? Nothing's fine about it.''

"Now we've been through this . . .'' Buster started.

That was enough. Valves blew inside. Pent-up springs let loose. Mose was doing a kind of mad dance in front of Buster's desk; he nearly jumped across it, ripping the stack of papers out of Buster's hands. ''You get him out! You hear me? Out! Now!'' he shouted. He kicked Buster's desk, hard, not even feeling the way he cracked into the wood with his bad foot. Buster's bulldog scamped toward the office door with a yelp. ''Get on that phone right now and see to it, goddamnit! Or you can take this here map and my job and everything else around here and shove it up your ass!'' He was out of control. Even Buster could see that much, and he scooted his chair on its loud wheels back against the windows to get out of the way. With one sweep of his arm, Mose cleared Buster's desk in a hurricane of papers sent scattering all over the room. ''What don't fit up your ass you can shove down that goddamn major's throat! You hear me! So get him out! Now!''

''Damn you, Mose. . . .''

''Fire me! Go on ahead! I dare you, damnit—see if you got the guts,'' said Mose. He was out of breath, calmer now, hardly able to believe the mess he was standing in and that he had caused. He took a short step back, his boot soles skidding on the papers so he had to grab at a chair to keep his balance. ''I mean, I've just about had enough. I need that man,'' he said, leaning against the chair, his voice quavering. ''The whole plant needs him. Who the hell else can I rely on like him? Who else? Who else?''

''I'm sorry Mose,'' Buster said. ''But I've explained all that to you. . . .''

''You got until tomorrow. I don't give a damn how you do it. He's either on that line tomorrow or I quit. Flat out. Quit,'' said Mose. ''Now you go on and get Bruce or Irwin or somebody to wash the place down and send them home. I'm taking the rest of the day off.'' He kicked a pile of pages flying with one toe of his boot, his bunion throbbing with an electric pain. ''That's all I got to say,'' he said then. He turned and limped out of the office past Carrie Whitcomb, Buster's secretary, who was looking on from the doorway with a dismayed expression. As he slammed the door behind him, she was already sinking to her hands and knees, sifting through the mess, Buster still backed up against his windows, rigid, not moving, as frightened as if someone had just tried to shoot him.

12

Spring 1944. A season of measured preparations on all fronts. Mose watched and read with increasing hope the newsreels and newspapers that showed how stone upon stone was piled up at Leningrad, the rubble dug out after the city's merciful liberation. Army and marine divisions were described as bobbing around gently on their troop ships, which cruised at half speed in a calm Pacific, waiting for the last big push at the Marianas and the Philippines. Routine in England took over with a mind-blurring repetition of field drills and boat drills and equipment checks day after day, the sky above darkened and droning continually with thousands of bombers, all of them ours by now, so it seemed there was no end of them.

In Wovoka County, trainload after trainload of gray screeching turkey poults began pulling in and unloading day and night. Dozens of farmers and farmers' wives sat in their trucks at the railheads every day, waiting in line to drive the wooden crates of them back to their farms, where they were sorted out into pens warmed by naked

light bulbs, little yellow chicks put in with them to teach
them how to eat, then they were doctored with medicinal
additives to their feed. Farmers walked their fields with
sticks in their hands, poking them into the ground, testing the consistency of the earth under the warming yellow sun to decide on the first day they could risk taking
their tractors out to start their planting without sinking
through up to the wheel hubs in the gray muddy clay
under the few fragile inches of their topsoil. Machinery
was tuned, accounts were settled, all the chairs at the
First Bank of Belle Fourche were filled with farmers
looking to roll over their loans. At the Nowell-Safebuy,
a temporary lull fell over the plant as the slaughtering
line was taken apart again and reassembled with German
ingenuity, which lengthened it another forty feet, then it
was sterilized, greased, adjusted, left ready and waiting
for the last big push of the summer campaign.

    Keller had come back to the plant in two days, and
Buster never once said a word to Mose about what had
happened in his office, or how he had gotten Keller out,
and Mose never ventured to apologize. Buster wasn't a
man to dwell much on his disagreements, especially if
he had lost one. Though Keller helped with translating
to Mose and Will McCarthy all of the prisoners' pro-
posed equipment overhauls, Mose didn't see that much
of him. There was so much to do, so many details, that
he felt he couldn't ever get anything completely done.
He was out of the plant more than he had ever been,
everywhere at once, it seemed to him, in town and on
surrounding farms, on the run fourteen hours a day. At
the plant building, he left the work mainly up to Will
McCarthy and the help of Keller's English to find out from
the prisoners just what it was they were doing in there,
with the machinery piled up in pieces all around them.
Will complained about having to change his schedule
mainly to days, but he was soon glad enough. Will was
exceptionally pleased with their ingenious work. "Don't
worry about a thing," he said to Mose. They watched a

team of prisoners arc-welding together a curving section of a new stretch of overhead turkey tracks. "I ain't never seen anything like it. The best we can do is just set back and leave everything to them. Maybe tell the rest of the night maintenance crew to get out of bed and come down here to watch. We all just might learn a thing or two from them."

Mose took Will McCarthy's advice and tended to other business, mainly keeping track of all the turkey poults coming in, seeing that the right farmers got the right numbers of them, and making sure those crates of gray screeching balls of down didn't pile up at the loading docks. Thousands of the tiny birds died of exposure anyway. Mose set crews of prisoners to work scrubbing down the railroad cars with iodine and wire brushes. Then he had to be running off to the turkey yards, monitoring the steady loads of grown turkeys still coming in, making sure they were sorted out, confined in pens, fed, watered, driven under tin roofing every time it threatened to rain so they wouldn't tilt their heads up at the sky and, amazingly, open their beaks wide to the falling rain and drown themselves. By now they were all that same White Holland hybrid turkey developed in Texas. With the exception of catfish and most kinds of chickens, these turkeys were the most efficient converters of feed to meat in the world. But they looked feeble to Mose, strangely dull-eyed. From farmers' reactions the year before, he knew what complaints to expect in the coming weeks. They still weren't accustomed to these strange new birds, maybe never would get used to them. Farmers would come to him in droves at first, complaining that these new poults seemed to reach the pullet stage much later than any other turkey they had seen. After that they would come to him again, complaining that these new birds had grown up to weights of thirty pounds and more so fast the legs couldn't keep up with the rate of weight gain. Mose envisioned a million of these strange new birds out here growing now, white-feathered turkeys in a single huge flock that filled his view to the horizon, all of them ricketing around on those collapsing, wheatstraw legs. But at least Mose's worries about the new poult shipments gave him whole afternoons working with farmers, off away from the slaughtering plant. He was grateful for that much. It even reminded him at times of what he used to feel like when he was just a yardman.

But all of it was too much to do for any man. The only way it seemed he could make it through the long hours of his day was to duck off to his little house for ten-minute breaks, fortifying himself with a few fingers of rye from his bottle, then lying down the way he had read in *Collier's* that Churchill was doing in his war room, for little five-minute naps. Then he hauled himself up, doused his head and shoulders under the kitchen spigot, shoved his work hat back on his head, and was off and running again.

Nights he was so wired from his days that he could hardly sleep. He sat at the end of the municipal bar and took his medicine, glass after glass, until Dolores Moss finally closed the place down. He woke up mornings feeling like his head was a wheelbarrow full of gravel. He was waking up later and later in the mornings. He snapped out of bed, threw on his clothes, bolstered his cowboy coffee with something stronger now and rushed off into the painful glare of morning. He thought of one of his Sunday lessons: *None shall be weary nor stumble among them; none shall slumber nor sleep; neither shall the girdle of their loins be loosed, nor the latchet of their shoes be broken. . . .*

Weeks passed like a whirlwind. Fields were planted. Turkeys were growing everywhere at a miraculous pace. The Nowell-Safebuy plant was slowly gearing up, moving again, working out all its new bugs. Keller was put on the job of painting cardboard safety warnings in German wherever Mose could see one might be needed. He also helped Mose clear up a misunderstanding about just how many prisoners were going to be needed at critical

stations, rearranging the crews. But the boy said little
else to Mose, and seemed to be keeping his distance as
much as he could. Aside from that, everything appeared
so right, maybe *too* right, which kept Mose stewing all
the more that something was wrong he hadn't seen. But
no matter his nightly worrying, the plant had never
looked better than it did that spring. This whole country
was strong and heated up and alive again. All the bows
were bent. Everything was ready for June.

The big push was suddenly on. The speedup of operations at the Nowell-Safebuy was phenomenal. Truckload after truckload of turkeys were unloaded in what seemed continuous convoys. Prisoner crews wielded long poles and whipped lengths of rope around at the flocks to keep them moving down the loading chutes and through the yards. Squat, fat-breasted hens were driven into one area of the holding pens. Larger and more gangly toms were marshaled off into another section. Prisoners rushed around in the loading chutes and at times leapt in to rip off the birds that clung on to the wire. Sometimes, when tom turkeys refused to be driven along, one of the big birds was picked up by the legs and dragged on the ground like a sack of meal ahead of the gobbling crowd. For some reason unknown to man, the rest of the flock then dumbly followed in its trail. The yard prisoners worked at a perpetual trotting speed under the hot sun, moving hundreds of turkeys an hour down out of the trucks and into the yards. The lots of birds were weighed, tickets written out, slips sent by prisoner runners up to the main office, where the checks were cut for the farmers. Each day, there were times when the yard crew fell behind and flotillas of turkey trucks began to back up on Main Street in numbers never before imagined.

Once off that beachhead of the scales and the holding pens, the panicked, gobbling flocks were pushed along through tall wire canyons by another crew. The birds were massed about fifty at a time into a funneling chute, at the mouth of which two prisoners, with one extra standing by for relief, manned a small sliding gate. Those workers each had ten to fifteen seconds to bend down, lift the gate, then reach into that chute mouth and snap up a turkey by its feet before the gate sprang closed against the crowd of birds. Overhead, wire clips moved steadily along on a clattering track. With the bird struggling in his hands, flapping its wings, slashing around wildly with its beak, turkey shit flying everywhere, the worker had to reach up and slip the big, sharp-clawed feet through the moving clips so the bird was fastened home. Two men five or six times a minute, six hundred plus turkeys an hour, five thousand birds a day.

The work was monotonous, repetitive, nonstop. It was full of nicks and cuts from claws and beaks. The strain in the back, arms, and shoulders was like that of lifting weights from the floor to over the head as much as a thousand times a day. Seconds were crucial. One foulup, one cantankerous or particularly strong turkey breaking loose, and precious time would be lost in trapping the bird and tossing it up again or, worse, chasing it around ridiculously in chaotic circles, white feathers flying in the cramped few feet of the concrete throat of the plant. Just a minute or two lost, and it might take a quarter of an hour of extra rushing labor for a man to catch up to his rhythm on the line.

Everywhere in the plant, it was the same; timing measured in seconds, the rush to keep the pace going or else lose the rhythm of the whole shooting match. The turkeys

passed through the eerie flashing blue glow of the
electric-shock machine, which gave off a charged smell
of burning feathers. Turkey throats were slit and the birds
were bled out by a shifting roster of prisoners, who had
to relieve each other so they could hose down their glass
face masks enough to see. After the steam defeatherer
with its pounding rubber fingers stripped the turkeys bald,
men with knives on the line had to use them in a few
precise instants, three or four cuts to each man on the
line, eight or ten seconds with the knife at most before
the next bird came swinging in front of him, and the
next, then another and another, over and over again thousands of times. The atmosphere there was hellish, noisy,
pressured almost beyond imagining. In the plant's harbor
mouth, where the birds were sliced open and gutted, their
parts pulled down through the cavity where their necks
had been, a putrid blood-hot steam rose up from the carcasses and joined a bath of steam that washed in from
the defeathering machine like a sauna. Added to this, the
heat of so many sweating men and the merciless summer
sun outside could raise the temperature in that section at
times to a hundred and ten degrees. That was the temperature Mose had clocked more than once by thermom-
eter, standing there helping his heat-exhausted prisoners.

From there the birds were pulled through into the
butchering room, chilled down in a cold-water bath, some
moved along to the wrapping stations, where giblets,
hearts, and livers rolled in paper were stuffed inside, then
the birds were shoved in net bags, tossed into foil packs
and hustled to the arctic atmosphere of Bruce Mc-
Govern's cold-storage room, where prisoners labored
away at the freezer racks, dressed in their ski caps and
parkas. Other turkeys were tracked along from the chill-
down tank up to the boning tables, where their firm fat
breasts were sliced off in seconds. Legs and wings were
pared out, the carcasses split, white meat separated from
the dark and tossed onto two different belts, which
droned along steadily into the canning room. The fat

drumsticks, wings, and carcasses were sent through a pressure steam bath until every bit of dark meat fell off the bones. All of this was accomplished by men standing shoulder to shoulder with deadly sharp knives in their hands. By the end of the first half hour of action on each shift, every time men moved, their feet slipped and slid around on the greasy and bloody and wet cement floors. The noise from the tracks overhead and the machinery all around them was as deafening as if they were sealed into the steel-armored echo chambers of tanks in battle. This whole section of the plant was refrigerated by diesel-driven compressors, so that those prisoners in the butchering room wore jackets most of the time. Moving from the gutting line to the butchering room, then from there on to the cold storage, station to station, often meant a body-shocking temperature change of more than seventy degrees.

The processed meat moved on into the canning room, where it was like a hell's kitchen with its low-steam ovens and huge twin cookers. Fast handwork was required here, fistfuls of meat stuffed into thousands of small cans by gloved fingers, boned turkey breasts shoved whole into larger tins. Prisoners working hand spray pumps filled the spaces left in the cans with a hot turkey broth agar. In the canning room, there was barely two seconds for each can at each station before it was belted along into robotic machinery that clapped on and soldered down the lids. Everything timed, rushed headlong, speeded up to the limits. The noise in there was stamped into the brain like into iron under thousands of pounds of pressure.

After the sealed cans were pressure cooked, rank after rank of them were tracked along like perfect close-order drills of shiny tin soldiers into the olive-drab spray-paint machine. Then they were quick-dried, run through the labelers, conveyed out into the boxing room. The prisoner crew there raced around, flipping open unassembled cartons as in a dance gone mad. Men with staplers fired them off like machine guns into the cartons. Other men

tossed the newly assembled boxes up on a belt just in
time for mechanical arms to stuff them full of neatly
stacked formations of larger tinned turkey breasts or
smaller turkey ration cans. One line for white meat; one
for dark. Forklifts whipped in at top speed, loaded up,
dashed off with their motors pushed to a high electric
screaming, careening around dangerously on their way to
the loading docks, where the prisoner crews labored out
in the open, no matter how harsh the weather, hefting
box after box of the finished turkey products into railroad
cars.

The Nowell-Safebuy was suddenly working at a capacity none of its designers had envisioned. How could any
plant keep up that kind of pace? Only if minute by minute, hour after hour, very few seconds were lost. No time
for thought. Not one wasted movement. Everything automatic, focused, intense and pressed to the limits of
human endurance. No time even for a piss break. Prisoners break time was radically scaled back to two ten-
minute coffee breaks, one at ten-thirty and another at
three. The prisoner lunch was pared down to half an hour.
The night maintenance crew was fleshed out by another
three dozen prisoners, enough to keep the overtaxed machinery clean, oiled, running, and ready for the next day's
action. That was the Nowell-Safebuy plan. That was the
program to make the plant the most competitive in the
entire turkey industry.

Things started going haywire almost from the start. It
was just damned near impossible to keep men running
that way. There was something else, too, that gave Mose
cause for concern. By the last week in May, just as the
Nowell-Safebuy was at the crest of one-hundred-percent
capacity, Hauptmann von Ujatz began to visit the plant
almost daily. The signs with their cockeyed German slogans—*Eigennutz vor Gemeinnutz, Freude durch Freude,
Freude durch Kraft,* and a new one, *Nehmt nicht zu viel
hin,* which meant something like "Don't Put Up with
Too Much"—now stayed hanging even when the shift was

over, because that man might be coming back in the morning. There was good reason for him to be there. Reorganizations of prisoner crew rosters were continually required, and that was part of what the Hauptmann's job was supposed to be. Some slower men were pulled off the line and sent out into the beet or hay fields. New prisoners were brought in from the Orman Camp to take their places, most of them trained now by experienced workers from the German crews instead of by Mose. But even considering the possible reasons, it still bothered Mose to see that man just sitting out there like a lone audience, a one-man show, smoking, hardly ever leaving his chair, calling in workers off the line as though for consultation, dealing out his orders it seemed to one prisoner at a time and as if he were the only man in charge.

The day the overhead turkey tracks were pushed to the highest speed that the steam defeatherer could handle, three serious knife cuts occurred in the gutting room. Shoulder to shoulder like that, rushed to extremes, palms sweating and slick against their knife handles, the workers suffered two cut arms and one long, ugly gash over the ribs in less than an hour. All three prisoners were sliced open by the workers at their sides. Mose wrapped up the wounds the best he could from the station's first-aid kit, then sent each man down the street, accompanied by a guard, to catch Doc Monahan at his office for stitches. The slaughtering line slowed, mercifully. Later that afternoon, one of the butchering room workers was running a tub of scraps toward the special vertical feeding barrels. He was moving so fast that his heel slipped out from under him on the slick cement floor. His tub went flying all over the boning crew as the man tried to cushion his fall, breaking his right arm at the elbow.

It had been Mose's experience that accidents usually happened in threes. First one man maybe cut himself badly, the end of a thumb or a finger sliced off. In minutes, everyone on down the line heard what had happened, and a darkly cautious mood descended on the crews. Mose would grow tense, waiting for the second one, as the noise of the plant machinery crashed over his men like a storming sea. Their movements became more erratic. Knives halted in midslice. Caution got in the way of a safer, automatic concentration. Mose would pace up and back along the slaughtering line, watching over men's shoulders, almost able to tell which worker it would be by the flicker of dark thought he detected in pent-up muscles or in a hesitant knife blade. Mose often pulled that man off the line, replacing him for a few minutes with a "rover." Or sometimes he didn't; sometimes that only made the scared man worse.

The second injury always happened, maybe that day, or it could be later in the week. And the second one seemed to have the opposite effect on the line. Brooding gave way to acceptance. Accidents happened; to worry about it only got in the way. It was as if accidents were somehow no longer in their control, were like a lottery picked by fate without regard to who or when or how, so men threw themselves mindlessly into their jobs to keep from thinking about the dangers. Mose would worry up and down the line now, watching for the man who was swinging his knife blade too wildly or for the one who didn't hear the whistle at the breaks or who was skating too fast through the hot putrid steam with a load in his arms. Somebody fell. Or careless human motion suddenly came up against the certainty of machines. Then, somehow, after that third injury on the heels of the other two, the rhythm of the line always seemed to balance out again. He didn't know why; only then could Mose breathe easy.

But this new phase of operations was different. Four in one day. The next morning, Hauptmann von Ujatz came to the plant again. After his usual delaying ritual in front of the plant building, the Hauptmann had his chair set up in a remote section of the turkey yards, which wasn't being used. He sat out there in the hot sun, chain-smoking, not even a hat on his head. In the bright white desert of the yards, he would have looked like he was sunning himself at a beach but for the corridors of wire surrounding him. He appeared thinner, more frail than Mose had ever seen him. The Hauptmann watched on like that for hours, allowing his orderly, Gruenwald, to go off and find some shade against the brick wall of the building.

By midmorning, there was trouble on the line. Dozens of hangers were coming through empty of turkeys. Mose tracked the problem back to the source. In plain view of the Hauptmann, Mose found several prisoners chasing turkeys in useless circles around the yards and through the narrow concrete alley of the hanging chute. *"Was ist los hier?"* he asked. "What in hell's going on?"

He noticed that the men hanging the turkeys up were prisoners he couldn't remember ever seeing before. "Where's what's-his-name . . . Gunther?" he asked. "Where's Wolfgang? Who in God's name put you at this station?"

The prisoners stopped in place, turning toward him with expressions of total incomprehension. One of them shrugged his shoulders. He fished into his pocket, pulled out a cigarette and lit it, then walked away from Mose to sit down. He leaned his back against the wall of the hanging chute, turkeys still jumping here and there, trying to fly in that clipped-winged tumbling through the air all around him. Another prisoner started gibbering at Mose in a dialect too fast to understand. Mose shut him up. The prisoner was grinning at him like a mischievous schoolboy, at the same time holding his hands up in a gesture of confusion like he didn't know how or in which direction to move turkeys into the building.

"Es ist Faulheit!" Mose shouted, appalled by their idleness. And they were smoking too. *"Und nicht rauchen! Rauchen ist verboten hier!"* He waved his stockpole through the air like he was ready to strike them. They backed away, grins no longer on their faces. *"Faulheit!"* Mose shouted again, still calling them lazy, though they had gone beyond that word. He crushed out the butt

that had been carelessly tossed aside. He stopped himself and took a deep breath. "You're all fired," he said then, calmer. He took out a piece of paper and pencil stub and marked down their numbers. All of them began with the prefix 81G, the rest of their identifies closely grouped in the 6700 range. Close enough to be in the same lot of numbers, the same prisoner shipment, and Mose wondered about that a moment. He folded the paper into his pocket and said again, "You're all fired. I don't want to see any of you at this plant again."

Mose took the five of them off to the company lunchroom, where they could be sat down with a guard. He hurried back into the turkey yards, gathered a few men from his experienced yard crew, men he had worked with for almost a year by then, and started them at their new jobs at the crucial hanging station. All the while, empty hangers were tracking by overhead, the whole line of workers idle at their stations. Prisoners were milling around, sharing rumors about what had caused this unexpected break time.

"All right, let's get moving," Mose said, working his way down the slaughtering line. *"Weiter machen! Alles ist schön in Ordnung! Weiter machen!"*

The line started up slowly but was soon moving again at its impossible speed.

"Where's my regular crew? Who in hell's making changes on me?" Mose asked Keller at lunch break. The prisoners all around him were shoveling food into their mouths as fast as they could. There were empty chairs at most of the tables. Some men were skipping lunch or carrying their plates off with them so they had time to use the crowded toilets, waiting their place in line while they were eating.

"Don't ask me," Keller said. "You are the one who should know. All work crews have been changed."

"What do you mean, changed? Who changed them?"

"Nobody tells me anything," Keller said. "Don't ask me, because I don't know."

Mose looked closely at the boy. Keller wasn't meeting his eyes straight on. The boy was all attention at his lunch like everybody else, spooning it in as fast as he could, talking as he chewed. He had kept his distance from Mose ever since he was clapped in solitary, even if it was only for two days. Mose understood that. He still blamed himself for getting the boy in trouble; also, he had never been the kind of man himself who got too close to his boss. Sure, Keller still helped with translation, or else Mose had him cruising around in the cool atmosphere of the butchering room as a rover, an easy job. But now that Mose really thought about it, it seemed that whenever he came into the butchering room, Keller was grabbing up a tub of something or was rolling out a scrap barrel in the other direction like he was downright avoiding him.

"Come on, boy, you can tell me," Mose said. "What in God's name is going on?"

Keller quit eating. He looked around at his fellow prisoners, hunched over their food. Then he quickly dug out a cigarette and lit it. Mose had never seen the boy smoke before. "Look, don't ask me, I tell you," Keller said. "Stop making trouble for me."

Keller whipped up his unfinished lunch and was suddenly gone, dumping his plate on the dish cart without even scraping it clean. He hurried out of the lunchroom, in the direction of the yards.

Later that afternoon, the steam defeathering machine broke down. An alarm went off. Valves blew in fire-hose jets of steam. Mose threw the main breaker switch on the line himself, and the whole works up to the canning room came to a stop like a freight train putting on its brakes. Mose called Bruce McGovern from his racks of frozen turkeys in the cold-storage room; he had had some experience with the defeatherer. The two of them ducked in under the blasts of scalding steam and unscrewed a big steel panel on one side of the machine. At least a dozen turkeys looked as if they had been intentionally dumped loose inside, jamming up the rubber fingers, blasted around in the chambers and cooked into a jellylike mess that clogged up the steam jets. About a hundred turkeys following through had come out with most of the feathers left on. "Anybody see who did this?" Mose asked the group of prisoners who had gathered around. "Can anybody tell me what happened here?"

Nobody could tell him. Nobody knew a thing.

"All right," said Mose. "Every one of you go get a chair from the lunchroom and come back out here. You're all going to sit down right here, and by God, you'll pluck 'em by hand!"

There was more milling around, all of them in lazy motion. A half hour was lost before ranks of prisoners were set up with their chairs, Keller included. Especially Keller. Each man had to pull a shock-convulsed turkey down off its hanger. The birds were dipped in steel barrels full of scalding water, carried in from the canning room. The prisoners sat with the turkey spread out over their laps. With the dull edge of knife blades, they started stroking and scraping at the birds until the feathers were off, wet messy mats of white down soon covering the floor ankle-deep.

But on the loading dock, looking for more men for the hand plucking line, Mose discovered that prisoners left idle there had made small shelters out of empty cardboard boxes. They were stretched out under the shade of them, dozing off. The tangled insides of an old radio was plugged in in the now quiet boxing room, easy swing music drifting out over the loading docks in the unnatural silence.

Mose kicked their box shelters aside. He pulled some men to their feet by their shirt collars, then herded them off through the plant to get to work on the plucking teams. Mose sent one of the army guards to rouse Will McCarthy out of his daytime sleep. For the rest of the shift, production was painfully slow because of the hand-plucked turkeys. A small team of prisoners worked alongside Will, laboring at cleaning out and repairing the steam defeathering machine until long past the day shift's quitting time.

Normally, Mose would have called for Buster Hill right away. Buster was off to Belle Fourche with Nowell-Safebuy consultants who were helping him complete the design for the new jobs project, the hatchery and research facility west of town. But what could even Buster have done? Besides, Mose had a good idea who was responsible.

He watched the box turtle's pace of the slaughtering line, only a few scattered birds making it through on the hangers, hardly enough to justify the electric bills for one day. Turkey deliveries had to be sent back to the farms. Mose went out by the loading chutes and passed the word along to the farmers and farmers' wives nervously wondering what had happened, some of them carrying buckets of water to their trucks and sprinkling it over their birds to try and cool them in the dangerous heat, others impatiently waiting in their trucks, which were stacked up clear to the corner of Grove and Main. On his way back, Mose made a detour in the direction of the Hauptmann's chair. Buster Hill had told him to ignore that man. Well, he would. He walked up to the man's chair like there was nobody sitting in it. Then he used the wooden rungs of its legs to scrape the shit off his boots.

"What is the meaning of this?" Gruenwald was hopping around, squinting in the strong sunlight, a look on his face like Mose had just woken him up. "What do you want with him?"

"What's he telling the men to do in there?"

"We make out a report of this at once," Gruenwald said. "This is interference and mistreatment!"

Mose was worrying his boots around on the chair legs now, scraping the hard-to-get-at edges. He spit on his scuffed leather boot toes and used the canvas seat of the chair to polish them. He felt the solid bone of the Hauptmann's behind through the toes of his boots. But it was ridiculous. That man just continued to sit there, staring out ahead of him as if into some distant space, not flinching, no reaction at all, even with two men raising their voices in argument ten inches from his head.

"When you finish with that report, you make sure to send me a copy for my signature," Mose said. "And you be sure and tell this hoity-toity jackass here that any more trouble with my crew, I'll have him and half his men sent off to federal prison. Including you." He looked down at his boots, clean now, even shiny in places, and turned on his heel to head off back into the plant building.

They were idle threats, and Mose knew it. Sitting at the municipal bar that evening, after three doubles, he even felt a little sorry about what he had done. Maybe he had jumped to conclusions. After all, wasn't it possible that the defeathering breakdown had happened on its own? A lot of the trouble at the plant was just as likely due to the incredible speedup. How much longer could that line keep working at such a speed?

The next two days, the whole plant functioned like a dream. No injuries. No slowdowns. No breakdowns. On Wednesday, they even beat their quota of five thousand turkeys a day by fifty-three birds. All his crews worked and strained and sweated like the disciplined soldiers they were, and Mose began to relax a little. He even allowed himself a drink on Wednesday afternoon. Lately, he had taken to stashing a few bottles around the plant—his regular one by the old feed bin, another shoved into a special place up under one of the loading chutes, and a half pint he laid out flat up on the water tank in the company toilet. He was always careful not to run into Buster Hill the afternoons he took a snort or two on the job. Drinking on the job had always been cause for firing at the plant. But hell, who in the world was hiring and firing these days but him?

The Hauptmann wasn't out there that day. Mose relaxed a little and sneaked himself a few swallows. He leaned against the wall of the plant building and watched

the action out in the turkey yards, the neat way all the
birds were being sorted out, moved in, slaughtered, processed. Happily feeling the deep vibrations of the plant
at his back like the humming of a well-tuned engine, for
a moment he couldn't imagine there had ever been any
trouble.

Thursday, Hauptmann von Ujatz visited the plant
again. He set his chair up in the lunchroom. He had never
done that before; he had never even eaten a company
lunch, so far as Mose knew. Mose had never seen him
so much as take a sip of water on a hot day. But there he
was, and he was reading, too, a high-brow *American Mer-
cury* magazine one of the guards must have bought for
him at the Rexall Drugs. Mose wondered how much English he understood. Mose had never seen that man do
anything other than just sit there, watching.

A few minutes before lunch break, Dale Rynning found
Mose out on the loading docks. "They're leaving the
guts in," said Dale. "Every time I turn my back. I gave
one of the little shits hell for it too. Didn't stop nothing.
Go on and take a look. I'd sure hate to eat what's going
in them cans. . . ."

At the gutting stations, Mose found a prisoner with his
shirt ripped open. His neck was bleeding from deep
scratches caused by the way Dale had grabbed him. Other
prisoners beside the man were still working away, like
they hadn't noticed. But Mose felt something behind their
concentration. There was an intensity in the room that
made him uneasy about turning his back on all those
knives.

"You've mistreated this man, Dale," was all Mose
said. He asked the prisoner how he was. The prisoner
nodded his head, feeling at the scratches on his neck; at
least he could breathe again. "Go on ahead to the lunchroom," Mose said. "Go on and sit there until quitting
time. And by the way, you're fired."

Mose saw what the problem was. The prisoners at the
gutting stations weren't reaching all the way in and pull-

ing everything down the way they should. Innards were
clinging to the carcass walls, some of them burst open,
letting loose a green putrescence that washed partly off
into the chill-down pool. The chilled birds were hitting
the butchering tables covered with their own filth and
only half cleaned. The ones that hadn't been caught by
Dale and tossed into the waste barrels had just been
pushed through the rest of the processing as though nobody cared. And it was too late now. They'd likely have
to throw out the whole day's production. Also, how long
had it been going on like that before Dale had finally
caught on to the problem? Pity the poor sailor or G.I.
who had to look that creamed turkey in the face.

"Damnit now," Mose said. "Shut her down! Shut her
down now!" he called out along the line. Somebody hit
the breaker switch. He sent everybody off to an unusually
long and early lunch. Everybody except for the crew at
the hellish gutting and canning stations. They wouldn't
get any lunch today. They were pulled off the line and
made to empty out the big chill-down tank, half disassemble the canning conveyor system, and scrub down the
boning tables with disinfectant, to be ready for the line
to start up again in the afternoon. He had other prisoners
sorting out the morning's production to a separate area
on the loading docks, hefting out boxes from the railroad
cars. Mose wasn't going to take any chances. He would
make sure when the line started up that he had replaced
every single prisoner at the gutting stations with rovers
or with men pulled in from the yards.

Mose stood in the sweltering, rancid steam of the gutting stations that afternoon, watching over the new men's
shoulders. Before they were even settled down to their
exacting jobs, just breaking into a decent sweat, about
half a dozen live turkeys were suddenly flapping around
loose and in panic inside the building. Turkeys ran gobbling straight into the gutting room. Whole teams of prisoners left their jobs to go chasing after them, laughing
and hollering the way city kids might after their first

greased pigs. Mose pushed his way into the thick of them, shouting, "*Weiter machen!* Get the hell back on line! Back to your jobs, damnit!"

It was all he could do to keep control when one of the prisoners came up to him, grinning, marching through the cheers of a small, khaki-uniformed crowd, holding out his live jittering turkey like a carnival prize. Just as Mose was ushering his prisoner crews back to their jobs, unleashed turkeys still trotting around all over the place looking for somewhere to hide, Charles Borchert suddenly walked right into the plant, clipboard under one arm, his big leather case with racks of test tubes and lab equipment swinging from the other.

Charles Borchert was a USDA inspector from Rapid City who came out to the plant at unannounced intervals to take laboratory samples for quality control and to check out turkeys for disease. Parts of the butchering room still hadn't been properly cleaned. From everything Borchert would see in the chill tank, in the gutting and canning rooms, Mose dreaded the certainty that he would order the whole damn plant shut down for a complete sterilization.

Buster Hill came in from his lunch and was called down to the shop floor immediately. Usually, Buster could manage to take care of any problems with USDA inspectors. It was even rumored that he had enough influence in government to get certain inspectors transferred all the way to Arkansas chicken factories inside a day. But no amount of influence could gloss over the unsanitary conditions that Thursday. Charles Borchert went immediately to the boxes full of that morning's production, and despite explanations from Mose, he opened dozens of cans and found feather bits, bacterial slime, and other unidentified impurities mixed in with the meat. Mose showed him the few cans from that afternoon, clean as could be, but that didn't help. Even the generally cooperative Charles Borchert couldn't overlook so many problems at once. How could he sleep nights thinking our

G.I.s might have to eat what was in those cans? The whole day's production ended up loaded onto trucks and shipped off to the county dump. Mose got the order that he would have to keep crews working for the next twenty hours with iodine, wire brushes and boiling water, washing down everything in sight.

After Borchert left, Mose told Buster what he thought was happening. "They're screwing things up on purpose," he said. "I don't know why, but they are."

"Damnit, that's hard to believe," Buster said. The two of them stood by, watching a crew of prisoners on their hands and knees, sponging down and scrubbing the floor of the gutting room. "It just might be our machinery isn't holding up like it should. Or it could just be honest mistakes. Five thousand birds a day, Mose. These men deserve the benefit of our doubts."

"Doubts? I don't have a single doubt."

"Leave it alone for now," Buster said. "Let's just get the job done, crank it up tomorrow and see what happens. The first sign of any trouble, you send for me, you hear? You should have sent for me long before this mess happened anyway."

"Yessir," Mose answered. That was all Buster was going to say about it. He waddled back out toward his office, looking as if he would see to it that Charles Borchert was sent off to inspect pigs in the Fiji Islands by the end of the week. But Mose had no doubts. Mose even thought he knew how that man was doing it. He imagined the several times a day that a different prisoner left his station, marched off with Gruenwald, then requested permission to move the Hauptmann's chair for him. While he was moving the chair, the prisoner and his Hauptmann exchanged words for a minute. When that prisoner returned to his place on the line, something went haywire. That must be the way it happened. It was clear as daylight to Mose that the Hauptmann was giving orders for sabotage.

Friday and Saturday came and went without incidents.

But deliveries were all fouled up. Some farmers who hadn't unloaded their trucks on Thursday were lining up with others who had been regularly scheduled. Arguments broke out among them over who was going to have to truck his birds back, unload them, feed and water them, then load them up again in the morning. Some of the unloading was held up two days, while Mose figured out new delivery schedules and gave them to Buster's secretary, Carrie Whitcomb, to get the word out on the phone. But at least the slaughtering line was moving. It moved as smoothly and steadily as it could under the circumstances.

After lunch the following Monday, with a pressing deadline hanging over the Nowell-Safebuy to finish filling its allotted railroad cars and not delay the whole damn train, the Hauptmann set up his chair in the shade of the boxing room. He smoked away, illegally. Nothing Mose said to Gruenwald could get him to stop. He put out his cigarette when asked, then when Mose's back was turned just lit up another. All of a sudden, through the huge arches of garage doors leading to the loading docks, Mose witnessed a scene of mass confusion. Boxes of cans were breaking open all over the docks. Prisoners were running around chasing the cans as though they were in a Buster Keaton comedy. They stooped around, some of them on all fours, trying to collect dozens of loose cans in their arms. They overloaded themselves, on purpose it seemed. Cans spilled out of their arms. No matter how much Mose shouted at them, not matter that he sent for Keller to make sure it was clear in their own language, they kept on that way, kneeling down, loading up their arms, spilling out cans, which went rolling all over the place. Mose tracked down the real problem. After inspecting the busted-open boxes, he figured out that almost none of them had been properly stapled. All the bottoms were breaking out of them. Forklift loads of spilled and crumpled turkey cans were scattered around all over hell and gone. The slaughtering line slowed. At fewer than three thousand birds that day, the line had already lost so many hours that week that the Nowell-Safebuy would miss filling its orders for the railroad; at least two freight cars would be pulling out mostly empty. In the middle of all this confusion, Hauptmann von Ujatz ordered his chair moved off to the other side of the plant, out into the sun of the turkey yards.

"It's possible," said Buster Hill, called down to inspect the cleanup in the boxing room and on the loading docks. Canned turkey crushed open under the wheels of the forklifts was already drawing flies. "It's possible that man really is screwing up the works. But why, Mose? Why?"

He followed Buster Hill out of the heat and back up to the plant office, where Buster had powerful fans going. Mose sat down and leaned back into the breeze, waiting for his boss to do something. Buster looked tired. Everyone Mose knew looked tired. But he was at least sure that Buster would take some kind of action now, something would be done, and he didn't feel so alone in his suspicions.

Buster Hill wasn't a man who wasted his time or capital. He was more than a millionaire by then, though a man would never think it to look at him. Divorced, he was usually alone in his small, three-bedroom house over on Grove Street. It was rumored he sometimes frequented the semilegal municipal cathouses up in Deadwood for recreation and that he was good to the girls, but that was about all the society he ever seemed to keep, other than the Belle Fourche Rotary Club or an occasional game of pool, at which he had grown bored because almost nobody ever beat him. Sometimes he gambled up in Deadwood, but it was the same there too, since he won ten times more than he ever lost. He still drove his same old battered Ford pickup, with a metal rig in back for antelope hunting. In his clean, orange-carpeted office, guarded for him by Mrs. Carrie Whitcomb, fastest secretary in town and sister-in-law to one of Buster's favorite bankers, Buster dressed casually in white short-sleeved shirts, gray work pants, and plain rough-out cowboy boots. Buster sat across from Mose, looking closely at him from behind his desk, piled high with disorganized clumps of paper, some of which were sifting to the floor under the powerful blast of his fans and covered the carpet underfoot like fallen leaves. Buster looked deep in thought, not quite sure what should be done. His dog was with him as usual that day, the bulldog he had bought after his divorce and that he had named Buster, after himself. Mose stared down at the little dog a minute, curling itself up now under the desk and around Buster's boots. The dog raised its head, staring right back at Mose with what looked like a worried expression.

"Mose, I'm tired," Buster said. "Sometimes I say to myself, Buster, what in hell are you in it for now?" The dog's bobbed tail started beating the carpet at the mention of his name. "When this damned war is over, I'm going to retire from the business," he said. There was an awkward silence as Buster rose heavily out of his chair and walked fatly over to his window, the bulldog dancing at his heels. Buster parted the venetian blinds and looked out at the main street of Nowell, that street he had lobbied hard not to pave to keep taxes down. "I just can't believe it's that man," he said. "Every report I've seen on him shows him to be entirely cooperative. He hates the goddamned Nazis. He was a big help all along at the prisoner distribution center in Virginia. And look what he's done in there! Look what he's done all over this county! Do you know that this county right now is producing six times what it did in 1939? *Six times!* Mose, think back now. How many breakdowns did we have in 1939? How damn many?"

"I don't care about 1939," said Mose. "And I don't give a damn what reports the army's got on him, either. He shouldn't even be out there at all, you know that. It's against regulations. He's supposed to be kept in his own separate compound, away from prisoners of the enlisted ranks. Why isn't he stuck away there like all the other officers at the camp? Why? That's the enemy out there. It's high time we started treating him like what he is. As far as I'm concerned, we either stick to regulations or I just might have to take this whole thing to some higher authority.''

''Higher authority?'' Buster turned from the window and laughed. ''Higher authority! What the hell do you mean?''

''The law. Some kind of federal authorities. Hell, I don't know,'' said Mose. ''The man is dangerous. I know he is. . . .''

''Federal authorities, huh? Jesus, Mose, what's gotten into you?'' Buster gave him a look that made Mose check his boots and jean cuffs like he might be tracking manure again onto the new office carpeting. ''Just don't you go flying off half-cocked,'' Buster said. ''Get a hold of yourself now. You go on and let me deal with this thing. I'll take a ride out to the camp this evening and have myself a little talk with him.''

''He won't,'' said Mose. ''That man won't talk.''

''Maybe not to you,'' Buster said. ''But I never really tried. Not more than to say a good morning or two. But maybe that's the problem. Maybe I should just go out there, have Major Pierce send for him, then get off somewhere without the goddamned army around and meet with the man privately. We just might figure this thing out together. Start off all over again from the ground floor,'' Buster said. He exhaled a big breath with a tired-looking smile, then he moved a fat hand in Mose's direction that let him know he had decided on something. It was as though whenever Buster made a decision in his life, it would be just as easy as that gesture. ''It's almost quitting time now. Why don't you get out there and blow the whistle. Call in the trucks and send them home early. Go on now and do it. Then you come up and see me first thing in the morning.''

14

At dawn the next morning, Mose was waiting at the main doors to the plant offices. It was Buster's habit to come in that early, shuffle through his work for the day all alone, then go off to eat his breakfast before even Mrs. Whitcomb arrived. Mose expected to have a breakfast with Buster at the Cove and figure out together just what would be done. The way Buster came sidewinding in at the wheel of his battered pickup and skidded into his parking slot, rage showing in the very posture of his driving, Mose was ready to give up on that expectation. Buster reeled out of the cab of his truck looking like he was maybe drunk, but Mose knew better. "C'mon up, goddamnit," was all he said at the office doors. He whipped the keys out of his pocket and socked them into the lock with a boxer's body punch. "C'mon there. We ain't got all day!"

Buster slammed the office door closed so hard that Mose thought the glass in it would break. Buster lumbered heavily across his carpet, feet kicking at piles of paperwork. A toe of his boot tripped up on a cord and the standing lamp went down, Mose jumping just in time to catch it before it hit the floor. Buster fumbled with the keys, then rested his forehead against the cool metal of his filing cabinet. He let loose a hoarse whistling sound of exhaustion.

After a moment, he unlocked a file drawer and pulled out a bottle of his expensive bourbon.

"You all right, Buster?" asked Mose. "Maybe we should have our talk later on," he said. "Looks to me like you should maybe head on home for some rest. . . ."

"Go to hell," Buster said. "Sit on down there now! Here's a heart starter for you. Or ain't you had your drink yet this morning?"

"No. I don't believe I will," said Mose.

"No?" Buster managed two coffee mugs with one hand. He splashed bourbon into both of them, streams of it running every which way over his papers in the open file drawer. He stabbed a sloshing-full mug out for Mose to take from him, fast, before it was slopped all over the room. "I ought to fire you. Right damn now. What do you mean, stashing a bottle out by that feed bin?"

Mose looked at the floor. He set his drink on Buster's desk, awkwardly sliding it around, looking for a place clear enough so it wouldn't tip over.

"Yessir," Buster said. He negotiated himself behind his desk, finally, buffeting off it and landing in his big overstuffed chair with his bottle and his mug. "Never knew I had such a drunk on my hands." Buster took a slow drink himself, letting Mose take that statement in. "You know, that man out there ain't half bad. One smart and ornery sonofabitch," he said. "You should have a talk with him sometime. You could maybe learn a thing or two. . . ."

"So he was talking about me," said Mose.

Buster closed his eyes and let out a huge breath. His face was pale, unshaven; he looked exhausted, the lines on his face as deep as if they had been carved by a knife.

For a minute, maybe longer, it seemed as if Buster would just fall asleep that way, his drink half raised in the air. He looked old. Buster wasn't wearing his cap, as he usually did. He was balding, a striper, as Mose called such men, the ones who combed what hair they had left across their domes in stripes. He noticed for the first time the stripes were mostly gray, wildly flung out every which way around Buster's full-jowled face. Buster clicked awake, sitting bolt upright like some kind of breaker switch had been turned on inside him. "Jesus Christ," Buster said. "What in hell are you yammering on about?"

"I asked what the man said, that's all," said Mose. "Or didn't you have that talk with him?"

"Course I did, damnit, what do you think? The man speaks English faster than a goddamned radio commercial. You ever heard him do that? You ever heard him speak English? Sounds like goddamn Roosevelt! Sophisticated bastard . . ." Buster took a long pull at his bourbon, grimaced at the mug, then set it down as if he wouldn't touch it again. More fortified now, he regarded Mose with an intensity as though he had just awakened from a bad sleep. "He talked some about you, Mose. Said you're turning into a drunk on us all. Tipping the bottle right in front of them. Bad for the men. Bad for everybody. Then he said, 'More people know the fool than the fool knows people.' Something like that. You know what that is? You know what?"

"No," Mose answered. He raised his own mug of bourbon to his lips, but his stomach turned. Drinker though he was, something about both it and Buster's tone gave him trouble swallowing it down. But it was there, in his fist, something to hold.

"Shakespeare," Buster said after a moment. "Goddamned Shakespeare. Never heard anything like it. Can rattle it off line after line like that. That was after I told him you're one of the best-known men in this county. All the farmers know you. Everybody in this town knows you. You're an important man, Mose. One damn important man . . .''

"Just what are you trying to say?" Mose felt himself breathing in tense rhythmic blasts through his nose, ready for a fight. He was squeezing his coffee mug so hard it was about to shatter in his fist. "Quit shittin' me now, damnit! Say what you got to say!''

"Hold on there," Buster said. "This is about you, buddy boy. That man wants you replaced. *Replaced*. Let go. Fired. . . .''

"I'll just bet he does!''

"Hold on now, hold on," Buster said. He began fishing around clumsily through his shirt, then his pants, finally dragging out a few wadded-up-looking papers from his hip pocket. "This here is a list of demands. That man is making demands. We're landing a million soldiers on the beaches of Europe right this minute—Ike is kicking their butts all over Normandy right this second—and that man is making *demands*. Can you believe it? Can you? Here," Buster said.

Buster took a long time folding the papers out in front of his face and getting his eyes to focus on them. "Lost my damn glasses to boot," he said under his breath. "Here. 'Number one. Because of serious cases of injury and mistreatment caused by production speedup and the civilian staff, outlawed by the Hague Convention of 1929, we demand that all civilian workers be removed at once from prisoner supervision. . . .' " Mose was about to jump up and say something, but Buster raised a hand to stop him. " 'Number two. Rehabilitation, reeducation, and reconstruction are the stated goals of the terms of our imprisonment. To better achieve these goals, we demand that we receive the full benefits of our labors over and above the expenses of our keeping of at least fifty cents per day per man as incentive for our labor. This money will be deposited in a common account at a bank of our choice. Access to such funds will be given solely to representatives of our own choosing.' Do you hear

that?'' Buster heaved around in his chair so hard, Mose
was sure the sound he heard was the wheels caving in.
"The rest of this, points three to six, has to do with
things like removing the ban on radios, more books allowed, classroom facilities, all kinds of things at the
camp. None of the rest is our problem. But look at this,
Mose. He wants an investment account. A goddamn pension plan! It's worse than the damn union.'' Buster let
the papers drop to his desk. He looked at them lying
there like they were poisoned. "Jesus, Mose,'' Buster
said after a moment. "How did we ever get so dependent
on them?''

"I don't know, but we are,'' Mose answered.

"Damn straight,'' Buster said. "We can't stay in business two hours right now without them.''

"You need my resignation, you know you got it,'' said
Mose. He swallowed the rest of his bourbon. It was
warm, and bitter, and somehow it was waking him up
like coffee. "No hard feelings. I never wanted this damn
manager's job in the first place. Go on and fill this up
again. Then I'll write out my resignation.''

"Resignation, hell,'' Buster said. "Here.'' He reached
his bottle out and splashed a small measure into Mose's
mug. He leaned his chin into one of his big hands and
stared off across his office for a moment as if the walls
were no longer there. "That man and I talked for maybe
an hour. He gave me these demands,'' Buster said. "I
left there so damn mad I didn't even stop to say a word
to Major Pierce. That greedy sonofabitch is scared to
death. Locked away in his office trying to figure how to
stay out of jail if one word of this thing, one damn word,
ever gets to Salt Lake City. The whole thing makes me
sick. I drove on out of there fast, half crazy. I drove on
out of there and I kept on driving. Miles and miles. I
drove clear on over to Wovoka Butte and got to thinking.
I parked out there, you know, up near the big fence at
the state park. Looking out over all that view. All that
starlit prairie, as far as you can see. As far as you'd ever

care to see, way out past the lights of Sturgis, the little yard lights of all the farms, way out into all that distance. I said to myself, Buster, I said, *somebody's* got to run this business. But why in hell does it have to be you? When this war is over, what are you in it for then? What for? What for?''

Buster waited as if he might hear an answer to that question. Mose didn't know what to say. He nursed his drink. How could he tell Buster anything like that when he couldn't even answer it for himself?

''I was mad. I tell you, I was damn mad. After a while, I got out of my truck and sat down on a big rock. I just sat there, thinking, all night long. Twenty years in this business. Twenty years. Every weekday morning of my life I've got the damn phone waking me up to tell me the price of turkeys in Chicago. Trade this. Ship that. Futures. Options. Jesus, every single morning. So what the hell am I in it for now? It's sure not the money. I've got plenty of money. Then to make the Safebuy richer? To keep my ex-wife and that mouthy idiot son of mine living in style? Hell, no. I said, Buster, I said, you've got money enough to last a hundred men the rest of their lives. You've got money and it's your born duty as a patriotic American to see you do something with it before you die. You're a rich man. And wealth is generally wasted on the rich. But what, Mose? What should I do? Go off and build a big ranch somewhere? Give it to charity? Quit my jack ways and become one of the elders of Mormon? Hell, the tabernacle'll get it all anyway, the Mormons are damned good at coming up with it all in the end. Or how about politics? Keeping the Republican cause alive? Run for mayor of this town. Or maybe even Congress. Something to do. That's all. Then I thought, You're fooling yourself, Buster. Nobody should get into politics just to give himself something to do. I was looking off southeast by then, toward the hills. The first gray light was showing, and those hills got even blacker, just like their name. I said to myself, Buster, Buster, there's no way out of it.

No way. You couldn't quit this business even if you tried. Jesus, if you ever did quit, all you'd do is sit there eating yourself to death. . . ."

Buster's voice trailed off, and the two men sat in silence together for a long time. Mose wondered what he should say, or if any words he could say would get through. The fact was he couldn't imagine Nowell-Safebuy Turkeys without Buster at the wheel. He had never considered that Buster might think of quitting. A yardman just didn't have those kinds of thoughts about his boss. The boss was the boss. What he did was what he did, and he told everybody else what to do. Behind him, Mose could hear the sounds of Carrie Whitcomb coming in, shaking out her keys, bustling around in the outer office getting the coffeepot going. Those sounds reminded Mose of all the work there was to do today. Or maybe not do, depending on what was decided.

"Where do we stand now?" Mose asked. "What are you going to do?"

"It's all so damn complicated," Buster said. "Mad as I was last night, I tried not to let on to that man. You know, good old boy, keeping it all as friendly as a barn dance. I told him the question of wages was out of my hands. Everything at the camp was out of my hands. As for my workers, and you, Mose, especially you, I told him I'd need some time to find something else for everybody. At least until the end of the summer. Give us that much time. But I don't think he believed me. And I know he doesn't believe one damn thing Major Pierce has been telling him. All the assurances. All the promises things are going to change. When you really think hard on it, that man is just testing us. He's trying to see just how much power we'll have to give him. He knows he's got everybody by the short hairs. Any fool can see the major's accounting just won't add up, that the major's let everything get too far out of hand, every blessed thing. Major Pierce is scared, damn scared. He's let things get way too far out of hand. Crops are waiting in the fields

and his guards are leaving rifles hanging on the fence-
posts. The major and his staff are goddamn criminals, if
there's ever any literal reading of the laws. Where the
hell's all the money? Where? That's what that man wants
to know. It sure as hell all hasn't gone for prisoner expenses. So the major's let things get too far out of hand,
damnit, Mose, you'll agree with me on that? Things are
just too far out of hand?''

"Yessir," said Mose. "Things sure are that way. Been
that way so long now it's hard to imagine anything different."

Buster pondered his foreman a minute, staring at him
in that way he had, which made Mose suddenly uneasy
again. Mose finished his drink in one swallow. He didn't
reach out again for more.

"We need a man like you out there," Buster said. We
need you now more than ever. We've got a job for you,
and we'll back you up on it one hundred percent. One
word from me and the major will put on extra guards, a
few at a time. We'll slip them in so nobody notices.
We'll keep them out of sight. Just add one or two more
guards every day and keep them ready up here, right here
in the offices. Mose, what I'm getting at is that we want
you to knock that man down a few pegs. You're the one
to do that. You're the one that man wants gone. You're
the one the prisoners see every day. But we don't want
you to do it without provocation. We want you to wait
until something happens, another slowdown like yesterday, or tampering, anything like what's been going on.
It's got to be a clear-cut case, plain to see for anybody.
We want you to do it so there are plenty of prisoners
around, as many as possible out there as witnesses. That's
important, because we don't think he really has all that
much of a backup from his men. According to Major
Pierce, numbers of them don't like that man one damned
bit. Because of his disrespect. Because of his disloyalty
to their values. There have been fights out there already.
Factions. Rumors. Secret gangs. Now might be just the

time to make use of that. Feelings are running mighty strong in both directions. The way things are going, this damn war might be over by Christmas. So you're going to wait for the slightest damn provocation. You're going to wait for just that much, then go ahead and kick that man's ass from hell to breakfast. I mean hurt him, show him just who's boss. Make everybody out there watch it happen. Then we'll bring charges against him, conform to regulations, and get him off our hands. We're going to ship that man straight to the high-security prison in Oklahoma and be done with him.''

Tense days passed, days of waiting. Days of struggling at the Nowell-Safebuy to meet its quota. Whistle to whistle passed so quickly Mose felt like he walked into the plant every morning, was spun around three times, then stepped out of it again dizzy, head pounding. He went to the Cove Café, the municipal bar until it closed. He couldn't sleep, hour after hour spent up and down in his stifling close bedroom. News was all over the radio, on lips all over town. Hundreds of thousands of our boys were bottled up in Normandy. They were over there fighting hedgerow to hedgerow, bog to muddy bog. Cherbourg was surrounded, a fortress under siege. The city of Caen was being savagely defended at a terrible price. Yellow telegrams were going out in the tens of thousands, pale horses knocking at the doors with everything that followed them. The Starbritt boy, Chic Bosserd, the second Hogan boy, making two in one year, not one son left to that family.

Mose paced up and back in his bedroom. Drinking

didn't do any good; there wasn't any punch left in it, like
hot water washing down his throat. What was he looking
for anyway? Was he lacking provocation so much as he
was unaware of what was going on? What was Buster
Hill really wanting him to do? And why? What was in it
for the company anyhow? Why not go after the major
instead?

All that Mose was sure the Hauptmann had done was
to make some demands. Anybody might have asked the
same, the way those men were working in there for a
dime a day under near-impossible conditions. It wasn't
the company that would lose out if they were paid any
more of what they earned. Sure, there had been moments
when he felt like going up to that man and just busting
him one. But just who was Mose to be holding the bal-
ances? As it said in the Good Book, a measure of wheat
for a penny. Three measures of barley for a penny. And
be careful of the oil and the wine. He had never wanted
this job, never once in his life; he was a yardman, that's
all, that was always enough. Then again, there was a war
on. He was smack in the middle of it without knowing
how. And he thought of Isaiah: *For every battle of the
warrior is with confused noise, and garments rolled in
blood; but this shall be with burning and with fuel of
fire. . . .*

The steam defeatherer broke down again. At first inspection, it looked as if somebody had tampered with
the screens so the traps had clogged with feathers com-
pressed as hard as bricks. When Will McCarthy was
called in, he said it might have been due to normal wear
and loose adjustments. Then again, it might not. Mose
knew that wasn't any real provocation. He hadn't seen a
sign of provocation for more than a week. The Hauptmann had been sitting out there only two of those mornings anyhow. Mose stood nervously in front of his
prisoners on those mornings, wondering when and how
it was going to happen. He waited. The extra guards were
all at their places, shuffling through decks of cards up at

the plant offices, rifles leaned against the hallway walls. The day the steam defeatherer broke down, trucks were stacked up and ready to unload more than an hour before the prisoners arrived. The breakdown kept the slaughtering line moving at a crawl until noon. Mose gathered all the available men and set them to plucking turkeys by hand again. He sweated in the steam with Will McCarthy, chipping with a hammer and chisel at the rock-hard feathers in the traps and drains. His prisoners sat in long ranks outside, in front of the plant building, slowly scraping away at the turkeys spread out in their laps, most of the men stripped to the waist and sunning themselves, a weak breeze lifting and swirling the white down in the heat of June like an exotic snow.

At lunch, things didn't look at all right to him. He noticed how ganged up the men were, all gathered around each other, muttering in low voices; others were off apart, in informal loose knots, deadly quiet. There was a mood among the prisoners, troubled and dark, even anguished. They had somehow gotten most of the latest war news. The effect on some was as if their shoulders were weighed down with great burdens; for others, there was a flinching of their jaws, a cold hard light in their eyes as with rebellious children, lying children who would never hear any law. A scuffle broke out on the line for the toilets. By the time Mose could get to it, the men involved had broken it up themselves and stood mutely there, covering it up, making a show of shrugging the fight off but with looks of contempt. When Mose pushed his way through to the thick of what had happened, he was stopped by what he saw on the toilet door. It was a deep crude swastika carved into the wood.

"I need your help, boy," said Mose, nervous, finding Keller off by himself. Keller was leaning against the wall in one corner of the crowded lunchroom, smoking, flicking the ashes into his full plate of hash and beans. "You got to tell me what's happening."

"Get away from me," Keller said. He stared coldly

across the room. Other prisoners, a few of them bunched together at a table in the middle, noted Mose's presence there. "Find someone else to be a spy for you. But not me. . . ."

"Meet me someplace then," said Mose. He looked off over his shoulder toward the seated gang of prisoners, men who were watching them both closely now. "Out by the loading chute. Like you used to. Like you're helping me. . . ."

"Go to hell," Keller said.

"Listen to me, boy," said Mose. "I mean it. You either meet me out there in five minutes or I swear to God I'll have you handcuffed by the guards and I'll drag you out there myself!"

"*Ja, ja, Sauficker.* . . ."

"What did you say?"

"I will be out there," Keller said. He looked up at Mose and grinned, maliciously. There was something about the boy's face that gave Mose the shivers. The tired, gaunt look of it; and the tight way his scarred upper lip had twisted into a bitter shape.

"Something's going on in there," said Mose out by the loading chutes. "You got to tell me. Right now."

"At least make it look like you are working me," Keller said in a low voice. "Please. . . ."

Mose looked around to see if anybody was watching. It was still lunch break, but a few prisoners were already straggling out into the turkey yards. Mose found a stockpole. He even made a little show of explaining how to use it, putting it in Keller's hands. "Are you in some kind of trouble?" he asked. Keller turned his back and clumsily began poking the stockpole toward a group of turkeys huddled in the pen. "Come on. You can tell me. We're friends, damnit. . . ."

"I have no friends," the boy said.

"I'm your friend," said Mose. "You just tell me, and I'll help you out of this. Now what in hell is going on?"

"This is not my life," Keller said. "None of this. This

is all over soon. If you are my friend, then you will leave me alone.''

"Something's happening in there," insisted Mose.

"Ja, ja," Keller said. "Don't ask me."

"I don't have anyone else to ask. And I need to know. I've got to know if I'm going to do something about it. Please," said Mose. He reached out then and grabbed Keller by the sleeve, turning him around face to face. "Please tell me."

"When I am with you, they say I am an informer," Keller said. "Is that enough for you? Do you see me with anyone? Ever? Nobody will talk to me. They have torn up my blankets. They spit into my food. Don't you see?" The boy's voice choked back; his fists gripped the stockpole, hard, like he was ready to start swinging. "Go to hell now and leave me alone."

"Is it the Hauptmann? Is it him?"

"You should go and ask him if you want to know." Keller began to use his pole on the lethargic turkeys, shoving them back from the wire, getting them up on their feet. "But no. . . . It is both because of him and not him. There are so many now against him. Only I must stand myself clear of everyone."

"I'm going to need you out there," Mose said. "Today. Maybe tomorrow. I don't know when. You stick with me, damnit. Nothing's going to happen to you. I swear to God almighty. All I know is that when I need you, you've got to tell them for me. All of them. You've got to tell those men just where they stand."

"Don't you see!" Keller shouted. "Don't you see? They are the ones who run this place!" He hurled his stockpole against the fence. "Damn you! All I want is to go home!" The boy sat down, crumpled up right there against the wire. He buried his face in his hands and started to weep. Mose stood over him—racked like that, sobbing—not knowing what to do. "All the same . . . all the same . . . all my life I have luck, so much luck . . . and still, look where I end up. . . .''

"Boy, boy . . ." said Mose. He stopped. There was nothing he could do. He looked out across the yards. In the distance, some of the prisoners were pressed against a corridor of wire, watching.

"I want to go home. Home," Keller sobbed. "My father's house. My house. To go home and shut the door. To shut my door and never again open it!"

The afternoon whistle blew, a high, wailing shriek that made the boy's muscles jump as with an electric shock. Gangs of prisoners began streaming out of the plant building and forming up their yard crews.

"All right, boy, get up now," said Mose. "They're watching us. Every move. Get up. I'll see to it they can't get to you. Come on now. You stay out in the yards today. You stay out here in the yards from now on. You'll be safe out here," he said. He helped Keller to his feet. He fetched the stockpole, hung oddly by its spike on a high strand of wire, then put it in the boy's hands. "Don't worry about nothing. I'm watching out for you. Nobody's going to get to you anymore. Nobody," he said.

That afternoon, Mose telephoned Major Pierce at the Orman Camp. He had trouble getting the major on the line, the master sergeant saying he was gone, until Mose threatened to drive out there right damn now and find him. Mose did his best to explain to the major about Keller. The boy's blankets were being torn up. He wasn't safe. "We'll get him on the informers program," the major said. "And thanks. We're glad you brought this matter to our attention."

"He's not an informer," Mose said. "He's never informed on anybody in his life. He's just my interpreter, damnit. . . ."

"What was his name again?"

"Keller. I told you that. K-e-l-l-e-r. . . . Prisoner number 81G-5377. . . ."

"Isn't he your interpreter?"

"Of course he is," Mose said. "That's the one."

There was a strange, unreal feeling in the pause that

followed. Mose thought he could hear air sucked through the major's teeth.

"Well, then," the major said. "Don't you need him? I mean, to get the job done?"

"We'll just have to get along without him," said Mose. "The boy's in trouble."

"But Mr. Johnson, most respectfully, when you accomplish your mission there, who's going to tell them? Nobody else around here speaks enough German. So who?"

"I don't give a damn who tells them," said Mose. "That's your problem, not mine. Not his, either. We'll just make do without him. Besides that, who in hell needs to tell them anything?"

"Well, then . . ."

"Don't *well then* me, goddamnit! Just get that boy out of there! Now! Or I'll damn well take everything I know straight to the federal authorities! You hear me, Major? Straight on up to the top!"

For a long moment, there was nothing but the sound of static on the line and a series of clicks, like maybe Jennie Anderson was listening in on the operator's circuit again. "Major?"

"We'll have to put together an official statement of this Keller's collaboration," the major said.

"What collaboration? I told you, damnit—"

"It's just a formality," the major said. "Nothing to it. We'll say he gave information on infiltration of the ranks, oh, say, by Nazi elements. Or factory locations or something. Weapons plants are always the best. Stuff we already know. We'll figure it out. Of course, the paperwork's going to look a bit unusual, since he's a former escapee, if we're talking about the same man. But we shouldn't have any trouble taking care of that. . . ."

"But, Major . . ."

"We'll keep him in solitary starting tonight. Then we'll give him a new name, a whole new identity, perhaps even a different branch of service. That's the way it's done. The next chance we get, we'll ship him off to a different camp, with his new identity. That's the way we do it. . . ."

"Are you sure? Jesus, Major, have you ever done this before?" Mose was suddenly unsure of everything. He had said too much. That was his trouble, he thought; he jumped in with his mouth wagging and caught a mess of flies in it every time. When had he ever heard of the army doing anything without getting it all in some snafu? *Situation normal all fouled up . . .*

"We'll make the arrangements," said Major Pierce. "This is an internal matter. We'll keep a guard on him during transport. We'll get him into our informer program at some other camp. Trust us to do our job, and we'll trust you to do ours. I mean, yours. That's the way. We depend on the civilian sector, you know," the major said in a lowered tone of voice. "And Mr. Johnson, we owe you one. We just can't afford to let them get organized like this. Without your courageous efforts, I don't know what we'd do in this crisis. I'll see you get a letter of citation for it. You'll be hearing from us. Just keep up the good work," the major said, then rang off suddenly, without so much as the formality of good-bye. For a moment, Mose thought the connection had been cut.

Mose went to find Keller and reassure the boy again. He said he would drive to the camp and see him off personally when the time came to ship him out. "Out where?" the boy asked suspiciously. "Where will they send me?"

"Just you listen to them," Mose said. "Do anything they tell you to do. Sign any papers they put in front of you. In the meantime, think of some things I might get you for the trip. I'm going to miss you, damnit, but at least you're going to be out of this mess." He threw an arm across the boy's shoulders and hugged him like a brother. "You're a good worker. My right-hand man," said Mose. "Nothing's going to be the same."

"*Ja, ja,*" Keller said. He was bobbing his head up and

down as if to say yes. But there was a tightness in his shoulders. And a look in his eyes as if two clear blue shades had been drawn down over them.

Mose sat drunk at the Cove Café that evening. He could hardly lift a fork to his mouth. He had a hip bottle, and he kept pouring whiskey into his coffee until it was gone. He couldn't take it anymore. The waiting. Everything. Everybody noticed. It was then that Carol McCann pulled him off his stool. She clutched him in her arms, hugged him close, and pressed her soft cheek against the sandpaper-gray stubble of his. The jukebox was going with a tune just in that day, a sad and evocative rendition of that old jazzy song "But Not for Me" by Judy Garland, belted out in her emotional vibrato voice like a fallen angel's.

Mose shuffled around, lost in Carol's big embrace, lost to everything. For a moment, nothing else in this world existed. Then, when the song was over, he stood back with a jolt, embarrassed, pulling his hand off her large, soft breast, dimly realizing how far he had let himself go. Carol was boldly wanting to pull him close again, not hiding her desires in any way, her body falling back against him.

"Sorry," was all Mose said.

He turned stiffly and walked out into the night. When Carol tried to follow him, he told her roughly to go home. Starting to cry, she leapt into her pickup and drove off crazily down the street.

Without a word, Mose watched her leave. He staggered off to the municipal bar. Alone, he sat there on his customary stool, hardly able to prop himself up. He was getting it bad, bad, and he knew it. How long had it been since he had felt that way? His mind uneasy, his body on fire, his blood pumping hotly with a woman in his arms. The wrong woman. A married woman. He knew her husband well, had unloaded his birds and talked turkeys with Jody many times. And look at him now. Look what he was doing. What would his Adelle think of him now? It would serve her right, stooping as low as she had. Then he thought she would have felt any sin of his as a kind of victory now, her own kind of twisted justice. But he had never been that kind of man. Never even once. Not in thirteen years. Mose sat there all night, drinking sadly, ashamed and defiled, not so much by the poor lonely woman as by something deep within himself. Everything was wrong. His whole life. All of it. Every move. And look at him now. Look at him now. How far could he really go? What was he really capable of doing?

A hunger was growing inside him, even as the lights grew dimmer all around him. He cussed his goddamn job. He cussed his men. He cussed his God. Nothing could save him now. A great darkness fell over his earth. Everything was trouble and darkness. He felt himself sinking toward the bar. He laid his head on his crossed arms and passed out cold.

16

There was an accident in the gutting room. Commotion broke out; loud voices called through the building. Mose rushed in and found a young prisoner moaning on the floor, holding a mean gash through his belly just under his belt buckle. No provocation. Just the prisoner next to him turning too fast with his knife in hand, shoes going out from under him on the slippery shop floor. Mose squeezed cold water over the prisoner's face and pressed a bundled shirt against the bleeding. He even tried to joke with him: *"Du bist sehr glücklich so kurz zu sein!"*

"Kurzfristig, oder?" the prisoner joked back, agreeing how lucky he was to be so short, but also so "short-term." The guards carried him out and drove him off fast to the hospital in Belle Fourche. The prisoner who had slipped with his knife had turned a greenish pallor in the steaming atmosphere. Mose gave him the rest of the day off. He tried his best to get the others back on line as soon as he could. Way too many prisoners had left their stations to file past the gutting room, muttering at all the

blood. But that was natural enough. Also, that it was hard to get them back to work on such a hot day.

As Mose left the gutting room, gently urging the men back to their stations, he imagined the phones already ringing in the office with complaints of turkey trucks stacking up again. Mose hurried out through the yards to help with the unloading. He shivered with sweat. The sun was high and blinding. Then he noticed something. He passed about a hundred turkeys packed carelessly into a sorting pen so small that they were trampling each other. Putting so many so close together like that could cause a disastrous pileup of turkeys, and his crews had been warned how to avoid it. Out across the yard, several wire barriers away, a number of prisoners were clinging to a fence, looking on at a violent disturbance in one of the pens.

"Was ist los darin?" he shouted, waving his arms at them. The prisoners still hung on the fence, looking on and doing nothing.

Mose ran out toward the pen. One bird had gone down. The others were leaping in and ripping at the blood spots. It was a sight in there, one of the worst pileups he'd ever seen, that mass of turkeys fighting over the long blood strings pulled from a carcass, blood showering them until in a grotesque dancing ritual the entire flock started going down, one after the other, all of them tearing at each other in reaction. Mose had seen this happen more than once; he had seen it until there was almost nothing left but a pile of dead birds and a cloud of feathers circling over the yards. There was no way to stop it short of men jumping in with their ropes and poles to beat the flock apart, separating as many as they could. Mose came up against the wire of the sorting pen.

"Springen lassen!" he shouted. *"Jetzt! Springen lassen darin!"* He was trying to get the prisoners to jump in with the birds. "Get in there!" he shouted again. He whacked a stockpole several times against the fence to show the emergency. But he was on the wrong side of

the pen and saw he would have had to run around it to
get at the gate. He climbed the fence, fast, reaching the
top and shouting, "Come on and get in there, damnit!
Jump in there! Right now!"

At the top of the fence, Mose looked around one quick
instant. The Hauptmann was sitting out there. He had
had his chair moved out there since morning. That man
was sitting in plain view across the yards as if in some
blind, limitless space.

Mose unhooked his pant leg from a twist of wire. The
Hauptmann was there, his head turned toward the commotion, his face pale and without expression. Mose
looked at the six yardworkers at the wire across from
him. There was something wrong; they just didn't fit.
Then Mose realized that none of them was from his regular yard crew. They stood back from the pen, horrified.
But there was something else, a childish amusement, as
if they couldn't hold back from grinning both in fear and
in amazement. The whole pen had gone wild by then in
a confusing violence of blood and feathers, beaks wide
with screams. Bald red heads tore at each other's meat,
trailing blood as the dust rose over them. The prisoner
crew just hung back there, fingers grasping through the
wire. Any regular yard crew would have known what
should be done. Mose swung himself over the fence. He
tore his leg open on the wire. He swayed around up there,
ripping himself free, painfully aware of the Hauptmann
in the distance, who was calmly looking on and doing
nothing. Then Mose jumped off into that crowd of birds.

Thirteen years spent working turkeys. Mose knew just
how to do it. He pushed his way through the mound of
large birds flapping up in the air all around him until he
reached the ones that seemed at the center of the violence. He started beating at them with his stockpole to
get them apart, all the while shouting at the prisoners:
"Kommen Sie hier mit! Kommen Sie jetzt! Wie diese hier!
Come on now! Come on, goddamnit! *Wie diese hier!"*
he shouted.

None of the prisoners made a move. Turkeys scattered every which way in panic around him. Mose could hardly see for all the dust, the flapping wings, the birds passing over him like a wind. Turkeys went down everywhere in high leaping fights, teams of them running in to devour each other in an instant, and Mose out there wading through them, throwing turkeys left and right up against the fence. His hands were cut and bleeding. Beaks tore at his legs and arms. If he lost his footing, he'd have to fight for his life. But he had too much rage for that to happen. With a blind strength, he sorted turkeys this way and that, flinging them around, tossing as many as he could right over the fence. He worked his way over to the gate and threw it open. Then he dove back in and started using his pole to divide the birds into smaller flocks, their feathers so soaked in blood they were pink, shoving them out into the open yard through the gate, dispersing them to where they scattered on the run and then settled down. On his way out through the gate, Mose grabbed a prisoner by his shirtsleeve and dragged and kicked him straight into the pen. That prisoner had a look of surprise on his face, bandy-legging around in front of Mose, helplessly waving his arms at the rioting birds.

"Sonofabitch!" Mose screamed. He kicked and shoved that prisoner back out of his way. He moved in again himself to finish the job, running two more small flocks out of the pen by grabbing up a tom turkey by its feet and pulling it along the ground in front of the others. Most of the remaining turkeys were already settling passively against the fence, hiding their wounds. Mose was angry enough by then. How much provocation did he need? His stomach fluttered. He began slowly walking around the turkey pens. He tossed his old wooden stockpole somewhere out behind him.

He rounded a corner of wire and turned in the direction of the Hauptmann. What was Buster Hill really wanting him to do? There was a sudden terrifying moment when he swore he heard the yard prisoners calling

out all around him, but then again, it seemed he had
always heard prisoners calling to each other in the yards.
Mose was sure none of them was following him. He
turned his head quickly once to look and there was no
one there. Ahead, he couldn't even find Gruenwald, not
anywhere in sight. All he saw was the Hauptmann, sitting there, his eyes staring straight through Mose like in
a trance. The Hauptmann was smoking. He showed no
sign at all that anything was wrong. His legs were
crossed. He looked relaxed enough, at ease and deeply
inhaling his smoke.

Mose came to within ten feet of that man and stopped.
The sun was scorching his cheeks. He opened and closed
his fists, deciding against hitting the man with his fists.
A flood of sweat gathered in his eyebrows, dripping,
blinding. He drew back a few feet and waited, just an
instant, a few pumps of his blood. His head felt like the
veins were bursting through the skin. Then he took that
step, just one step, forward. A small, surprising shout
escaped him. He took a slow running leap and flew
square into that man, knocking the chair right out from
under him.

"Guards!" Mose shouted. "Guards! Guards!
Guards!" and he kept shouting the word, aware that a
crowd of prisoners was already streaming out of the plant
building. He looked quickly around. A dozen of their
faces were pressed against the wire behind him. Prisoners started climbing the fences, running around for the
open corridor, all of them coming at him at once. Mose
drew his pistol. He stabbed the pistol out level with his
waist, pointing it at the Hauptmann, who was rolling
over to his side on the ground.

"Guards! Guards! Guards!" Mose shouted, desper-
ately now, trying to make himself heard over the shouts
of the prisoners. He looked down at the Hauptmann. It
didn't seem like he had done much damage to the man.
Mose would always remember that man as grinning at
him through the dust. Then Gruenwald was suddenly

there on the run. Mose turned and aimed the pistol at his face. The orderly froze there, raising up his hands.

"Guards!" he shouted. "Guards!"

He took a few steps backward and jammed the gun barrel hard against the Hauptmann's head.

The Hauptmann, without so much as turning his head, picked himself slowly up until he was standing. He slapped the dust from his pants. Then he took one short step from Mose and bent over, picking up his chair and starting to fold it out again.

Mose couldn't believe what he was doing. Cymbals of the sun clashed inside his skull. Sweat ran into his eyes like a gouging into them. Awkwardly, Mose kicked out at the Hauptmann with his boot. He reached for the chair, pulling it free of the man's hands. Then he kicked the Hauptmann hard enough in the backside to knock the man face first to the ground.

"Guards!" Mose shouted again, his voice hoarse and losing volume. He was surrounded now by his prisoners. He reached his pistol up in the air, and the trigger gave. The heavy butt jogged his palm. The sound was like a whipcrack that echoed and reechoed against the building. He spun on his heels, surrounded, everything reeling. With all his strength, he flung the chair end over end into the crowd. Where in hell were all the guards?

The Hauptmann was on the ground in front of him. He propped himself up on his knees, ready to make an effort to stand back up again. Mose was terrified. Every nerve in his body was a steel spring. Now he would have to hurt that man, not wanting to hurt him. But it was like the sky cracked in two, nothing could stop it, not if he was pulling himself up that way. Mose stepped back, cocking his whole body. With all his strength that remained, he kicked that man hard in the face, his boot cracking into it like into the red core of a summer melon.

That man was hurt. He lay crumpled over his knees. Slowly, he sat up just enough to begin spitting teeth. He finished. He pulled his shirttail out and wiped his face, wavering around, straightening his body up as much as he could. Then the Hauptmann extended his legs out painfully and crossed them, the same posture on the ground as if he were still sitting in his chair. His body stiffened, pulled itself straight. He sat that way, not moving, looking dazedly ahead until he saw something. He reached his arm and hand out for it, slowly, pinching it still burning out of the dust. His fingers trembled as he brought it to his lips and drew in a breath. With a defiant expression, tilting back a face that was no longer like any face, the Hauptmann let a blue stream of smoke out toward the sky.

"Whatsa problem here!" shouted Sergeant Hormel. Guards were running in disarray out of the plant, with rifles raised. Some of them started to shove the prisoners back in groups, using their rifles like stockpoles, herding the men roughly against the building. The sergeant was out of breath and still buttoning his shirt. When he pushed through and saw the Hauptmann, in part hidden by Mose's body, his face went slack. "Holy cow," he said. "What did you do to him?"

"This sucker there . . ." Mose took a few long strides toward the sergeant, his gun wavering in the direction of the Hauptmann like a witching rod. "I just took him down a few pegs here," he said. "We been at it out here! We all been at it now!" he said, louder. The gun was pointed at the sergeant's chest now, making him slowly back away. "Why don't you just ship them all back where they belong? Get 'em out of here!" Mose shouted. "I don't want to see them back in the morning! You send them out in the beet fields from now on! Yessir! You give them hoes been sawed in half! Make 'em *bend down* for it! Then we'll see. . . . *Verstehen Sie!*'' he screamed. *''Verstehen Sie!''* he screamed again, turning around full circle and taking in the crowd of prisoners that surrounded him.

The guards, the prisoners, everyone had stopped there, shocked, watching. Even the Hauptmann seemed to turn his head a little, as if he could see, raising up his hand in a gesture that halted Gruenwald from lifting him to his feet. Some of the guards were very carefully starting to turn their rifles in Mose's direction just in case.

"Like this!" Mose screamed. "Like this!"

In a mad-looking dance, Mose pantomimed weeding with the short hoe. He nodded at his prisoners, just once, *ja, ja,* the way many of them had done to him when they understood what he told them. Then Mose dropped his pistol back in its holster and buttoned the flap. Turkey trucks stacked up down the street were honking their horns. Mose reeled around half crazy, starting out of the yards in the direction of his house. His head ached. His ears rang out with noise from inside his head. Groups of prisoners made way for him like the parting of a sea. A quiet had descended over them. Nobody said a word. He was staggering, the muscles in his legs gone to mash, not sure he could even make it the short distance to his house.

He fell into his bedroom. He reached up on the small oak chest for his bottle, tossing aside scraps of paper and dirty clothes. He sat down on his big bed and took a swallow, closing his eyes for a moment as though that could shut everything out. "You're a goddamned fool," he said out loud. "One damned stupid fool. . . ."

Mose clasped and unclasped his hornlike fingers around the bottle, for an instant feeling the missing end of his left thumb against the glass. He rolled his head around, trying to ease the tension in his neck. That's where the noise was now. That's where it was painfully shouting out. He opened his eyes again, staring blankly ahead, using his shirtsleeve to wipe off the burning sweat flooding into them. He took another drink, in long, hot swallows. There was no place he could go now. The Cove Café, the municipal bar, his house, especially his house—anywhere he went, Buster Hill would shortly find him. Then the questions, Buster noting down all the details, pumping out of him just what exactly had been the provocation. Thinking this, Mose imagined he could hear the sound of Buster's pickup engine already starting up in front of the plant building. But where could he run to now? Where could he hide?

He hauled himself up and began moving quickly around his bedroom. He threw off his stiffened work clothes, ripped his legs out of his underwear. The pistol dropped to the floor with a thump. He reached into the closet for his best clothes—new brown cotton pants, his black Mexican cowboy shirt with pink and yellow flowers. He rushed into the bathroom and sprinkled shaving lotion over his face, under his arms, ruffling a palmful through the graying weed patch of his hair. He reached under his bed for his dress hat, a large brown Stetson with double peaks in the crown, its wide brim bent to his own odd style. Mose whipped the hat around frontways on the axis of his hand and put it on, tilting it back until he felt his ears against the brim. He ruffled through a tangled drawer for his money, a heavy roll of bills he shoved into his pocket.

He left his house, out the back way. He climbed into his car, an old blue De Soto, in a panic pumping his foot on the accelerator and listening to the battery winding down from how long it had been since he had started it. The engine caught, rumbled, threatened to stall, but he gave it gas, shoved it into reverse, and spun the tires until they were smoking on his way out the driveway. As he rounded the corner onto one of the unpaved side streets, in the rearview mirror Mose thought he saw Buster's dark-green pickup pulling to the curb in front of his house.

By the time Mose reached the highway, he had finished

his bottle. In a shaky pattering of his hands all over the
front seat of his car, he searched anxiously for another.
But he knew. It was rolling around under the front seat. He
pulled it up like a prize-winning fish, still sealed, full,
the face of old Mr. Overholt on the label like his best
friend. He rolled down the window and tossed out the
empty, hearing the glass on the pavement like a shot he
left behind. He slapped his open hand on his car door
with an uneasy joy, released, and surprised himself by
hooting like a range boy into the green summer fields.

The land spread out flatly all around him. It seemed
there was no horizon, the horizon simply faded into a
dark shimmering heat mirage. Crops were growing full
swing in the hothouse of the earth. On both sides of the
road, the fields were filled with movement. Mose passed
crew after crew of prisoners of war, stripped to the waist,
dark-tanned bodies shining with their labors as they bent
over thinning beets, their hoes flashing up and down, up
and down, chopping at the rows and tossing up a storm
of green chaff into the air all around them. Farther along,
Mose passed Will Hartley in a sunlit tornado of dust
straddling the seat of his old orange Allis-Chalmers tractor pulling its sharp harrow teeth, which weeded out the
soil between his shin-high rows of corn. The highway
was busy with trucks, a lot of them with women at the
wheel, trucks that whipped by him filled with the huge
white cotton fluffs of turkeys on the way to the plant he
had just left. Other trucks strained under loads of feed
and pulled implements that swung crazily back and forth
on their hitches as he jammed the gas pedal down and
dangerously passed them. Mile after mile whistled by
under tires of wind and alcohol. Ben Hogan and his girl
were out along the road with their stockpoles, looking
hot, out of breath gathering their white-feathered turkeys
back from chasing grasshoppers in the fields. The girl
reached up her thin arm and waved, and Mose cut through
the wind with his hand just once, waving back. The sight
of her out there made him think of Adelle, the way she

used to haul herself out into the fields with him, hatless, sunburned, her face set and determined from working. It was a thought like a honeycomb sweet in his mouth and bitter in his belly. She would never let go of him; she was and was not and yet still was. He broke the seal on his bottle, twisted the cap off, poured a golden cupful down his throat. For a moment, he was both enraged and ashamed at the direction he was driving.

The McCann farm was a small homestead with only one corner butted up against the highway. To get to it, Mose had to pull off the road onto a rutted track, stop his car and open two of Jim Fuller's barbed-wire gates, drive through, stop again, get out and stretch the gates back across, leaning the weight of his body against the posts and squeezing them back into their wire halters. One of them was so tight he wondered how a woman could ever manage it alone.

The lane of the McCann farm was badly potholed. His car jumped and bucked over the lane; it had been a long time since any man had shoveled the holes full of gravel. The fields on either side were badly overgrown with weeds, yellow sprays of sweet clover choking out whole rows of stunted corn like underbrush. Dark thorny patches of thistles here and there had already opened up their lavender crowns. They should have been cut out long ago; somebody needed to have run over the whole place with a cultivator at least by last week. The barbed wire was down in places along the lane, posts broken off at the ground and held up only by their sagging wires, staggering in the breeze at odd angles like a row of drunken men. The small, low house at the end of the lane showed the gray patchy weathering of its siding, the white paint chipped away. Bucking up over the sun-hardened mud ruts of the drive, he didn't see any pickup there. Maybe she was gone for the day. And maybe he would wait. Mose turned off the engine and felt his car rolling to a stop, branches of the overgrown hedges scraping its side. The sun glared blue on his windshield.

He sat there a moment, taking in the silence broken only by the hot ticking of the car engine and the sounds of birds.

A rumbling caught the air in the distance, a pickup engine starting up. Mose got out of the car, pulled his hat brim down closer to shade his eyes, and started to move his boots through the weeds in the direction of the turkey barns. He stopped. His mouth was dry, his throat suddenly closing down. He almost turned and climbed back into his car, meaning to drive right out of there as fast as he could. He swallowed hard. He rounded the corner of a wooden fence behind the house and saw Carol in the distance, that big pretty girl with her hair in braids. She was struggling with a heavy sack of feed in the bed of her truck. He saw right away what she was doing. Backing her truck in every few feet along the feed troughs, she dragged the heavy sacks of grain across the pickup bed and out onto the open tailgate, then tipped them over so the feed spilled through gaps in the fence into the troughs. Masses of white turkey pullets were rushing in from the pens. They were climbing all over themselves under their little tin rooftops to get at their feed. The birds filled the air with a chattering, happy noise.

"What brings you out here?" Carol said flatly, out of breath, dragging at the burlap corners of a feed sack. It occurred to Mose that she must have heard him driving in. She hadn't so much as walked back to the house to greet him or even see who it was.

"Let me do that," was all Mose said. He shouldered in beside her and showed his strength, whipping the sack up like it was as light as an overstuffed pillow, then he poured the grain out into the troughs with one easy swing of his arms. Carol stood back, watching him, her wrist raised up to her forehead to shade her eyes from the sun. "You shouldn't be doing it like this," Mose said. "You should get yourself a wagon. Dump the feed in, pull it along behind the truck, and just shovel it out. Easy as tossing snow."

"Never did have a feed wagon on this place," she said. "Jody always did it this way."

"I'll bet he did," Mose said. He stood there awkwardly, heart racing, not knowing what move to make next. "New to the business, I reckon," he said. Carol had an expression on her face as if he might be out there collecting bills. Whiskey was rising like a vapor bath behind his eyes and like pressure cooking at his brain. He could taste it and smell it now, strong and sickening as vinegar, and he stepped back a little, aware she might be knocked over by his sour breath.

"You just come out here to tell me what I'm doing wrong or what?" Carol said. She had a way of talking with her mouth turned down at the corners, tough and frowning, her blue eyes suddenly as empty of expression as a goat's. Mose felt like a torch was lit in his throat, welding it shut. Insects hummed. Turkeys gobbled at their feed. He looked away from her hard-set face and down at the stitching of his cowboy boots. He moved the pointed toe of one boot around, drawing little circles in the dirt. "Well, what then?" she said, harder. "I'm too damned busy out here to go wasting my time."

"I just . . ." He choked a little. "Maybe I might take you out or something. For supper. Down to Spearfish maybe. Or over to Belle Fourche. That's all. Just to be friendly, that's all. If you'd like. . . ."

She looked into his face for a long time. She still squinted toughly into the sun and at him. But something settled over her; her mouth went softer, her strong, full body shifted its weight as if some gentle force was drawing it closer to the ground. "There's some lemonade in the icebox," she said then. "You best make yourself real comfortable. It's going to take a damn long time to get ready to go out anywhere."

"No, you go on," Mose said. His stomach was turning nervously, maybe at her answer, maybe at the thought

of lemonade on top of everything else. "I'll finish here.
You go on and get ready. I'll join you up at the house,"
he said. But she didn't move for a minute. She just stood
there, facing him, her eyes full of questions. She decided
then. She nodded her head once. Without a word, her
body brushed close past his and he caught the clean smell
of her hair. He watched her moving easily toward the
house, her hips swaying gently; big as she was, her coveralls were too large for her, rolled up and flopping at
the cuffs and at the sleeves. Mose swallowed hard. As
she swam past him in her loose coveralls, he saw all the
more how generous the shape of her was, and in all the
right places.

Sitting in her kitchen, he listened to the sounds she
made. Her bath. Her distant little song as the water ran.
It had been so long since he had been alone in a house
with any woman. While she was getting ready for her
bath, he filled a gold-rimmed glass with ice and poured
her out a stiff drink. He knocked on the door to the bath
and left the drink out for her, too shy to reach in and
hand it to her but his mind alive with the sweet, alluring
odors of what he imagined was inside. He sat back down
at the kitchen table and took in his new surroundings. To
the same degree that her farm was wildly overgrown and
untended, her house was a woman's house. Everything
was clean and in place: spotless embroidered tablecloth
under his drink, yellow-flowered curtains at the kitchen
windows, through which the hum of a single fan blew in
a cool and sensual breeze that held him fixed in its fingers
like a trance.

He felt unreal. For a moment, everything that had happened that day was gone from his mind. He was somewhere else and somebody else. He drank down cool water
and whiskey from one of her gold-rimmed heirloom
glasses and felt like a king. Then a shock of memory hit
him. The chair shifted under him and he felt like dou-
bling over with a stab of pain. He closed his eyes. He

sipped a coolness down his throat, breathed in, then gave himself over again to a kind of oblivious spell.

She bustled out of the bath with a whipping of steam and towels, a delicious perfume following her into the house like the first sensed sureness of a change in weather coming from the hills. In her bedroom, she put on music, that fine Glenn Miller number "I Dreamt I Dwelt in Harlem." Why did she choose that one? It was drunk music, the way its big-band rhythms swayed and frothed and jumped under his skin. He felt he was sitting in a palace. Its fountains washed over him and made him even drunker. . . .

She came out into the kitchen dressed in a soft red robe embroidered all over with the purple shapes of flowers. Her makeup was on, a glow in her cheeks, her eyes lined darkly, deep red shining on her lips. She opened the door to the icebox for ice in her glass. Then she held the glass out to him, meaning for him to fill it again so she could nurse it while she dressed. A necklace of pearls glowed like a string of moons against the sun-gilded skin of her neck. Gold loops dangled from her ears, a circle of gold around her wrist, a loop of gold wedding ring glittering against the glass. She smiled at him, a secret knowledge in her movements, and something stirred in Mose, two minds like two horns cracking his head in two. What was she doing alone like this with a man? No shyness. No sense of shame. How many other men had she been with like this? Maybe dozens, he thought. Multitudes. Likely every hired man. Her hair was let out, wet and hanging in tangled snakes down her back. He had never once thought such things about her, but there she was, acting like she knew what he was thinking. She seemed so sure of herself, the way she held her glass out with one hand and her robe bunched closed with the other. Right there. In front of a strange man. A man not her husband. Just a twitch of her fingers and it would all let go. A piercing, druglike bath of her perfume filled up the space between them. The gold on her wrist and ears and finger shattered the sunlight like knives. All of it made him see in that instant someone else. Never the way she had been when they were so poor yet alone together under their patchwork quilts, simple in their love, forsaking all others in each other's arms. But the way she must be now, wanton, loose, given to wildness, the riches of her body, her lips the color of blood, perverse stabbing desires of her flesh like a black joy in her eyes. A voice rose inside him like the cries of a wounded and desolate coyote; fires leapt up with a wrathful pain. He was about to double over, gritting his teeth and letting loose a shout. Then a balm of her music washed over him like silver and spice, precious stones and silk, palaces of ivory and marble. He was alone with this woman. He was rich; he was wretched. He was God-fearing; yet he plunged blindly, willingly into her cup. She smiled at him huskily, painted with that whore's mouth. And she held out her glass. . . .

He found himself next to her, pouring from his bottle. Their faces met, and he felt the heat of her kiss. Right there in her kitchen, his hands tore in under her robe and ripped it off her shoulders. Maybe she tried to let out a sound; something gurgled in her throat. Her fists pounded at his back, but he couldn't let her go until she gave, easily, pulling him in. And he was strong, strong. He would have her one time, then many times, then half a time more. He would carry her in his arms to her bed, drunk with the whiskey of her fornication. Then he would hurt her. Slap her. Suck in the hot coal of her tongue. Bite at her shoulders and neck and breasts until he tasted blood. Flip her over like a sack of grain, whipping at her pink flesh until she screamed. They would shout and cry and fight at each other like dragons. He would pour himself into her like a spilled-over glass. Having her, every part, all of her, once and for all, that's what he wanted. To fly into her wilderness. Open the teeming mouth of her filth and corruption. Feed her from his face. Take her great wings in his hands and spread them out, pinning her to the bottomless earth.

There was a loud knocking outside. Mose awoke from a sleep like a poison gas to the sound of bootsteps. The curtains of the room were closed. The woman beside him turned and moaned, and he realized who she was with a shock, her shape under the sheet washed by a hazy light through the shades. She flung an arm out with a grumbling, and it slapped his face. The noise grew in intensity to a steady pounding that shook the house.

"Open up in there! Open up!" It was a man's voice. "Goddamn you, Johnson, open up right now or we're coming in!"

Carol raised up on an elbow with alarm. She jumped out of bed and threw on her robe. "Oh, Jesus, stay right there!" she hissed. "Don't move!"

"All right! We're coming in!"

"Wait!" she called out. "Just a minute!"

"I'm not here," he mumbled. "I don't care who it is. . . ." She was already on her way through the door, checking her puffy face in the hall mirror once and run-

ning a quick hand through her hair. Then she was out
and in the living room, bare feet trotting over the floor.
Mose pulled the sheet up over his body and wrapped the
pillow around his ears. An empty bottle clinked against
the metal bedstead at his feet. He closed his eyes. What
had happened last night? He took in a deep breath and
let it go. He rolled to his side and lay there like a sick
dog, shutting his eyes, hard, as if their pressure alone
could ease the hammers in his head.

Boots slammed into the room like an earthquake.
Shades rattled. White light blasted him like the flash of
an explosion. His body was rudely exposed in the wind
of sheets ripped off the bed. He sat up, dazzled by the
sunlight, pitching himself forward and swinging his legs
around in a reflex to jump up and fight.

"Goddamn you, Johnson!"

"Take it easy now, Major," said the voice of Buster
Hill. Mose slowly focused on double images of Major
Pierce and Buster Hill. The major's young face was
twisted, ugly with rage. Buster was holding on to the
major's jacket sleeve as if reining in a horse. Carol was
in the doorway, looking scared, her face a mess of dark
smears, her pretty robe bunched up to her neck so tight
she must have been choking.

"Sheriff!" shouted Major Pierce. "Where is he,
damnit!" Carol turned quickly in the direction of her
living room, then stepped aside as Sheriff Meeker, hat in
hand, peeked his head around the doorframe. "Arrest
this man," ordered Major Pierce. "We've wasted enough
time already!"

"Hold on, hold on now," Buster said. "Give the man
a chance. Mose? Mose, get up now," he said. Then he
waved a fat arm in Carol's direction and said, "You there.
Go get some coffee on. . . ."

"What in hell's . . . ?" Mose could hardly speak.
Words seemed to be caught in some kind of fur in his
mouth. Sheriff Meeker came into clear focus then; his bushy
gray mustache and the uncomfortable twist of his

mouth. He stood with his eyes averted from the bed, hat held low over his belt buckle as if he might be trying to act proper in the presence of a lady. The realization hit Mose fully that he was lying there completely naked. He curled up like a salted slug, covering himself with his hands.

"What . . . can . . . ?" His tongue cracked. He coughed and tried to clear his throat.

"Hey, Mose," the sheriff said. "I'm damned sorry about this. Really I am. This here, well, it ain't right, that's all. None of our business being in here."

"We don't have the time for pleasantries! Let's get moving, Sheriff!" Major Pierce's voice sounded like it was squeezed through a half-blocked valve.

Buster leaned in closely over Mose, handing back a bunched-up sheet that helped cover him like a kind of loincloth. "Get your clothes on," he said.

Mose made a mess of unfurling the sheet and got his legs tangled up in it trying to cover himself the rest of the way. Buster leaned over closely as if to help and whispered just intensely enough for him to hear, *"Do exactly like I tell you, damnit!"*

"Over there," Mose said, pointing. Dazed, he watched Buster straining to bend over and grab up the pants and shirt left in a heap. Sheriff Meeker nodded his head once in the major's direction, excusing himself, backing sheepishly out through the door. The major, watching him leave, looked stupefied, his face pale as a swamp haunt. As Mose started to lift himself up, the major's head jerked quickly toward the open window as if he expected a sudden artillery round from that direction. Mose hopped to his feet, struggling for balance. He turned his back to them as best he could, hiding his parts. Like a scratching pullet, he hopped from one foot to the other, drawing on his pants and socks. He saw by the window light that he had maybe slept as late as noon.

"Listen to me one minute," he said to Buster. He dragged his shirt on and fumbled trying to snap the pearl buttons, stalling for time to find the words. "Listen. I decided. I ain't going back on the job. I quit. I mean it now. I flat out quit. . . ."

"Just you hurry up," Buster said. "The major here don't like to be kept waiting."

"The major can go to hell," Mose said. Now that he had clothes on, he felt he could turn and face them down. "And so can you. Go to hell. Now just get out of my way!"

He pushed past the major on his way to his boots, one of which he found tossed over behind the door. "I ain't going anywhere," he said. "I'm staying right here. Now why don't you just get the hell out and leave us alone!"

"Charges will be read to you soon enough," the major said. Mose stopped in midpull, balanced on one foot, drawing on his boot. He looked over at Buster then, who nodded his head like bad news. "Just thank your stars you're not in the army. I'd have had you taken out and shot five minutes ago."

"Hold on now, Major, hold on," Buster said. "Come on, Mose. No arguments."

Something in his tone made Mose follow the two men out into the living room. Sheriff Meeker was sitting on the couch, hat between his knees, an expression on his face like that of a visitor at a funeral. Carol was bringing in cups of heated-up coffee. Somehow, she had managed to find a pair of jeans and pull them on under her robe. As she whipped by him, she looked quickly in Mose's direction, a flash of hatred and blame. On the carved wood box of the windup organ, the framed service photo of Jody in his navy Cracker Jack suit looked out over the living room with a pimply grin.

Sheriff Meeker took a cup of coffee, then Buster took a cup, and on her way back to the kitchen, Mose raised his eyebrows at Carol, asking her a silent question that she completely ignored. He would have given anything for coffee. He felt that if he could just get some coffee in him, everything would be all right. But there was to be no coffee for him. The sheriff downed his cup fast and rose to his feet. He took two long strides in Mose's direction. "I'm damn sorry about this, Mose, but I got to do it," he said. "Believe me, I ain't even sure it's my jurisdiction. Seems like more of a federal problem." The sheriff slowly put one of his bony hands on Mose's shoulder. He reached the other hand behind his back and unhitched his set of handcuffs. "You're under arrest. Put your wrists out in front of you and hold them together for me now. And you be sure and let me know if I get 'em on too tight. . . ."

Bracelets flashed, ratcheted shut. Wrist skin caught in their teeth with a needle-sharp pain. The chain between them clicked heavily as Mose raised his hands up; somehow there was the feeling that they weren't really his hands. Muzzled in the dull white sheen of nickeled steel, his body just ended at the wrists; the rest was no longer a part of him, a shackled will, palms pressed together and fingers interlocked like some stranger's decapitated and helpless prayer. Maybe it was this sense of heightened strangeness, a sudden dull ache in his ears like diving into a deep hole in the river; he couldn't surface, his body sagged and went limp with the pressure and his thoughts whirled in a tumbling current over the falls. He couldn't speak. He couldn't even ask why. He stood in shock and for the first time saw things for what they were, the men around him suddenly as distant from him as a totally different breed of animal. He was at their mercy, all of them, a deprivation of his liberty that, it hit him now, he somehow felt he deserved. He must have wanted this; he had even fought hard for this condition, a workhorse that had all too willingly broken itself to harness. After that moment, all he could do was look at Buster Hill like a dumb punished child and say in a weak, cracking, stupid voice, "My . . . my car . . ."

"We'll take care of it for you," Buster said. "Come along now, Mose, we'll get you out of this in no time. Come on now. . . ."

Outside, a husky, tough-looking soldier leaned against Major Pierce's army-green staff car, smoking. He straightened up to a vague attention and opened the back door. Mose looked around at Sheriff Meeker, climbing into his county patrol car and starting to talk on his radio. Why wasn't he riding with the sheriff? "I'll follow you all in," the sheriff called out to them, grimly, then started up the engine.

Mose was scooted into the back seat of the army car, sandwiched in between the major and Buster Hill, feeling like a criminal. The big-shouldered driver nearly covered the whole back seat in shade. He made rubber burn as he speeded over the bumpy lane toward the highway.

"Tell us what happened, Mose," said Buster gently. At the same time, Buster squeezed Mose's leg above the knee as if with some secret communication.

"What happened where?"

"You know, yesterday. What happened in the yards. Tell us exactly what you did."

"Well . . ." He tried to think of what exactly had happened. It wasn't easy. His headache rolled and crashed and heated up like some busted canning machine. And he wasn't himself, Mose, not anymore. "They were packing them in too close. A pileup. Bad one. Turkeys going down all over hell and gone, and it was him that let it happen. I mean, I did like you told me. But I didn't mean to really hurt him like that. . . ."

"But what did you do?" asked Buster.

"Do?" He couldn't figure it. What was he supposed to have done? "I . . . I took him down. A few pegs. Kicked him, I guess, like you said. . . ."

"Damnit, Hill, you should have found another way," said Major Pierce.

"What in hell happened?" Mose asked. "Jesus, what? I did everything you told me, Buster. . . ." He stopped. There was a weight against his chest. He was shaking all over; he felt like he was ready to cry.

"The major's in a whole world of trouble, Mose,"

Buster said. He spat out his open window. "Ain't that right, Major? And he's aiming to drag you, me, and everybody else in with him if we don't watch out."

The major was looking out his side of the car, listening but making no move to answer. His silence alone seemed to confirm the truth. "There's thousands of acres of beets out there that need thinning and weeding," Buster continued. "Cornfields that need ditches dug to get watered. There's tons of beets still piled up in storage right now, tons and tons of them, wanting to be made into sugar. Ain't that right? Ain't it, Major? Not to mention turkeys. A quarter million of them, and then more, all of them getting ready right damn now for the line. We've got a contract that says they'll be in cans or cold storage before Thanksgiving. Ain't that right? None of that's getting done now. Not one whit of it. All because some greedy sonofabitch in a uniform thought he might get just a little more than his piece of everything. Get his piece and then some. Then buy himself a damn construction business and fill up on his government feedbag for the rest of his life. But that's all over now. All of it. And as soon as word gets out, maybe every one of us will end up in jail. That's for damn sure. Mose, how many turkeys do you figure you and me and Dale and the boys could butcher all by ourselves before Thanksgiving?"

Mose nodded once, and a sense came over him that maybe he understood. He settled deeper into the car seat and looked around out the windows for the first time. The car was on the highway, racing along in the direction of Belle Fourche. Nothing was moving in the fields. Nobody was out there. Not one man he could see. It was a working Saturday. And not one prisoner in sight out there working. "Buster, none of this is my fault," he said. "None of it's any fault of mine."

"The fact is, that man is dead. All night at the hospital, they thought he might make it. He died early this morning. Bleeding. Pressure on his brain. And they say it was you who killed him."

"They're leaving us with little choice, Mr. Johnson,"
said Major Pierce. There was a pleading in his expression, an intense look both fearful and aware of his one
last chance. "They say it's my duty to see you prosecuted
to the full extent of the laws."

"Major, you couldn't prosecute a dog for a chicken
thief," Buster said. "Don't you worry about a thing,
Mose. We got us a lawyer and we got us a courtroom
doctor'll say that man died of complications from his
previous wounds. He was sick anyway. Just falling over
might have killed him. Doc Monahan said he'd never seen
a body in overall worse physical condition. The Doc
knows what's what. He's the one we'll get to write out
the autopsy, so don't you worry about nothing. . . ."

Mose was hardly listening. He was lost to them, no
longer present in that car. All he could see was a vision
of the way the Hauptmann would be sitting out there,
day after day, weak, sick, like some misery was tearing
the meat off his ribs from the inside. Then Buster Hill
threw an arm around Mose's shoulders, looking strangely
pleased, his face bearing the same expression as it did
on his way home after shifts when five thousand birds
had been slaughtered, processed, packed without a hitch.
"We're going to be all right," Buster said. "Don't you
worry one bit. All of us. All of us except maybe for
him," he said, jerking his thumb rudely toward the major. "The fact is, the major here's been shitting in everybody's nest right from the beginning. Ain't that right?"
Buster chuckled a little, a strange sound, his lips pulled
back, his teeth bared like a grinning dog's. "Ain't that
right, Major?"

Major Pierce kept his gaze fixed, steady and unmov-
ing, out the window. He leaned into his fist and said
nothing more. The whole rest of the ride, he didn't answer so much as a word.

Mose was hustled out of the car, up some back steps,
and through a back door into the Belle Fourche courthouse. Nobody was waiting there. No police. No crowd.

It was as if everything had been arranged so there would be no publicity. Sheriff Meeker even attended himself to the fingerprinting, the paperwork, the quick flash photo against a lined and numbered screen. Mose didn't know what he expected: maybe that he could stand in front of a judge, a gavel would come down, Buster would fork over rolls of cash, and Mose could be set free again. All he wanted at that moment was to go across the street and get himself feeling straight for a minute with a drink. He was sweating, first cold, then hot, his head pounding, a dazed, shuddering sensation moving through his head like a thick fog.

It was Saturday afternoon. No judge could be reached to come in and set bail. Mose learned from an apologetic Sheriff Meeker that he would have to cool his heels in one of the basement cells of the building until Monday. The sheriff led him down there himself, through a long cement-block corridor to a tiny cell off alone in one corner of the basement. The door to it had no bars; it was a heavy steel door with a small, thick window in it that had mesh like chicken wire reinforcing the glass. There was a single window, high up, almost higher than Mose could reach, through which a gray-blue light entered. Before the door slammed and a tumbler slid home like a dropped weight, Sheriff Meeker slipped him a half-pint bottle of bourbon. "They could have my badge for this," he said. "You just hold tight. You'll be out of here in no time."

That little bottle had the effect of what two aspirin might on the way his body felt. Sitting alone that night, the bottle long empty, Mose wrapped himself in his blanket. He sat on the cot, gritting his teeth through violent sweats and shiverings as if he had a case of malaria. Sick like that, for the first few hours, he was hardly conscious of where he was; a part of him was sure that any second, something would happen, some agreeable surprise.

Then the bad thoughts hit him: what he had ruined; a deep self-hatred at the pit of his sin with Carol, at what his arrest there and the rumors of its news would surely do to her life. He wrapped his arms around himself and gripped his ribs hard, letting out a tiny anguished moaning. Then, like a blast furnace in his chest, a series of pounding shots of fiery pain that pummeled every sense he had ever imagined of his soul, the thought struck home that he had killed a man. Murdered him. And he wept, drowning in his cries, bereft and alone, smothered in the smoke of a burning landscape of his entire being. He wailed at its loss, destroyed and heaped up and blown away like a bombed-out city, gone, all of it gone, and all of its people vanishing forever. He sat doubled over like that all night, weeping in a pain so terrible he heard himself begging for his own death, pounding himself with his fists, slamming his fists into the brick walls until he might have broken bones. Nothing was left of him. Not one idea. Not one hope or prayer. Everything wiped out, slaughtered, gone. All the fruits he had ever wanted from this life were gone. All the things that were good and right and happy had left him behind. Gone from him. Just gone. Everything. And he would never find them again.

19

Alas for the seed of men. For the anger of nations. Rivers turned to blood. Everywhere that summer there were lightnings, voices at full cry, thunderings, earthquakes, great hail. The ruin upon ruins of Rome was retaken after campaigns that cost 189,000 men. Blood from the wine-press. Battles on the tiny flecks of earth called Saipan and Guam, 58,000. Dust cast upon their heads. Normandy, Saint-Lô, Falaise, breakout into France, 248,000 dead, wounded, missing. A millstone cast into the sea. V-1 bombs over London, 24,000 casualties, most of them women and children. Voices of brides and bridegrooms heard no more. Warsaw, 200,000 starved and slaughtered like trapped animals. Candles burned no more. More than six hundred thousand succumbed to weakness and disease in China. Islands fled away. Mountains were not found. One million innocent Jews that summer alone. Such riches come to naught. One million two hundred thousand Germans. Holds of foul spirits. Cages for every hated bird. Great cities lost in their burning. Two million

187

Russians in a breakthrough into Poland on tracks of blood. The harvest of the earth was ripe that summer. The high-water mark was reached. And the beginning of the end. Soon enough, its final sickle would come down from a white cloud crowned with a golden light fiercer than the sun. The final inventory, one hundred million wounded, maimed, missing; forty-nine million killed. And millions more who could never be counted. God only knew how many there were and would be and wouldn't be. *And all the fowl were filled with their flesh. . . .*

The way Mose Johnson would later tell it, Hauptmann Hartmut Christian von Ujatz was given a ceremony with full military honors on the morning of June 27, 1944, at Camp Orman, South Dakota. No matter the strong regulation prohibiting the display of any enemy flag or insignia at prisoner-of-war camps, a flag was draped over the Hauptmann's simple polished casket; it was a tricolor flag, red and white with a black two-headed eagle, its talons poised, grasping, painted by a prisoner artisan at its center. It was the flag he had requested in writing, the colors of an imperial banner long obsolete but under which generations of the men in his family had first sworn their commissions as officers in the German army. Along with it, because of fierce protests among factions of the prisoners, a smaller red banner with a white circle at its center filled with the black, stark reverse-wheeling cross was draped at the last minute at the foot of the coffin. An oration was read in German by a chaplain. Two other prisoners spoke briefly, a thin and ravaged-looking enlisted man who had once been a gunner in the Hauptmann's very company, then an infantry lieutenant from the officers' compound, named Schnurre. Stories of bravery were recalled. The men he had saved. His numerous wounds. Then an anecdote about how once he had driven too far into the British lines. Seeing he might be captured, he leapt out of his half-track and walked blithely straight into a small garrison of the enemy. In his excellent English, he told them they were surrounded, pointing out the imaginary positions of German tanks, and the whole unit of British soldiers, convinced, surrendered to him. The assembled prisoners laughed grimly at this old bitter taste of minor victory. Lieutenant Schnurre then recounted with emotion the details of the Hauptmann's most recent great action, the ultimate sacrifice he had made for their general welfare. There was a moment of silence. Then, at a signal from Gruenwald, his bereft and loyal orderly, and by a highly unusual agreement with Major Pierce, U.S. Army guards fired a volley of seven rifle shots in salute.

The casket was carried solemnly to a makeshift facility, where it was burned, as requested, the ashes then either spread out on camp grounds or, as was later rumored, scattered on the surface of the tiny lake the prisoners had constructed at the camp. A few years later, that big pond became the basis of a U.S. Soil Conservation Service study, its location and design found to be ideal for expansion. The U.S. Army Corps of Engineers drew up the plans, then in came the fleets of trucks and bulldozers that built a large concrete dam to replace the earthworks of the prisoners. An ample reservoir of irrigation and drinking water named Lake Orman slowly flooded the basin and the spit of prairie where the prisoner-of-war camp had once stood. It was even planted with rainbow trout. White beach sand was imported, spread out in the shape of a gleaming scimitar, and swimming was allowed on the edge farthest from the river. In all ways, Lake Orman became a great boon to this county. Long after the war, it was only Mose Johnson who oddly maintained to people here that every single drop of their tap water and the water for their livestock and their corn and alfalfa fields contained a trace of Nazi ashes.

The Hauptmann's funeral took place nearly a week and a half after his death; it was a tense ten days, during which, all over the county, not one prisoner of war presented himself for work. The morning the Hauptmann

died, they formed up to be counted as usual in their
khaki-uniformed ranks in the desertlike, almost chilly
summer dawn. When the army guards ordered them into
their trucks, they simply sat down in place, all of them,
disciplined rows of men sitting with hands wrapped
around their knees on the packed clay parade ground.
Looking on from a distance, behind the wire partition of
their own separate compound, a few dozen German officers did the same, though they had never once been
asked to climb into trucks and be shipped out as laborers.

Major Pierce was beside himself, deciding what to do.
Since the Hauptmann was dead, he didn't even know who
it was he should appeal to for a solution to the crisis.
None of his guards spoke German well enough to make
more than simple inquiries. Who was in charge of them
now? Who could he appeal to for reason in this emergency?

The major put all his guards on full alert, in helmets
and field battle dress, lining them up around the parade
ground with bayonets fixed on their rifles. Then he remembered a strange-looking prisoner with a mashed-in
face, named Keller, the closest thing he had to an informer, and had him marched at bayonet point from his
solitary confinement. At first, Keller was reluctant to get
involved at all. Finally, he gave over the information that
the infantry lieutenant named Schnurre was the one to
be contacted; he would be next in line of authority among
the officers.

Oberleutnant Schnurre had been well briefed; he was
waiting for the guards to take him to the major's office,
under his arm a leather folder that contained a list of
demands. The major had seen that list before. It was
exactly the same litany of requests for money, factory
and work-detail slowdowns, educational benefits, and
camp improvements that had been submitted to him by
the Hauptmann himself. Added to this was an immediate
demand for the arrest and punishment of the murderer of

their commander before any negotiations would take place. Through Keller, Oberleutnant Schnurre informed the major that the demands were inflexible. Until the major acceded to what he considered to be absurd demands, not one prisoner at the Orman Camp was going to move. Not one. Factory and fields would stand idle.

The major immediately began a search for Mose Johnson, and under the circumstances, he felt it pressing to join in that effort himself, here and there all over the county until he found him. But news of the manager's arrest wasn't enough for the prisoners. More serious measures would have to be taken. So at first, despite the gross infractions of international laws regarding prisoners, the major tried coercion. He ordered a team of guards to start moving into the ranks of sitting men, threatening them with billy clubs, actually hitting a few of them and dragging them off to a barracks building quickly refashioned into a kind of jail. These examples had no effect. Not one of the remaining prisoners so much as moved.

Next, the major tried locking the prisoners out of their barracks. If they wished to sit there not moving, well, then, he would let them. They would sit there as long as it took to break them down. Without food and water. Without shelter. No matter if it rained or if the almost unbearable sun at that time of year made them drop from its stroke. The first two days and nights, an unhealthy stench took over his parade grounds, like that of an open sewer. The men had prepared themselves with tin plates and mess utensils. Deprived of access to toilets, they carefully passed these containers man to man, full of piss and excrement, to what seemed to be the strongest among them, sitting at one edge of their perimeter, who flung the filth as far as they could, much of it landing up against one wall of the major's own office barracks, which overlooked the grounds. After three days and nights, locked out of their barracks, cut off from their daily needs, even as used as they were to heat and cold, to being without water and food, as accustomed to such desertlike conditions as any men in this world could possibly be, the first of them started dropping. One by one, the first two dozen or so fell over like hunched-up trees blown down in a forest, passing out full length on the ground. But Oberleutnant Schnurre was still inflexible, heartlessly watching on as the guards moved through the ranks of prisoners, picking up such men and delivering them to the camp hospital.

Major Pierce revised his program immediately, fully aware that if too many of them actually died of exposure and deprivation, he would have a team of army intelligence men crawling all over his camp and through his file cabinets and his account books, especially his account books, before the week was up. Somebody was sure to begin asking questions, trying to make sense of the creative bookkeeping, the mazes of complex figures from combined receipts and payrolls, which were, of course, way over and above the camp's real expenses for keeping prisoners. Who knew but that the major might be jailed or, worse, busted in rank and shipped off to the Marshall Islands to dig graves.

It was only then that the major resorted to real negotiations. He ordered the doors to the barracks unlocked. He brought in barrels full of lemonade, and truckloads of the finest fresh-slaughtered beef for a conciliatory meal. He ordered a day of rest for the next morning, "a day of cooling off," he called it. He left the prisoners to wander their camp at will, as they always had. That way, at least they wouldn't be sitting out there on the gumbo anymore, in plain view of motorists on their way to Belle Fourche, who could see them all sitting and suffering out there from a high bluff on a spur of the highway.

People were already talking enough. An excuse had been printed up and circulated in newspapers such as the *Nowell Enterprise*; due to a measles epidemic, it said, prisoners at the Orman Camp were to be quarantined from their work crews until further notice. But that kind of excuse was only good for so long. Already, one ambitious cub reporter from the most important paper in the state, the *Argus-Leader*, in Pierre, the capital, had been caught nosing around the camp perimeter with an antique Speed Graphic, trying to get pictures of the scene. The major had had to enlist Buster Hill's help in seeing that the young man was fired from his job, then followed all the way to the Nebraska border by the state patrol.

That night, the major tried to revise the demands on the money issue to thirty cents; to get Schnurre at least to abandon the requests for classroom facilities, more books, newspapers; not to mention the high cost of hiring an additional civilian doctor for the camp, since it would take ten reams of paperwork and up to a year for the army to be able to provide one; and to protest strongly that he, a mere major in the backwaters of this war, personally, unfortunately, had absolutely no sway at all over what and how the prisoner work crews were directed by the civilians in factories and on the farms that hired them. The major sat for hours wheeling and dealing with Schnurre, who refused to use English, even though it seemed clear the man understood far more words than he let on. That morose and slow-speaking young informer, Keller, acted as an interpreter, hour after hour, until all of them were so highly strung on coffee nerves that their voices had risen to the pitch of shouts without their even noticing. But there was still no progress. No movement at all. By the end of nine exhausting days, there was no choice left but for Major Pierce to give in to all demands. His only victory was a little additional time to be able to see the demands carried out. In exchange for that much, he was forced to grant yet one more day without sending his prisoners to work, a time they would devote entirely to the observance of their Hauptmann's funeral.

After the funeral service, Major Pierce addressed the prisoners in the main compound. He delivered an official apology on behalf of the United States Army for the atrocity of the death. He pledged that he would see to it that the man responsible was brought to the swiftest jus-

tice. At the same time, the major announced an increase
in prisoner wages to sixty cents a day, fifty cents of that
to be set aside in trust at the First Bank of Belle Fourche,
exactly according to Hauptmann von Ujatz's request.
"After this understandable period of grief for a beloved
commanding officer," Major Pierce intoned with elo-
quence, then he waited, listening to his words repeated
in that guttural tongue he had grown to dislike so much
over the past ten days, and by a young man who spoke a
strange, throaty dialect to boot. ". . . and in light of the
concessions granted you with the full support of my command and my government," he said. The prisoners before him listened politely, but he sensed a certain
heightened defiance in the way they remained at attention
even when he'd let them know they could stand at ease.
". . . we trust you will all decide now to return to your
work before any further disciplinary measures must be
taken. Thank you very much for your forbearance during
these critical times. There will be trucks waiting for you
in the morning."

The major dismissed his prisoners. But they did not
move. They stood at attention as if they might stand that
way until the war came to an end. Then, as the major
turned and started for his office, some of them broke into
a song behind him, violent and rousing. Others scattered
from their ranks and tried to leave the assembly in ap-
parent disgust. Fights broke out among them. Scattered
gangs of the prisoners, pent up, deprived, tense for days
on end, simply let loose. Guards, wielding rifle butts and
billy clubs, tried to wade into the knots of wrestling men.
But the prisoners were too many, their rioting too violent
as they battled in confusion among themselves, strains of
that song still rising over them: "Raise high the flags!
Stand rank on rank together. Storm troopers march with
steady, quiet tread. . . ."

It was Keller who translated the words for him, as both
of them stood back, behind a line of guards, from the
scattered outbursts of human fray. Tear-gas canisters went

off in their midst, and the song died down, prisoners finally dispersing into their barracks and breaking up fights mainly on their own. "It's that dirty pimp's party song," Keller said. "You can see how it is. Gangs of them bullying the others. And now it will only get worse."

Major Pierce watched as the compound slowly cleared, only then comprehending what he was seeing, just how deep the divisions were in the prisoner ranks. He regretted that he hadn't found a way to really use that somehow; but it was too late. All that was left for him was to restore some sense of order to his camp before headquarters in Salt Lake City found out. If that happened, as it did whenever there was trouble in camps such as this, the whole operation would be disbanded and the thousands of prisoners reassigned to other camps across the nation. He would surely lose his command. And up until now, he hadn't done at all badly for himself and his select group of staffers. Everyone in this county had made out, as long as they could, the way he had it figured. His best course at the moment was not to make waves. He would let the situation die down, then slowly look for means to begin chipping away at the absurd promises he had made. Perhaps the logic of their collective action had only that one moment of unity before it failed. And if that turned out not to be true, at least he might make it out of this war with an intact reputation; not to mention the significant money and contacts he and his friends in the 10th Services Command had arranged for their civilian lives. He was thinking of a contracting business. Or a consulting firm for the federal prison system. The possibilities seemed endless. As he mulled over the situation, making the best of this minor defeat, the young interpreter at his sleeve interrupted him. "Maybe you can send me to another camp now, like you promised," Keller said. "With things as they are, it is maybe not so good for me here."

The persistent throaty sound of that young man's voice

was getting on his nerves. The major had planned to delay several weeks before Keller was given a new identity
and shipped out incognito to a camp in Arizona. The
paperwork itself was complicated; and he was busy, worried, his job a mire of details, his desk a continual shuffle
of confusing and often fouled-up forms to deal with.
Also, there still might be a use for this prisoner. He had
served a few times as a clerical helper with the papers
regarding prisoners and transfers, and the young man had
done a bang-up job. And once a prisoner like him was
in, cooperative, a source of information, he was in. Any
warden would have to be a fool to let him go easily. But
it was clear his use was limited now, since it wasn't safe
for him to rejoin his fellow prisoners. And there was that
strange dialect he spoke; the major wasn't sure the man's
German was even all that comprehensible when he translated. So take an inch, give a mile. That was the way
things were going. Major Pierce signed the young man's
transfer order to another camp that afternoon.

Mose was out on bail for the three weeks it took for both sides of his case to be prepared. He was relieved, with pay, of all duties at the Nowell-Safebuy plant. He was advised by Buster Hill to make sure he stayed out of any possible sight of the prisoners. He wasn't supposed to be around town very much, or even on the roads during working hours. So he mainly drove by a back route into Belle Fourche and warmed a seat at the Poplar Bar until it closed. After that, the nights awaited him, haunted by forebodings of the coming days. He was scared. Even with Buster's assurances, he felt sure he would be severely punished, and that might be nothing less than what he deserved.

The way Mose would remember it, what took place at the courthouse in Belle Fourche couldn't exactly be called a trial; it was a hearing and an inquest, held under federal jurisdiction, with district court judge William "Link" Schmidt presiding. Though "Link" Schmidt was known as an honest judge, he wasn't above being influenced by the winds of local power and expedient opinion. The courtroom itself was hot; a huge ceiling fan moved the stifling air around like a stalling propeller. The venetian blinds were down over the windows, which for some reason were kept shut. Mose had been prepared by Buster Hill and by his Nowell-Safebuy lawyer, Harold Rosengrin, brought in all the way from Chicago, that no matter how much he might want to speak out himself, he shouldn't. "Just don't talk except to answer direct questions if you're asked. I don't think they will, not if things go right. Even then, we might take the Fifth. If not, answer in as few words as you can. You won't do anybody any good by talking."

There were no members of the press present; and no spectators. To Mose, the courtroom felt like a deserted church. There was a clerk of the court, who was a total stranger. Major Pierce, decked out in full-dress uniform with his few service medals, sat at the table with a federal prosecutor named Killburn. Killburn, who had come all the way from Rapid City, was a young man who had made a reputation by prosecuting draft evaders hiding out with a few maverick Sioux down on the Rosebud reservation. There was also Buster Hill, sitting in the pew directly behind Mose. That was all the people there were in the room. All except for the witnesses, who were called one by one, led in by a bailiff from somewhere off to one side, a direction from which Mose thought he could hear the continual sounds of scraping chairs.

Most of the defense witnesses spoke about Mose's character. All of them were friends, ushered in and out quickly. Mrs. Nilsen said that Mose was a regular customer, was always giving nickels out to keep the jukebox going, and he almost always cleaned his plate. Then Jim Fuller was called and gave an account of the time his whole flock had been wiped out by the turkey blackhead disease. Mose had helped him rebuild his stock with prize-winning birds and money loaned to him out of his own pocket. After him, Reverend Ott took the stand, sweating profusely in his summer-white ministry suit. The white collar at his throat was somehow tipped and loose; he had missed fastening its little brass stud. The reverend described how Mose was often a lay reader at the Church of Christ Reformed, that he had steadily attended the recent military funerals and been helpful to the bereaved. Rosengrin asked the reverend if he thought Mose Johnson was the kind of man capable of committing murder. Reverend Ott answered firmly, ''No more than a cat can play the fiddle.''

On his way out of the courtroom, Reverend Ott took a few steps over to the defense table and said quickly, ''Bruce McGovern is sick. He won't be reading for us this Sunday. We could sure use you again. We've missed you. I'm planning on Luke fifteen.'' The reverend winked at Mose, cuffed him on the shoulder in a fatherly way. It was clear that Judge Schmidt was becoming impatient; the bailiff was about to come out and escort the reverend from the room.

Mose listened to the testimony with a detached feeling; it was, of course, interesting to hear himself talked about, only it seemed as though he was forming a picture in his mind of someone else. Like a friend he might have been close to once, described by people who had known him only years before they met. Then, strangely, that was all there was for the defense.

There were two key testimonies from the other side. Doc Monahan was called in by the prosecution. Mose was surprised the Doc would be called against him. He started to say something to Rosengrin about it, until the lawyer squeezed his arm, hard, stopping him. The prosecutor stood up and began rattling off a series of factual statements about the results of the Hauptmann's autopsy. Certain things emerged. The man's liver was just about gone from hepatitis. He was at least partly diabetic, aggravated by the damage done to his pancreas by a bullet wound; and he was taking no insulin, evidenced by his enlarging heart and the beginning of damage to his retinas. There were at least six other wounds: Vertebrae in his spine had been smashed, and pieces had healed badly, "floating," the Doc said. "A bone fragment could have severed his spinal cord just by him moving his head." And shrapnel. "A piece about the size of a pencil eraser lodged against his carotid artery. And another, sharper, about the size of a pin, and pointed like one, buried in the membranous tissue between the axis of his spine and the stem of his brain, too dangerous to remove. It's a miracle the man was still alive at all," the Doc said.

Then the prosecutor, in an oddly subdued tone of voice, without gesturing, without seeming to make too much of it, asked if, in the Doc's opinion, death could have been caused by physical blows received from Mose Johnson on the day in question. It was then that Mose realized nothing would ever be said here about the cause. Not one word. He had assaulted a man; everyone was assuming he was guilty of that much. As though unprovoked. As though there was no reason, and no orders at all that he had followed.

The Doc was wearing his best blue suit, the one he usually wore on Sundays or when he had business meetings at the hospital. One of his hands fell quickly, nervously, into a rumpled pocket. He seemed to be rummaging around in it for something. "Could be," the Doc answered in a weak voice. The Doc looked directly at Mose, a flickering glance, then away from him somewhere at his feet. "Could be not," he said. A moment passed, the time it took for one full cycle of the big wooden fan blade stirring over them. "Like I said," the Doc added, then licked his lips, "in my opinion, the man could have killed himself just getting out of his bed."

The prosecutor didn't pursue any more questions. Mose felt one of Buster's hands fall on his shoulder from behind, patting it twice, reassuringly. The Doc almost started to stand up, as if he might be finished. But Harold Rosengrin was on his feet. For the defense, he asked the Doc also to describe Mose Johnson's character. "Well, as far as anybody in Nowell will tell you, he's an all right fellow. Works damn hard. Keeps his lawn mowed. And another thing,'' the Doc said, a flash of a smile crossing his lips before he remembered where he was sitting. ''He's always paid his bills right on time.''

The prosecutor then called his only eyewitness. It was a surprise to Mose to see Gruenwald dressed as he was, in a German army uniform, no paint across his back, only a white armband with POW on it indicating that he was a prisoner.

Judge Schmidt looked a bit amazed as well. The judge was a tall man with clean-cut features, clear blue eyes, a bushy gray mustache, and thick snow-white hair. He looked intelligent behind his half-frame glasses. Despite the burdens of his office, he seemed a likable kind of fellow, bird's-feet wrinkles at the corners of his eyes making him appear on the verge of pleasant laughter most of the time. But when Gruenwald came in, Judge Schmidt's mouth took on an ugly twist. Gruenwald was decked out in the sharply tailored field gray of his regiment, with stark death's-head emblems on his collar patches, black epaulets, his tunic edged at the shoulders by his lance sergeant's insignia braid, even a knight's cross fastened at the throat of his tunic. The judge surveyed him from his disturbing collar to his polished black boots, as if he were the real criminal.

Seeing Gruenwald dressed like that, one could easily imagine how these soldiers could be such formidable enemies. Mose knew from stories the prisoners told that their uniforms were long ago stripped from them. Usually, the very soldiers who had captured them rifled through their clothes, their belongings, cut the buttons off their tunics, ripped off their insignia and epaulets and medals, especially the medals; everything the enemy had or wore was meat for sought-after souvenirs. Where had Major Pierce come up with a full-dress German uniform?

Gruenwald spoke eloquently in his British English. At times, the voice took on a clipped and angry rhythm, and his face went cold, his jaw clamping so tight that he was just about speaking through bared teeth. The prosecutor even seemed to be urging him to anger, waving his arms a little, heating up his gestures every time he pointed across the empty polished space in Mose's direction. Gruenwald described the afternoon his Hauptmann was beaten: according to him, brutally murdered while he was doing nothing more than sitting as an observer, as had been his assignment.

"Without provocation?" the prosecutor asked him for the third time.

"Certainly not," Gruenwald answered. "No one could have been more cooperative than our Hauptmann."

"No action or words of any sort provoked this brutal treatment?"

"None whatsoever!" Gruenwald said with some astonishment. "I've told you!"

"None then?"

"None!" The voice had risen to a shout. The sound of it cut through the silence of the room and echoed back through the empty gallery. It was like listening to two drums speaking.

"That will be all," prosecutor Killburn said.

Gruenwald sat there a moment, bewildered, an unspoken question on his lips. Judge Schmidt reached for a pen and scrawled out a brief note for himself, an expression on his face as if he were sucking on a piece of lemon. Rosengrin rose to his feet and greeted the orderly with a smile, politely asking him to restate his identity for the court's records, his rank—lance sergeant—and also the army unit in which he had served, whose smart dress uniform he was wearing, the 2nd battalion of the 125th Panzergrenadier regiment of the Afrika Korps. It was the unit that had almost single-handedly held Hill 28 at El Alamein against forces ten times it strength. Driving back the full weight of Montgomery's frontal assault, and suffering under air raid after air raid, it had fought to its last tank and working gun, then held out it seemed on spirit alone until even its infantry ran out of bullets. It was Rosengrin who recited this service record, which by implication was the Hauptmann's as well. The tone Gruenwald used in speaking the name of his regiment showed his pride in its fame. "You consider yourself a good soldier?" Rosengrin asked flatly.

Gruenwald paused a moment; something had changed in his expression. He was cagey now, nervous; the fan slowly turned overhead like through a wash of steam. "Yes," he said. "We were all good soldiers."

"Do you consider yourself a good soldier now?"

Gruenwald looked at the judge, then at the lawyer, then all around the room. A muscle in his cheek was ticking steadily. He swallowed.

"Yes," he said.

"Under the rules of the Geneva Convention, you have been provided with a so-called Memorandum Addressed to German Soldiers? And it is a direct communication to captured soldiers of your army from your superiors in Germany?"

"Yes," he said quickly.

"What does this memorandum order you to do?"

Gruenwald thought about this for a moment.

"As I remember it, we are to keep physically strong, make ourselves familiar with our rights, and take every opportunity to escape," he said. "That is the duty of all soldiers in captivity."

"No other duties?" Rosengrin asked.

"No," Gruenwald said. "I know of no others."

"Not even to obey orders, if you should get them, from your superior officers?"

"We are still soldiers," Gruenwald said.

"Any orders at all?"

"We are still soldiers," Gruenwald repeated.

"German soldiers," Rosengrin said.

"Yes," answered Gruenwald.

"*Any* orders at all. To form escape committees, for example. . . ."

"We had none of those," he said.

Judge Schmidt leaned over and reminded Gruenwald that he should only answer the questions, not volunteer information. Then he scratched another note. Rosengrin paused, politely observing the judge until he finished.

"Let's say, if you were ordered to *destroy* something," the lawyer said. "Like factory equipment, for example. Or the cut the bottoms out of boxes in a factory. Or simply to slow your work down, perhaps to impede production at your job. . . . What would you do?"

Gruenwald didn't answer at once. He turned toward the prosecutor's table as if expecting help from that direction. The prosecutor folded his hands, looking into them as if he were considering a manicure.

"We are soldiers," Gruenwald said, finally.

"Loyal to your country? To Germany? To Hitler?"

Sweat was making dark stains under the arms of his uniform. Gruenwald reached out slowly for his water glass. All eyes in the courtroom were focused on his throat. He drank, set the glass down. Then all he said was: "Yes. We are still German soldiers."

Mose Johnson was exonerated of all federal charges, not because, as Judge Schmidt made clear, he was deemed to be blameless; the prosecutor simply had not prepared a strong enough case. Buster Hill drove him back to Nowell in a mood of celebration; at the municipal bar, Jim Fuller, Pearly Green, the Doc, Ben Hogan, and several others were waiting for him, expecting good news. A crowd had gathered. Dolores Moss had hung red, white, and blue streamers, and even young Ron Ballock had come in unexpectedly, home from New Guinea, limping from his million-dollar wound and soon to be discharged. Shouts went up as Buster ushered Mose in. Drinks stood in a line on the bar for him. Men crowded around, slapping at his back and shoulders, reaching out to shake his hand. Mose drank three quick shots down; then he couldn't stay there any longer. He couldn't cheer, couldn't reach out and shake their hands. He slammed back through the door and into the street. Nobody seemed to consider the fact that he had killed a man.

There was no question that he would go back to work at Nowell-Safebuy Turkeys. Buster Hill relieved him of his manager's job for the duration; Dale Rynning was the one promoted to fill his place, giving up his union stewardship and crossing over. Mose was to go on a month-long vacation for himself, anywhere he wanted, with full pay and Buster buying the tickets. The plan was that, eventually, he would take over some of the direction of the new jobs project west of town. But Mose didn't go anywhere that required tickets. He spent his month mostly alone up in the hills, driving around in his old De Soto. He seemed to live for a while in the famous numbered saloons of Deadwood, in the mining bars of Lead, checking into hotels for three-day stretches, avoiding Nowell as much as he could.

No matter how much he tried to stay away, though, the town's news somehow always found him, like a lost dog returning miles to its home. All through that summer, rumors were flying about Carol McCann. They grew more and more harmful. One morning late, a time between breakfast and lunch when the Cove Café was usually empty, Mrs. Nilsen off in back washing sinks of dishes, the radio on full volume, Mose thought to duck in and grab a quick breakfast before heading for the hills again. He sat down at a booth in back, then Pearly Cyrus Green came in and sat down beside him with a loud "Hey, Mose."

Pearly called out his order, then sat there with a snickering look on his face like he had just shot a fox in his turkey barns. It was natural enough he'd try to rib Mose just a little about that McCann girl. Nobody had any secrets in Nowell. Everybody knew exactly who was making money, who had nerves and who was plumb crazy, and, in those days, what woman might be shaming some poor sailor or soldier over there fighting. "Hell, you ain't the only one!" Pearly said, trying to unclasp

Mose's fingers from his shirt. "They say she's sacked with that half-breed Charley Gooch! Even Maggie Rynning's been out to the farm looking for her 'cause of some talk about her with Dale! Can you imagine? And just yesterday Clyde Bosserd said he seen her riding all over out in the gumbo with Sheriff Meeker. . . ."

"That's a goddamn lie," Mose said. "You take that back right damn now or I'm going to drag you out in the street and make you eat it!"

He grabbed Pearly's shirt collar so hard he ripped off one side of it.

"Damn, Mose!" Pearly said. "What in hell are you blaming *me* for? I'm your friend? Your friend!"

"She ain't like that," Mose said.

"I'm sorry," Pearly said. "But it ain't just me. Have you gone crazy or something?" He got up out of the booth just as Mrs. Nilsen was bringing his hamburger over. He waved it out of the way and tossed a quarter on the table quickly, feeling at his neck and his torn shirt as he headed for the door. Opening it, he turned and said back in at Mose, "If you don't believe me, go on into the municipal bar some night and see for yourself!"

Mose drove out to the McCann farm that afternoon. He stopped his car at the barbed-wire gate and sat there a long time before driving in. What was he after anyway? What business was it of his? Wasn't it better to cut off that one offending hand and just go on from there? But he wanted to know. After what he had done to her, she'd likely shoot at him before he could get out of his car anyway. That was fine with him. He opened the gate, then started up his car again and drove along toward the McCann house over the bumpy lane, still not knowing what he should say.

The farm was deserted. He cupped his eyes to the glass of the porch windows and looked into the house. Dishes were piled up in the sink, and empty glasses were scattered around on the chair arms in the parlor. Flies were everywhere. Something was sitting out on the kitchen counter and drawing them as if it had been left there for days.

Mose took a walk back around to the turkey barn. What he saw there made him stop short. Hundreds of turkeys were flocking to him along the fence, piling up at each other over the empty feed troughs, most of them looking half dead from lack of water. Mose spent a good hour or so running up to the house for a bucket of water to prime the barn pump with, then hand pumping the watering troughs full. Everything was wrong out there. Jody just never had set the place up the right way. Well, it was none of his business. Mose even felt like a thief as he looked around the barn for the feed crib, then scattered what little corn there was left in there for the hungry birds. He finished, climbed into his car, and headed back to town.

It wasn't until about a week later that Mose saw Carol McCann. She came into the Cove Café early one morning, her piled blond hair half in tangles. Her pretty pale-blue print dress had a long, dark stain down one sleeve, and the cuff was ripped open. She looked tired, and puffy in the face, her eyes bloodshot and sunk in deeply. When Mose first saw her come in that way, he looked down into his coffee, avoiding having to meet her eyes. One of his fingers was drawing circles on the countertop, around and around. But he could hear and sense her every move. Her footsteps hesitated a moment behind him like maybe she was going to turn and leave once she saw him there. Then she just kept on walking in, unsteady in her high heels, taking the farthest booth in back. Mose was about to get up and leave. What could he say? Nothing could ever take back what he had done. Then he thought of the way she was neglecting her farm out there, the way she looked coming in, and he stood up and went back to her table.

"What do you think I'd want with you?" Carol said sharply. "Some kind of dinner date?"

"A cup of coffee," said Mose. "One cup of coffee's

all I ask. Then you can go on and do whatever you please and I won't care.''

"Sure," she said. "Just like you ever did."

"Maybe I'd best not then," said Mose. "I'm sorry."

She leaned back in the booth and crossed her big but shapely legs like she was making a show of them for him. She lounged there a moment, her lips curled at the edges in that bitter way they had, tough and frowning. He was about the try to sit down with her again, then she took a long inhale on her cigarette and let the smoke out into his face like a blast of an acid gas.

"O.K. then," said Mose. "I'll get out of your sight. If that's what you want. . . ."

"Suit yourself," she said. "But I ain't going anywhere either way."

"All right," said Mose. Finally, he sat down across from her and signaled to Mrs. Nilsen for cups of coffee. The café was about a quarter full that morning; Anita Foos was in there, and Andrea Scott, off at her own table, reading some Mormon religious pamphlet called "The Cornucopia of Gabriel." Bruce Gamble sat with a couple of farmers, talking hardware over at a corner table. Mose felt their conversations slowly changing as they noticed him sit down. More talk to fuel the fires. Like there hadn't already been enough damaging news. He self-consciously lowered his hat brim a little and sat at the edge of the booth, as far away and unattached from Carol as he could.

"You going to just let all them turkeys out there starve to death or what?" he said then. "Looks pretty damn sorry out there to me."

"What in hell business is it of yours?" she answered. She started to say something more, then stopped short as Mrs. Nilsen served their cups. Carol breathed out a long sigh of smoke and swirled her spoon around, mixing in the cream. "Don't seem like it's any of my problem now anyway," she said. "Won't be long before Jody's home, and that's the end of it. Then I don't know. I just don't know. . . ."

"It's not too late yet," Mose said. "You can still save things."

"What? In this town?" Carol laughed, a sharp sound of contempt that came out through her pretty nose like a sneeze. "They all got me marked as one thing and one thing only in their mind, and that's it. Jesus, even Jody knows about it. He'll be in San Diego next month and take his leave coming due. Never thought the mail could move so fast. Airmail. All the way to Hawaii, then back here and back again. You'd think it ain't possible, not with the war and all. But that's that. I just wish I knew who in hell it was that wrote him abut it," she said. She noticed a stray lock of her hair hanging wildly and tried to neaten it with a quick push of her hand. "So why not? Why not just let it all go to hell?" Carol looked up from her coffee at him, her tired eyes filling, then her body shook once deeply in a quiet sob and she brought her hands up around her eyes like the blinders on a horse. "Oh, God, what am I going to do? . . ."

Mose started to reach out across the table to hold her somehow, then stopped. She wouldn't want his comfort, not his, and people might see and make things worse. Instead, he reached into his back pocket for his handkerchief. Then he saw how dirty it was, carried back there and used for who knew how long by now. Clumsily, he reached into the napkin holder and pressed a few napkins into her hands. He noticed how long and slender her fingers were, and how she had painted her nails, which were just starting to grow out. "Damn them," he said. "Just say damn to all of them. Go on. Let loose."

"I'm not going to cry," she said. Saying that, she took her hands down, wiping her eyes with the wadded napkins. She pulled her plain cloth purse up off the seat beside her and found her own lace-edged handkerchief, which gave off a smell of lavender. She blew her nose and straightened up in the booth, making a show for him, and for anyone who cared to look, of that same tough and frowning expression.

"And they twain shall be one flesh: so then they are no more twain, but one flesh," Mose said.

"If you're going to go spouting that stuff off, you should be over there with Andrea," Carol said with a forced laugh. "You really just don't know, do you?" she asked. "You surprise me. Of all the men in this town, I'd thought you'd be the kind who understood."

"I do, I *do*," said Mose. Then damn everybody, he reached across the table and took both her hands in his. He was amazed at the way she let him take them, her fingers even squeezing back a little. "I'm sorry. So terribly sorry," he said. "Me . . . there ain't nothing I can say. Something just happened to me. Out there. On the job. And . . . that night . . . Then what happened later . . ." He stopped. It was too much to explain to her now, and all of it beyond what he could put into words. "But this," he said. "You. This way. This just can't go on."

"But that's what you don't know," she said. "It can. It can and it will. And there's nothing you or me or anybody can do about that now."

"Go. Just go," Mose said. "Meet him. Clear over there in San Diego. You love him. You know you do. Just a kid half horse's ass when you married him, and you still love him. So get the hell out right now and go and meet him!"

"All he thinks about is that piece of ground out there. . . ."

"He ain't any farmer! You know that!"

"All he kept writing about in his letters: How's the well holding out? What's the corn like coming up? And don't forget to get after them fences. Jesus, just keeping it all in one piece has been . . ."

"Stop it. Stop it now," said Mose, and Carol did.

"Your coffee's getting cold," she said. Then, after a moment, "Thanks. Thanks for sitting here with me. I mean, I don't blame you anymore. You're a sonofabitch.

But there's no shortage of them, not in this town. So it would have maybe happened anyway,'' she said. She smiled again, but differently now, wiser, even some kind of woman's teasing in her expression. ''If not because of you, then someone else. . . .''

''That won't matter to him now,'' said Mose. ''I know it, I *do*, so you just believe me. You go on out there right now and meet him. Here,'' he said, and he pulled out of his pocket a roll of bills that looked as fat and heavy as a baking potato. Under the table, he wrapped the roll in his dirty handkerchief so nobody would see what it was. Then he reached that fist-sized bundle across the table and dropped it into her open purse. ''Take it. I mean it. It don't mean nothing to me. There's more if you need it. Get yourself a train ticket. Today. Right now. And a nice room when you get there. Best damned hotel in San Diego. Then you go on down to that boat of his and meet him and take him straight there. Believe me. Please. You get him to forget that scratchy farm out there that already killed his dad off with work. Soften him up some. Work on him. You know what I mean. Get him to just sell it off to Jim Fuller or to Jake Ballock or to anybody. Long-distance. It's all just papers to sign. There's plenty of buyers in the market. I hear the Nowell-Safebuy's even planning to start buying out their own farmers soon. Listen to me, Carol. Please,'' he said. He searched his memory for the right words.''*Behold, the bridegroom cometh; go ye out to meet him.* That's what to do. That's all you *can* do now. Then don't either of you ever come back here again.''

Carol stood up at the table and looked in her purse, then at him, then she reached in for a dime to put on the table by her cup. She closed the clasp on her purse. And in front of everybody, no matter who might be watching at the Cove, tall and dignified, even with that rag of a stained sleeve on her dress, Carol reached one of her long-fingered hands out and touched his face. That hand was strong, and he gave in to it, letting it lift his face.

Then she leaned over Mose and, for a long time, a moment so long it was fixed and branded and gossiped about by almost everyone in town, just where her fingers had been, Carol pressed her sweet scented lips together and left them there, on his cheek, kissing him.

After Carol had gone, Mose drove off to Deadwood and holed up in a motel cabin there for a week with his whiskey and his loneliness. Just as Buster had told him to do, he spent the rest of that embattled summer avoiding Nowell as much as he could. He dropped in every once in a while, checking with Buster, meeting at his house a few evenings. Buster talked about his new job starting up but always managed to put off saying exactly when. So the summer went on like that, Mose generally off alone, carrying himself along on his boot soles of alcohol and grief.

Only once did Mose enter the turkey yards, the week after Carol left town. It was late, long past midnight. His flashlight streaking around eerily through the tunnels of wire, he made his way slowly out to the little breeding pen. He was concerned about the birds left in there. Though someone had been feeding them, he could see that as many as half of them had died of neglect. The pen had filled with straw and refuse, which covered the ground like a deep compost. The once tidy wood brood houses were spilling over with black moldy straw, so that the hens would no longer set in them. The turkeys that were left were pulling their own feathers out because of the unsanitary conditions, nobody even bothering to delouse them anymore.

There was something else. Mose didn't notice it until he was in the pen with them, kicking his boots around trying to clear refuse away from the feed trough. He was dragging out a feed sack to give the few dozen birds that remained a little extra grain. The birds still enclosed in the pen had been allowed in the past few months to breed with each other as they willed, none of it accounted for, as he had always done by his careful record keeping on

graph-paper charts. Mose poured a small yellow stream
of cracked corn into the trough, and six or seven scrawny
pullets scratched around his legs in a little gang, peeping. A beam of his flashlight fell over them. He stopped
pouring feed. He snatched one of them up, cradling it
under his arm as it struggled, its small head craning
around, beak wide open and black eyes darting not so
much with fear as with its frenzy to get to the trough
with the others. Mose ran his fingers over its young
growing feathers, ruffling them up, examining the colors
in them under a stronger light. They were like nothing
he'd ever seen before; they would grow into bright-copper
feathers speckled with green, like a combination of the
dark-green English and the copper Narragansett, with
long reddish legs, big breast, and a crop like the Bourbon
Red. And the bird he held, at least, seemed like it would
grow more than sturdy enough. He set it down on the
ground and snatched up one of its brothers. The same.
All of them were the same, and looked as though they
had the kind of sharp, aggressive qualities that would
make them a perfect type of backyard breed. Mose stood
among them in astonishment, raking them over with his
light. "By God, you're it," he said with a sad little laugh.
"The Johnson."

For a moment, he stood proudly watching them, filled
with something close to hope. He thought of making arrangements with Pearly Green to come and pick them up
in the morning. Take them out to his farm, where they
could be kept in a decent pen, coddled, watched, raised
up properly. It would only be after a few generations that
he would really know if they had breed integrity. He
imagined himself out there, working them, checking their
vitamin supplements, weighing them every week to keep
track of their gains. Maybe even showing them, entering
his best in county and state exhibitions. But what good
would that be? With Nowell-Safebuy policy what it was,
who would ever raise them? He couldn't even say for sure
where they had come from.

Mose switched his flashlight off and stood in darkness. He listened to their sounds, growing fainter without light, their scratching around no longer interested in feed but looking for places to roost. It was all by accident; nothing here had been by his choice or selection. Somehow, he had planted them, they had taken root, but he saw them like a field of wheat that could yield only thorns. He was about to catch them up and begin wringing necks; at least that would be more humane than leaving them in there like that, on their own and dying of neglect. Then he thought, What the hell. He would phone Pearly in the morning. Give them over to him for what they were worth; watch them for a while anyway, just to see what might happen.

Late the next morning, hardly sober, Mose telephoned Pearly; in talking over the matter of keeping such birds with him, Mose found himself agreeing to take a drive out to Pearly's farm to help him and one of his boys change the rings on a tractor engine. It was good to be out in the open air, breaking into an honest sweat as they wrestled with the heavy engine head, pounding the half-locked pistons into line with a rubber hammer. Machinery always seemed to be what most defeated Pearly on his farm. But he always had good luck with his livestock. Mose kept up his patience and helped get the job done. Later, they walked around the turkey barns, and Pearly marked out a place where Mose might set up a small pen. Because they were in a mood to celebrate the deal they had made and the smooth repairs on the engine, Mose drove Pearly off to Belle Fourche, buying the drinks until the Poplar Bar closed down.

The next afternoon, Mose discreetly ducked into the Cove Café for a late lunch after sleeping in so long. As he was eating, he heard the distant sound of a bulldozer. He didn't think much of it then. But that evening, just as he was driving around the back fences of the turkey yards, his car loaded with several boxes for his birds, Mose saw the bulldozer parked out there beside a huge mound of

dirt, manure, scrapwood, and crumpled-up sheets of tin.
Nothing was left of his small enclosure. Where it had
stood, along with the narrow lot behind it, which was a
dumping ground for broken parts, rolls of wire, and sur-
plus metal drums, only a leveled, cleared dirt area remained. Mose was beside himself; he tried to find Buster,
then Bruce McGovern, and finally found Dale Rynning
at the municipal bar. "We been needing that space out
there as long as I can remember," said Dale. "We're up
to near six thousand turkeys a day now, you know. Where
else can we put 'em? Hell, I just figured clear it out once
and be done with it. The birds in there didn't look like
much, so we just tossed 'em in the scrap barrels and
ground 'em up with the feed. Dammit, Mose," he said
then, as close to an apology as he would ever get for
anything. "Nobody ever told me they was still yours."

Later that night, Mose wandered around in the cleared-
off dirt, stumbling over his own feet in the darkness. The
wire yards stretched out against the deep-gray horizon,
and he looked off into them, some of them filled with
huddling fat white turkeys that seemed like a faint yet
hateful source of light. There were distant noises from
inside the mostly darkened building, the sounds of high-
pressure hoses blasting against sheets of steel. He was
empty and alone. He thought of the job ahead, the building to help oversee, and then what? Then what else but
be put out to pasture there. Watching over a small crew
working along, shift after shift, shipping off crates of
day-old Nowell-Safebuy poults to local farmers. Then
again, after what he had done, what more did he deserve?
There was nothing in that for him. It all seemed desolate—the bare ground under his boots, this town, even
the whole land around him—because there was nothing
left in any of it he could take to heart. That night was
the end of it for him. He was through with working turkeys. None of this would ever again be a part of his life.

21

Our boys started coming home. They came gradually at first, single men in uniform hobbling off the buses of the Jack Rabbit Line that had pulled up in front of the Cove Café. Some were wounded, shell shocked, and told stories of heroism. Most had simply put in their time and been lucky. They fell into the arms of their joyous families. But they all seemed awkward looking around at the familiar sights of this town like foreigners after their journeys; it was as if they still couldn't believe that where they had landed was home. Then that day came when the front pages of newspapers across the land filled with the stark photos of a massive cloud billowing up on its sturdy mushroom stem as though angelically to final victory, as if a God-sent miracle, the A-bomb, which shut down the last theater of the war with swift retribution. Happy music filled the air again. There was dancing in the streets. Our boys started coming home in droves, with new leases on life, energies fixed in youthful optimism on securing their futures, their homes, their loves, and on building themselves a different world. As many as two hundred came back to Wovoka County during that final year of war and in the months that followed its prophetic victory.

Nowell-Safebuy Turkeys was working in an even higher gear by then, ever expanding, two full shifts of prisoners of war processing up to six thousand birds a day. Jobs were at a premium for returning soldiers. There was some time for them to look around, modest severance pay, and the "fifty-two twenty club," as it was called, a weekly cushion of twenty dollars a week for a year to help them back into civilian life. The Nowell-Safebuy entered a busy period of work projects, hanging out a sign over the doorway to Buster Hill's main offices that read: WELCOME HOME VETS. Almost one hundred new men were hired, then put to work laying bricks for the new Nowell-Safebuy hatchery and research facility west of town, digging and pouring the foundations of its huge feed-storage silos, paving its roads and its parking lot. There was plenty of work to be done, and there were more than enough men willing to do it. The company's policy was to hire workers on for construction first, which was mainly not covered in the area by any union, then gradually to transfer these workers to the slaughtering line when the construction was finished. That was the company's plan. Wages were set at somewhere about thirty dollars a week to start, with a company lunch thrown in. The Amalgamated Brotherhood of Butchers and Meatworkers sent in representatives all the way from Chicago to study and then protest this new policy. But during the tough transition from war to peace, with so many boys coming home, a strike action would have to wait. Buster Hill was approaching returning veterans with offers of immediate jobs; and the young returning soldiers seemed grateful enough for just that much, as satisfied as they could be, at first, with the prospect of earning almost any wages at all to begin rebuilding their lives. Thirty dollars was thirty dollars. At least that was something.

Meanwhile, hundreds of German prisoners of war continued working turkeys at the Nowell-Safebuy and refining sugar at the Great Westward. Crews of them went out each day as usual by the thousands into the surrounding fields. It must have seemed unjust, even irrational, to witness them laboring away month after month, still like chain gangs. But the careful machinery of peaceful occupation moved far slower than that of the wartime emergency; whole zones of Europe had to be reorganized and secured before the prisoners of war were sent back overseas.

When they finally were shipped home, during the spring of 1946, they left in better condition than many of the nearly 400,000 German prisoners in this country at the war's end. Also, most fared better when they did return. Many of the prisoners first sent back overseas were detained when they landed in Europe and were forced to remain in the French or British occupation zones, laboring in the ports or on farms, often under brutal conditions. In Britain, some were fed miserably and slept in unheated warehouses on fog-covered docks. In France, some were whipped and otherwise abused and insulted by the country villagers who had suffered under the Nazis. Many remained prisoners in the occupation zones until 1947, a few even longer. The prisoners of Orman benefited from their later departure and from the lucky fact that they had money in their pockets, provided by the fund set up for them. So some were able to negotiate bribes and false documents when they landed in Europe; others somehow weren't detained at all and returned directly home. They went back to find a Germany still dazed and ruined and hungry, shivering in its rags in the hovels the war had made of its houses. The prisoners of Orman must have come back feeling like rich men, hundreds of good American dollars in their pockets to help them make fresh starts and different lives.

There was only one other disturbance at the Orman Camp after the prisoner strike. In late January of the final year of the war, two prisoners simply vanished, leaving

their bow saws behind in the snow while on a woodcut-
ting expedition in the hills above the town of Spearfish.
Alarms went up all over the county and throughout the
Midwest. Cars full of army guards combed the roads.
Police stakeouts were set up at train stations, bus depots,
intersections on suspected routes toward Canada and
Mexico. Wanted posters were sent out by the thousands.

The prisoners blithely walked out through the woods
toward the highway. Their comrades in the barracks had
prepared grain sacks that they cleverly stuffed and dressed
in prison clothes, painting faces on them. They carried
the two man-sized dummies out through the snow-blown
mornings and held them erect while waiting in line to be
counted at roll call. Each night, they arranged them in
cots and tucked the blankets in. In was three full days
before the slack guards at the camp even noticed.

The two escaped prisoners thus had plenty of time.
They were both young enlisted men, and their plan was
so boldly outrageous that it astonished the federal authorities who later investigated their case. In a travel ar-
ticle in *Collier's*, one of them read about the huge party
in the city of New Orleans called Mardi Gras. They
shared the glossy color photos with each other, talked
the party over; it seemed like an extended version of the
Fastnacht festival, a pre-Lenten revel in their beloved
Black Forest. In the wind-blasted winter boredom of
camp life, they were seized with the crazy idea that
somehow they should go. Why not? What better way to
see this America?

So they stuck their thumbs out along wintry highways
all across the very heart of the country, hitchhiking their
way into Louisiana. Neither of them spoke more than a
few words of halting English. And neither of them so
much as bothered to change his clothes. The letters POW
stood boldly on the backs of their prisoner coats for anyone with half a brain to notice. When later questioned,
they said at least twenty-two different cars picked them
up and let them off along their route. They were very

friendly, these Americans. The two young prisoners were fed, given cigarettes, everything. Nobody called the police. Not one of those generous motorists.

The two young prisoners actually made it all the way to New Orleans. They panhandled on Bourbon Street, sat in bars listening to jazz. They joined in with the reveling throngs of carnivalgoers decked out in festive costumes; in their POW outfits, they blended right in with the crowds. They were gone two and a half weeks. Finally, they were arrested by a passing highway patrolman just north of St. Louis, bags full of Mardi Gras hats, horns, masks, and souvenirs over their shoulders. It was discovered that they were actually hitchhiking back to the Orman Camp to turn themselves in. What must those good American motorists have been thinking? What must it have been like in their cars as they sped along through the midwestern days and nights with these thick-tongued German soldiers on the seats beside them?

Mose Johnson remained mainly aloof from the news of this escape, as he did from the changes going on everywhere around him. He elected to retire from Nowell-Safebuy Turkeys, living on the money he had saved and from the modest pension Buster Hill arranged for him. At first, he spent a few days trout fishing with Doc Monahan up in the hills. Other days, he puttered around his house, his lawn, his garden, and carried out a few odd jobs for his church, until his drinking got the better of him. Mose also wrote and sent packages to Keller, or to Obergefreiter Gunther Niemmer, which, as he found out from Major Pierce, was Keller's new identity. Keller's cover story was that he was a captured U-boat sailor. He was interned in a camp at a place called Papago Park, Arizona.

For three months, Mose didn't hear anything back, but he figured that after so much time his gifts must have gotten through. Then one morning he found the packages crumpled up and stuffed in his mailbox, their brown paper stamped in post office red ink, with a tiny hand pointing its finger to his return address and the words *Undeliverable. Addressee Unknown.* Mose grabbed up the packages, climbed into his car, and drove out to the Orman Camp to find out what had happened.

Major Pierce was busy. Engineers from a U.S. Army unit were poring over blueprints of the new river basin dam in his barracks office. Members of his staff were pounding out calculations on an adding machine. He was already the owner of a brace of Caterpillar dozers, parked like a squadron of gleaming yellow tanks outside. The major expected his discharge in a few months. He had already drawn up limited-partnership papers and had himself bonded as a subcontractor on the massive dam and irrigation project for the army. To get in to see him, Mose had to shove aside a master sergeant and storm into the major's office with those packages in his arms.

Six weeks later, a big olive-green envelope arrived in the mail. In it was a quick note from Major Pierce, stating that the file inside was a copy of the official inquiry into an incident that had occurred at Camp Papago Park a few months before. The file concerned a U-boat prisoner named Niemmer. The covering letter and supporting documents described in detail that there had been disturbances at the camp. The way Major Pierce explained it to him, pro-Nazi factions among the prisoners had formed a commission to purge the "traitors," that is, men they said were "disloyal to Germany." The principle of their action was called *durchhalten*, meaning something like "holding fast." It was a term they knew well, from the mouth of their Führer himself, from the hysterical orders some of them had brought with them, carried with their capture, from Germany. Even as it grew daily more clear that the war was surely lost, these *durchhalten* gangs were becoming ever more violent and desperate to hang on to whatever power they had until the end. Even at the Orman Camp, Major Pierce had some trouble with *durchhalten* gangs; but that was nothing like what was happening at the German sailors' camps, where many fellow prisoners were beaten even for minor infractions, such as refusing to give the Roman salute.

At Papago Park, Arizona, a seaman named Werner Drechsler had been murdered the past year. Then another sailor, whose name was Niemmer, was charged with treason by his fellow prisoners. Six hours after he arrived at his new camp, he was court-martialed in absentia and found to be an informer, the evidence against him only the rumors that had followed him along a kind of cross-country prisoner grapevine. Seven elected prisoners from the "court" followed him into the barracks. They jumped him and covered him with a blanket. Witnesses to his shouts and struggles did not intervene. The following morning, camp guards found him hanged by his neck from an electric-light cord in the shower room.

Mose looked over the pages of documents with a weight growing in his chest; then he flipped to the last page, a copy of the standard prisoner-of-war personnel form, including a botched-looking photograph that dropped out into his lap. He sucked in his breath. He held the small photo in his palm and raised it up to the window light. It was a straight-on portrait of a man with a numbered placard around his neck. The man in the photograph had husky shoulders. Brown eyes. A dark goatee-like beard and mustache, the kind most of the U-boat sailors wore at the time of their capture. Above that sparse black moss of beard, this man had a well-formed, shapely nose that stuck out at the camera as handsomely as a romantic actor's in the movies.

"Well, I'll be damned," Mose said out loud, much relieved. Then he looked over the file of papers again and wasn't so sure. It was possible the army hadn't switched file photos when they had given Keller his new identity. Mose wasn't sure how such a system worked. Wasn't the army famous for getting its paperwork all fouled up? Besides that, how much sense would it make to transfer an Afrika Korps artilleryman like Keller into a camp for naval prisoners? What could that boy possibly know about U-boats? How could his barracks mates not catch on to his cover?

As Mose thought all of this over, he considered that what might have happened to Keller was that the sheer stupidity of some army staff somewhere or the bungling of red tape or, worse, the desire to get rid of Keller had sent him to his death. Who would have known more about Major Pierce and his dealings at the Orman Camp? Or then again, as in the Drechsler murder, Keller might have been set up by his most vengeful fellow prisoners; in which case, the army would more than likely mix up and confuse and alter any files it needed until they conformed to its own convenient version of the truth, absolving itself of any blame.

Mose spent months pestering Major Pierce to get more information, photographs of the body of the man who had been killed, anything. Before the year was out, a message came back that no further information existed on any Obergefreiter Niemmer, and all personnel files on Oberkanonier Walter Keller were now considered classified. It was as though he had simply vanished into the system. Missing and gone, like so many millions.

Years later, in 1950, Mose learned about an execution of prisoners of war at Leavenworth from a former army corporal he met at a bar in Sturgis, who had served as a guard at the Papago Park Camp. The seven men who had assassinated the prisoner named Drechsler at Papago Park, Arizona, had been tried by a U.S. Army court and convicted of murder. International appeals were filed for clemency, all of them rejected. They were finally hanged at the federal penitentiary at Fort Leavenworth, Kansas, in August of 1945, the last mass execution recorded in American history.

Mose pressed him about it again and again, but the former guard at Papago Park insisted he had never heard of any seaman named Niemmer; since he had helped to process new arrivals, he should have known. He also had never heard so much as a rumor of a second murder at the camp; the only one to his knowledge was the U-boat sailor named Drechsler. Mose kept drunkenly pushing him to remember, to be sure, until the man walked out on him, thinking he'd been called a liar.

People in town seemed barely to remember the prisoners of war by then. A whole new era and yet another bloody conflict overseas filled the news. Houses were going up everywhere. The streets were finally paved. Nowell-Safebuy Turkeys had continued its period of steady expansion, even vertically integrating to the point where it owned and operated tens of thousands of acres of surrounding farms. Television came to this part of the country. Prosperity and babies boomed. The whole world seemed to be moving to a different pace and rhythm than anything it had known before.

By then, Mose Johnson had become almost a town fool, staggering drunk much of the time, his old blue car found banged up and nose first in ditches all over the county until his license was taken away. Boys growing up here knew him only like that—sour-breathed, unshaven, his house like a haunted house, the shrubs overgrown, the lawn turned to weeds. Kids played jokes on him. They watched him stagger up on his peeling wooden porch in the afternoons and fall into his house. Hearing his old bedsprings creaking as he lay down, one of them climbed up on his roof and dropped a lit cherry bomb down his stovepipe. They hung cats by the tail from his back doorknob, live and screaming. They egged his mailbox. Soaped his windows. Toilet-papered his trees. Once they even filled a paper bag with dog shit, doused it with gas, set it on his porch, pounded their fists on his door, then lit the bag. Hiding in the bushes, they watched Mose stomping out the fire, cussing loudly, stumbling around and falling all over himself. Then they sprang out at him in a laughing, taunting gang until he grabbed up a stick and chased after them down the street. He was their fool.

The town wino. A man their parents pitied even as they
warned them to stay away from him.

At the municipal bar, men barely tolerated him, with
his morose weaving silence, or his slurred yammerings
on, still caught somewhere by his past, never able to get
out of it, like a soldier who would never recover from his
memories. Some of his old friends would sit talking with
him at times, for what it was worth, and later on, even a
few of the boys left in this town who had grown into men.
They were years when Mose was almost continually sick
and silent, all notions of time confused, his brain gone
wet, his body all bones, his skin sagging like a wrinkled
blue turkey throat, his black rheumy eyes fixing with a
primitive glare any newcomer in the bar. He drank mostly
in silence, one of those used-up, drunk old men who
guard some small secret portion of history the rest of the
world has forgotten.

Mose Johnson went on like that for about fifteen more
years, until, one winter, he finally died of alcoholism.
People thought it was a miracle he had hung on that long.
So long, in fact, that only a few people he had known
were left in Nowell. Mayor Buster Hill had died by then,
while chasing the newest bulldog pup he had named
Buster down the street. Doc Monahan was still alive, but
just barely. And Reverend Ott was hardly able to get
around enough to perform the funeral service. He
propped himself up in front of a sparse group of his congregation at the Church of Christ Reformed. There was
no mood of loss, no evident signs of grieving; Mose
Johnson had passed away after so long a period of public
dissipation and embarrassment that, if anything, his death
was considered a relief, even a blessing. It was as if he
had wandered off into a personal desert of his own making, and somewhere out there, beyond reach of anyone,
he died alone. At his funeral service, there were only a
few faces of people who had known Mose in his early
days: Pearly, Will Hartley, Jim Fuller, Anita Foos, and
Marge Hogan. Two of the men acting as pallbearers were

enlisted at the last minute, never even having met him. Reverend Ott delivered a brief and respectful few words describing Mose as a hard worker, a man who had once been of valuable service and a credit to his community. Nothing was said about his later, sadder years. Except maybe in closing, before the final prayer for his soul, when Reverend Ott opened up the big Bible and read in a parched voice, *"Lo, this only have I found, that God hath made man upright; but they have sought out many inventions. . . ."*

Mose was buried in a little cemetery behind the Church of Christ Reformed, his grave marked by a simple wooden cross. A few years later, the church was closed as a place of worship and turned into a warehouse for beets and potatoes, its graveyard wildly overgrown with weeds that stood taller than its headstones. That happened after this town's prosperity had gone boom and then bust. Nowell was on its way to becoming little more than a ghost town. It took its first few steps on its one-way journey back into a new kind of prairie wilderness when Nowell-Safebuy Turkeys shut down its operations, moving them to turkey facilities in Minnesota. Then, after a prolonged and painful labor dispute, which drew adverse publicity all over this country, workers striking for months against accepting four dollars less per hour in wages and benefits to keep Safebuy "competitive in the industry," the company shut down its operations even there. It moved its turkey-processing business all the way to a brand-new plant already under construction outside São Paulo, Brazil, where thousands of dark-skinned men waited eagerly in line for jobs with wages set at an astoundingly high equivalent in cruzeiros of $120 a month. Safebuy stock rose dramatically on the American Exchange. Farms went broke. Banks failed. Schools closed. People moved away for parts unknown.

One afternoon, just after the Cove Café had been taken over by old Pearly Cyrus Green as more of a hobby than a business, something happened that Pearly would remark on to people and wonder about for years. A young man with a blond beard and a briefcase under his arm pulled up in front of the café's big picture window in a bright-orange Volkswagen Beetle. The car had a luggage rack on its turtlelike roof, heaped high with a rolled-up tent, packs, camping gear, which were slipping over to one side. The young man, dressed in a flowered shirt, jeans, and sandals, had a beard and hair that was long and unkempt, and wore a necklace of pink coral shells. Pearly thought he was just another one of those hippie riffraff traveling all over in those days and was likely so stoned on drugs he had lost his sense of direction. Just for spite, Pearly liked to misdirect these hippie types miles out of their way. But there was something familiar about the young man. Milky blue eyes. A clean, boyish look under all that hair. Something about him Pearly just couldn't place. The young man had a fancy-looking camera over his shoulder. He came in like he knew the joint, taking in the whole room for a moment, its tables, counter, booths, and jukebox, with a strange, wide-lipped smile of recognition. He grinned and bobbed his head at Pearly in a familiar way. Then he sat down at the counter and asked Pearly in heavily accented English if a man named Mose Johnson was anywhere to be found.

"That is too bad," the young man said after Pearly told him just where he could look for Mose. He seemed to hesitate then, thinking a moment before he asked, "And what of his family?"

"Right here is about all the family he ever had," Pearly said, pointing at himself. He never liked to talk much about Mose Johnson; if folks couldn't speak well of a man, then they should just keep their mouths shut. "What's it to you anyhow?"

"Nothing to me," the young man said. "But my father in Germany, he tells me to stop here. When I am on my vacation abroad after schooling. So then," he said after a moment, scrutinizing Pearly closely. "If you are such as his family, perhaps I should leave this with you." The

young man reached into his briefcase. He pulled out the
kind of furry gray box expensive jewelry comes in and
set it on the counter. "My father wants Mr. Johnson to
have this. Or maybe someone in his family. So then I
guess you may give it some use."

Pearly looked at the box sitting on the counter like
some kind of strange animal he would be careful to touch.
The young man noticed this for a minute, then opened
the lid on the box to show him. "It is only a watch," he
said. "Not expensive. My father worked many years for
the company that makes them. There is something he had
written on it. Here." He looped his finger through the
black leather band. He lifted the heavy silver watch out
of its satin-lined cradle, unbuckling the strap and holding
it up to show off the ornate Old German lettering en-
graved on the back of its casing. *"Ruhe in Leben,"* he
said. "Don't ask me what it really means. Maybe to rest
in life. It sounds odd even in German. Most odd in particular on a watch. My father has many odd ideas. He
spent much of the war in this place. So here it is. My
father would want somebody to have it."

He held the watch out for a long moment before Pearly
finally took it out of his hand. He examined it, then instead of strapping it on his wrist, Pearly closed it in its
box and shoved it away in a drawer behind the café
counter. The young man watched him do this, shrugged,
then buckled his briefcase closed. He asked directions
for a place called Orman. Pearly thought he must mean
the lake and recreation area, so as he did with anyone
heading there, he quickly pointed out for the young man
the almost empty display of plastic squeeze bottles of
suntan lotion up near the cash register. They had been
sitting there so long the stuff inside had hardened like
glue. As though out of politeness alone, the young man
bought a bottle anyway. Pearly showed him the little
wooden animals he carved as curios, and the young man
bought one of those too, pulling out a wallet that was

thick with cash. Only then did Pearly give him directions out of town to get to Lake Orman.

Pearly watched out the big window. He wondered why there wasn't a girl. The young man looked like there should have been a girl with him. Before climbing back in his car, he walked a little ways out into the main street of this town. He gauged the sunlight, stood back, focused his camera at the Cove Café, and snapped a picture. Then he wandered up the street about two blocks to where the old Nowell-Safebuy turkey plant stood abandoned, its wire long ago down, troughs turned over in its yards and peppered with bullet holes. All the glass was out of the windows. The tall brick smokestack was broken off at its top from the prairie winds. The young man took a few steps into the old turkey yards, looked around for a minute, shrugged, raised up his camera, and clicked the shutter again. He ambled slowly back toward his car and stopped. He stood there awhile, not moving, white sun bearing down on the tufts of browning weeds that grew up all around him in the street. He looked like a man deciding something, searching his memory for the right keys. Then he squinted one eye and brought his camera to it again, aiming it quickly at the long rows of boarded-over shopwindows that lined the street. But he must have thought better of that, letting the camera drop back against his chest. He walked on more quickly, squinting against the sun, and with a strange, taut expression of distaste. At his car, in front of the big window of the Cove, he spent a few moments wrestling impatiently with the equipment on his luggage rack, trying to shift it straight again. He fought with it, muttering, unbuckling straps, loosening ropes and shifting things around until, finally, the rack moved just a little, more firmly, something better than it was before. He pulled a pair of sunglasses out of his pocket and put them on, adjusting them on his face. He stood back a few steps and inspected his work. He shrugged again. Then he climbed back into his Beetle and drove away.

About the Author

Douglas Unger was born in 1952 in Moscow, Idaho. His first novel, LEAVING THE LAND, was a winner of the Society of Midland Authors award for fiction, an ALA Notable Book of 1984, and a finalist for the Pulitzer and Robert F. Kennedy awards. He is also the author of EL YANQUI. Unger teaches in the Creative Writing Program at Syracuse University.